CLEAN KILL

NICK EVERARD

The Book Guild Ltd

First published in Great Britain in 2022 by
The Book Guild Ltd
Unit E2 Airfield Business Park,
Harrison Road, Market Harborough,
Leicestershire. LE16 7UL
Tel: 0116 2792299
www.bookguild.co.uk
Email: info@bookguild.co.uk
Twitter: @bookguild

Typeset in 11pt Adobe Garamond Pro

Printed on FSC accredited paper
Printed and bound in Great Britain by 4edge Limited

ISBN 978 1914471 667

British Library Cataloguing in Publication Data.
A catalogue record for this book is available from the British Library.

CLEAN KILL

For dearest Kiki, who told me to get on with it.

CHAPTER ONE

John Gault gazed wistfully at the framed photo of his wife on his bedside table.

Jenny was smiling happily at him in the picture, taken twenty years ago at sea, and he remembered that blissful summer weekend well. He'd been out sailing in the very same boat that day, which was intended as a tonic, but instead he'd simply felt lonely and conspicuous. The combination of fresh air, sun, spray and an hour's drive back from Burnham-on-Crouch had left him tired, albeit virtuously so. He longed only for a large whisky in front of the TV.

She had died two months ago: cancer. Though it was kind of the Vennings to ask him out, frankly he could do without it. But he understood: fifty-five was very young to be a widower, and people wanted to help.

Furthermore, during those final days Jenny had made him promise to accept invitations. He blew her an ironic kiss as he headed out.

'I'm going,' he said affectionately, before turning from the photo. He still talked to her.

'Satisfied?' he said, glancing over his shoulder.

John was ambling downstairs as the bell rang: Cathy Venning in front, with James hovering behind. He'd somehow expected that, he realised as he opened the door.

'Ready, John?'

She was ash blonde and pretty in her designer jeans and cardigan. Mid-forties, he supposed. There was genuine concern beneath her greeting as she offered her cheek for a kiss.

'As I'll ever be,' said John, with a grin he didn't feel.

He stepped outside the farmhouse door, gently discouraged his disappointed cocker spaniel Barney from coming too and headed towards the Vennings' car. James clapped him manfully on the shoulder and said nothing.

He was something senior in the City and looked it; he commuted weekly, and John wondered vaguely why he was home on a weekday. They'd moved to the village where the Gaults had farmed for generations about ten years ago and, with children the same age as Tom, had soon become close, Jenny and Cathy particularly. He liked them in a superficial sort of way, though they weren't really country people.

'Just the pub,' said James over his shoulder as be buckled his seat belt. 'They've got a new chef, apparently.'

It sounded as if sampling a new chef was a regularity for him.

'Great,' said John, as the swish BMW moved off towards his gateway. Small talk.

He'd been married to Jenny for twenty-nine years, and it still felt very strange to go out without her. She'd always been the one to lead on that. John had contented himself with ironic and amused interjections as she sparkled, more and more so, he now realised, throughout the years of their marriage. He was sociable enough, and by no means an introvert, but he'd always lacked her easy ability to oil a conversation.

They pulled into The Swan's car park in silence, and John climbed out of the car to open Cathy's door rather clumsily.

'We've got someone joining us,' said Cathy, breaking the awkwardness as she uncoiled her long legs.

'Please tell me you're not trying to pair me off already, Cath,' John smiled.

God, what if she was? James seemed to sense his unease.

'No blind date, old man,' he said, with his normal smooth amiability. 'Besides, you know her.'

* * *

'So, who?' muttered John to James over his shoulder, as they followed Cathy into the smart bistro pub. 'I've got a bloody awful memory for names at the best of times; everyone knows who I am at the moment, and I haven't a clue who most of them are.'

'Thought Cath had told you – sorry,' said James. 'Awkward. Sarah Hall. You know…'

He trailed off in embarrassment and pushed past John gratefully as Cathy looked back for him to confirm the reservation.

John was surprised. He did know. The Halls had been a feature of the village for a few years a while ago and then had moved away. They were a friendly, undemanding and attractive couple whom he'd liked. No children. He'd never quite understood why they'd left or indeed cared greatly – not his business. It was not something to be discussed, Jenny had

3

inferred, and that had been good enough for him.

James indicated for them to follow the waitress he'd spoken to and assumed command as she took their drinks order. They settled down at a table for four.

'So,' said Cathy, brightly, 'how've you been?'

John was getting used to the way people skirted around the unmentionable, whilst trying to express their sympathy. He'd just lost his wife. How was he expected to be?

'Everyone asks that,' he replied wryly and regretted it as he saw Cathy's face fall. He knew she meant well.

'Sorry, uncalled for,' he said. 'OK, I suppose. Different.'

'Well, after so long together… bound to be…' James ventured, tailing off. The same awkwardness.

'Exactly.' John smiled as best he could.

'Anyway,' said Cathy briskly, 'Sarah Hall.'

John waited expectantly as she took a sip of her drink.

'It's not a set up.' Cathy waved her other hand expressively. Perish the thought.

'I just bumped into her the other day and thought…' She left her sentence hanging, and John's smile remained fixed. 'Well – why not?'

She looked at him defensively. James came to his wife's rescue.

'You know, after what happened to Peter.'

John looked askance at both of them, his query unsaid. James and Cathy glanced at each other: the shorthand communication all long-married couples evolve. John recognised their unspoken worry.

'You don't know?' said James, with mild incredulity.

John shook his head. The Vennings exchanged that look again.

4

'About Peter. Her husband?' Cathy's turn to express disbelief. They looked at John expectantly, double-checking.

He shrugged. 'No.'

'Well, you've got to know before she gets here,' said James decisively. 'Killed himself. Suicide.'

John gaped at them, shocked.

'What… when?'

Cathy laid a hand on his arm quickly.

'Shhh – she's here. About a year. At least you know now.'

John looked over his shoulder to see Sarah approaching; he hadn't seen her for at least three years, he guessed, but her diffident smile and natural grace were immediately familiar. Her auburn hair was shorter than he remembered, and she looked as if she'd lost a little weight too – not that she'd ever had much to spare. A nice person, he thought, sometimes you can just tell.

'Sarah.' James bent slightly to kiss her on the cheek, and Cathy pecked her too; they were about the same height and age.

'You remember John Gault?'

Sarah looked at him steadily, with friendly grey eyes. Too long ago for a kiss, John thought. They exchanged an awkward handshake.

'Lovely to see you again, John,' she said in her soft voice.

John inclined his head. 'Likewise.'

'And I was very sorry to hear from Cathy about Jenny.'

She hadn't danced around it. Should he reciprocate? But he had no idea of the circumstances. Better not.

'Thank you.'

* * *

5

The evening went well, after a slightly reserved start, and John soon found himself enjoying it.

James was witty in a rather 'hail fellow well met' way; he and Cathy teased each other gently, as happy couples do, and Sarah soon relaxed. She was living in a village fifteen miles away now, apparently. But John's situation eventually cropped up, as it was bound to. Cathy started it, jumping into a gap in the conversation.

'So, John…'

Here it comes, he thought.

'How are you going to keep busy?'

John raised his eyebrows. He hadn't expected that. 'Well, I'm not exactly at a loose end at the moment. Probate, generally sorting everything out—'

'But then?' interrupted James. 'Farm's handed over, isn't it?'

John took a sip of his wine. 'Yes. Tom took it on a couple of years ago; that's why we swapped houses. Jenny's idea when he married Emma. But he's only twenty-seven. Got a lot to learn. I'll probably help him out a bit.'

It was a bit feeble; he wanted to change the subject. There was no escape though.

'What you need is a project,' said Sarah, quietly firm.

'Why? Do you have one?' He regretted it as soon as he said it. There was a pregnant pause.

'I'm new to this situation, you see,' said John, trying to dig himself out of the mire. 'Being alone, I mean.'

Sarah said nothing, though flushed slightly. For Christ's sake shut up before you make things any worse, thought John.

'You should write,' said James, breaking the uncomfortable silence. 'You've always wanted to.'

'Too late,' John replied. The others stayed silent. He shrugged helplessly. 'Maybe.'

'I never knew,' said Cathy. 'What would you write about?'

John felt sheepish and regretted unburdening himself to James over that third pint a few years ago.

'Oh – thriller. Murder mystery perhaps. But it'll never happen.'

'Why not?' said Sarah. 'You'll have the time.'

There was no avoiding either the challenge or the sympathy in her cool gaze. John shook his head but made no answer.

'Well – that pint at the beginning has gone right through me,' he said, more to break the pause in conversation than out of dire necessity. He headed off towards the gents.

When he came back, all three of the others went silent and smiled as he approached. John knew what that meant.

* * *

Out in the car park, John lingered by James's car as Sarah finished her farewell kisses with the Vennings. She turned to him.

'Well – goodbye, Sarah,' he said. 'It was lovely to see you again.'

Rather to his surprise, he realised he meant it.

'Yes, you too.' They both leaned in awkwardly for a kiss on the cheek, going the same way and muddling it. Sarah laughed.

'Look, Sarah,' Cathy interrupted the moment, 'perhaps you could give John a lift home? It's on your way. We'll be in trouble with the childminder as it is.'

It was very obvious. Sarah looked uncertainly at John. He could hardly say no.

'Sure,' he said. 'That is if you don't mind?'

She turned to unlock her zippy silver Golf GTI, parked alongside James's BMW. 'Fine. No problem.'

John said his own farewells; they both climbed in, and Sarah opened her window.

'Well – bye again,' she said to the Vennings. 'And thanks.'

John leaned across her. 'Yes, thanks once more. It was kind of you to organise it. Really.'

James and Cathy waved back, staying fixed in that position until the Golf had turned out of the car park.

'Childminder, eh?' said James, turning to his wife. 'I think we last had one of those about five years ago.'

Cathy got into their car with a smile of quiet satisfaction. She said nothing and didn't need to.

* * *

It was only a couple of miles back to the farm.

'Nice couple,' ventured John.

'Yes,' Sarah replied. 'They've been very good to me.'

He wanted to know how, and what about, but there wasn't time, and his gateway was fast approaching. Which raised a problem, he suddenly realised: should he ask her in or not? To his surprise, he recognised a feeling he hadn't had since university, when reflecting upon whether to ask a girl up to his room for coffee. They'd always seemed to get the wrong idea. Which was the right idea.

'Left just here, by the white gates,' he said, thinking that she probably wouldn't remember that he'd mentioned his move earlier. 'Tom's in the main house now.'

She said nothing and turned through the gateway.

'So… would you like…?'

It felt stilted and was. The car drew up.

'Erm, no, I don't think so, do you?' She was amused.

'Well, thank you for the lift.'

He got out of the car, shut the door and waved at her through the window. Sarah flashed a smile at him as she drove off, a genuine one, it seemed.

John unlocked the door, greeted the ever-loyal Barney and headed to the whisky bottle he kept in the kitchen: one of the few changes he'd instituted around the house since Jenny's death. He poured himself a decent measure.

'Hmm,' he said bemusedly and raised the glass to his dog.

'That was unexpected, Barney.'

CHAPTER TWO

The big, metallic blue Bentley Continental Flying Spur with blacked out windows swished up the three-hundred-yard gravelled drive, over the crest in the middle, and a sprawling mock Georgian mansion came into view. Neither were quite the trappings of a gentleman, but then Carl Barrow wasn't one.

The four-pillar portico, almost side-on to the left as the car approached, was much too big for the house, but Carl was a man large in every way; he had wanted it like that. Likewise with the huge drawing room, jutting off at an angle from the main house, with its French windows opening out from the side, which faced the car head-on as it approached the gravel turning circle – it was a completely different architectural style.

Sod what people thought; it was his money. Carl was out of the near-side rear door before the chauffeur had a chance to open it.

'Thanks, Woody,' he said to the crestfallen driver, who'd wanted to show what he'd learnt on that expensive course.

'No problem, boss. Glad it went well.' Carl nodded back.

From the other rear door, a third man joined them. At fifty, Frank Paton was a few years younger than Carl and of much slighter build. His hair was rather too dark, and he sported a thin pencil moustache. Carl had never bothered to conceal his greying hair; he just wore it in a tight crew cut these days. Frank looked natural in a dark suit, as solicitors tend to, though his brown shoes weren't quite the matching thing. His slim brief case completed the professional image.

Carl bounded up the steps to the elevated front door, with Frank a pace or so behind him. Woody drove around the house to the purpose-built five-berth garage at the back, where the Bentley lived between a Ferrari (red, obviously) and a grey Range Rover, also with blacked out windows. They all had matching personalised number plates, in sequence. There was a white Audi A5 convertible there too, which belonged to Carl's wife.

Cynthia was waiting in the hall. She was blonde, expensively dressed and heavily made-up, probably too much so for mid-morning in her own home, but she wanted to show her husband that she'd made an effort. At fifty-one, she still carried herself with the confidence of the busty swimwear model people sometimes said she'd been in her youth. Her mood was brittle.

'You got off, then?'

Cynthia looked her husband coolly in the eye, arms folded across her still spectacular chest. Carl was momentarily taken aback but glowered back at her. She pointedly did not offer herself for a kiss.

'I don't think that's quite how to put it, Cynthia,' said Frank, in patronising lawyerly fashion.

She paid him no heed, looking stubbornly at Carl, who held her gaze calmly.

'I'm innocent of all charges if that's what you mean. I thought you'd be pleased.'

She turned on her costly high heels without a word, her steps echoing loudly on the chequered mock marble floor till she vanished through the swing door. Beyond it, Frank knew that stairs led down to a huge, all-mod-cons kitchen. He could hear her muffled descent.

'Welcome home, mate,' he said, turning to his client with heavy irony.

Carl bridled, but Frank sensed his hurt. 'Silly cow. What does she think pays for all this?'

He gestured vaguely around. 'Come on. Let's have a bottle of bubbly; it's been a good day.'

Carl went off to find one. Frank waited contentedly in the sunshine on the terrace at the back of the house, overlooking extensive lawns. When he returned a couple of minutes later, Carl was grumbling about it being the maid's day off and having to do everything himself if he ever wanted anything done.

Frank put on what he hoped was a sympathetic expression but was pleased to see that Carl held a cold bottle of Taittinger (vintage, of course) rather than anything cheap, plus two glasses. He flattered himself on being a bit of a connoisseur these days.

Carl opened the champagne expertly and poured.

'Cheers, old mucker,' he said, raising his glass. 'And thanks.'

They both took a more than genteel sip. Carl poured again.

'Well, it's certainly the result we wanted,' replied the lawyer, smugly.

Frank basked in Carl's gratitude. A man like him needed a canny legal adviser without too many scruples and paid well when he found one. His client smiled in agreement for a moment, then his face darkened.

'Yes. Lot of crap aired in court though,' he said and looked up expectantly.

Frank pursed his lips before replying. It was true. Whatever the legal technicalities, his client had certainly not emerged from the trial with his good name untarnished. Not that he had a good name.

'Might be an issue there.' He looked at Carl and took another sip. 'I was going to leave it until tomorrow, give you a chance to celebrate the acquittal.'

Carl hadn't got where he was by avoiding problems. He dealt with them, and the sooner the better.

'Go on.'

He waited calmly as Frank gathered his thoughts.

'You remember we had that *Panorama* crew nosing about last year?'

Carl nodded. 'Sure, wanted to interview me. Told them to piss off, didn't you?'

Frank winced. 'In so many words, yes. But we know they're still digging. And they're contacting a few inconvenient people.'

Carl raised his eyebrows. 'Who?'

He refreshed his glass again, the end of the bottle. There was none left for Frank.

'Jimmy Laing, for one,' said Frank.

Jimmy Laing ran a rival operation, largely based south of

the river, whereas Carl's main interests were in North London. There was an uneasy truce between them, and even occasional cooperation, though either would exploit any weakness in the other if it became apparent.

'Jimmy won't talk,' said Carl decisively, after a pause to reflect.

'No, he won't,' said Frank. 'He doesn't like the attention. But others might – anonymously perhaps.'

Carl paused to think again and drained his glass.

'Can't you get an injunction or something? Tell them to lay off? I'm an innocent man, after all.'

The irony of using the law in his defence was lost on him.

Frank shook his head.

'Free speech at this stage. We might be able to do something afterwards, depending on what they say, but that's dangerous territory. My guys reckon they've got a lot of film already in the can and only need to shoot a suitable ending after the verdict. The acquittal makes it worse.'

'How?' said Carl.

Frank smiled thinly. 'Guilty bastard goes to jail isn't much of a story. Guilty bastard gets off is.'

Carl got that; he was no fool. 'So, they'll make it. When?'

'Whilst it's still topical,' said Frank. 'They'll probably air the programme within a week.'

* * *

Cynthia sat alone in the big kitchen with a glass of wine, her second; she'd already fortified herself before Carl returned. With shaking hands, she lit a cigarette; she was supposed to have given up, but if today didn't justify one nothing would.

14

She'd been sure he'd be found guilty – damn it, he *was* guilty! And if he had been, he'd have been put away for a long time: five years at least. That would have been her moment to get out, and she had her reasons, which Carl understood full well. Family reasons.

And now?

She stood up and looked at herself in the mirror critically. A little thicker around the waist perhaps than she'd been before the children, but still a figure to make a cardinal kick in a stained-glass window, as Carl had once memorably put it.

Good Catholic stock, the Barrows; notionally Carl still was, in deference to his formidable Irish mother.

Cynthia raised a glass to her reflection, exhaled and turned away. Time for a rethink.

* * *

In the evening Cynthia fed Carl a TV supper in the den off the kitchen and turned quickly on her heel without a word. Football – his beloved West Ham. They seemed to be losing again, judging from the language floating through to the kitchen. She'd said nothing to him since the morning.

'Thanks, love, looks great,' he called after her, eyes still on the screen.

He was trying to make up. She knew where that was going.

Cynthia went early to bed and watched a romantic film there – not a very good one, as it turned out. Her husband came up within the hour, predictable as ever. She listened to his footsteps on the stairs and braced herself. It was no later than 10pm.

Carl's head came round the door, with that smile she knew so well. Once it had charmed her. She knew now that it was just a tool he used whenever he needed it, and since the scales had dropped from her eyes it had entirely lost its effect.

'It's nice to be home, doll,' he said softly.

Cynthia stayed focused on her uninspiring film, propped half up in bed, though she wasn't taking it in. She suddenly realised that it might have been wise to have chosen a less revealing nightdress. Too late. Carl moved round and sat on her side of the bed.

'Why don't you turn that rubbish off?' He took her hand in his. She pulled it away irritably.

'Because I'm watching it.'

'Come on,' he was wheedling now, moving in to nuzzle her neck.

'Carl – no.' She pulled herself away forcefully and stared at him in defiance.

'This is my bed.' Not so charming now, indignant.

'Spare room's made up.'

'You're my wife.'

Cynthia said nothing and fixed her eyes on the screen. If she stood her ground, he wouldn't force her; she knew that.

'Oh, screw you,' Carl said, pushing up from the bed and heading for the door.

'That's one thing you won't be doing,' Cynthia shouted after him.

The door slammed. She was pleased with her quick reply and aware of her heightened heartbeat.

She listened carefully in case he'd paused outside the door, but his steps thumped heavily down the passage.

Cynthia dozed briefly, but all too soon she was wide awake, adrenaline still coursing through her body. Her main worry was what the children would think when she left – if she ever did.

They were all so different.

She was least worried about the youngest, Robert (or Bob, as Carl insisted on calling him). Like the others, he'd been privately educated, but he'd seen how his older brother in particular had struggled to relate to fellow pupils who were more naturally privileged. Somehow, Robert had been better at it and made the most of his opportunities. He was naturally bright and got into Durham University (a long way from Hertfordshire – probably no coincidence). Now twenty-four, he seemed to be heading for an academic career, specialising in astrophysics. He seldom came home, and when he did, she found him hard to talk to, though there was still a strong mother-son bond. Robert had little time for his father, and Carl simply didn't understand the world his youngest son now moved in; like herself, Cynthia thought he was probably a bit intimidated by the boy's intellect. She was certain she could rely on Robert's support, albeit from a distance.

Mary was a daddy's girl, and Carl spoiled her shamelessly; he'd even insisted on naming her after his old boot of a mother, now thankfully dead. The name was all Cynthia's daughter and her mother-in-law had in common. She'd boarded privately at a famous girls' school and could pass for the upper-middle-class Sloane type it specialised in producing, though Cynthia noticed that the accent slipped easily when she was joshing around with Carl, as she often did. Mary had never brought friends home from school, though had been quick to take up the many invitations to glamorous places she'd received. As far as Cynthia could see, she'd done very little at Bristol University except party. However, with her mother's figure, and an easy social manner, she'd waltzed straight into a well-paid City PA job at the age of twenty-two. Four years later, she had graduated to a management consultancy role in the same firm. Cynthia found this astounding; she had never met a more disorganised person in her life than her daughter, though perhaps she just kept that for home. Carl paid a steep mortgage on the flat he'd bought for Mary ("Mags") in Fulham and gave her a generous allowance on top of her salary. There was the little Mazda sports car too, with its personalised family plate. Mary would know which side her bread was buttered if push came to shove, thought Cynthia.

Then the eldest, David – "Davey" to his father – the enigma. He had gone to university too, the first on either side of his family to do so, but nearby in Essex. He'd read Accountancy. Carl approved: 'Understand money and you'll make money,' he'd said. Cynthia had hoped David would then embark on a conventional professional career, and he could look and sound the part when he wanted to. But all he had ever wanted to do was to work with Carl, and he'd never made close friends from different worlds at school or university, unlike Robert and Mary. It made Cynthia cringe to see how David had initially tried so hard to fit in with the characters who surrounded his father: the laddish behaviour; the swearing; the affected East End accent. It had brought him nothing but barely concealed contempt, tolerated only because he was the boss's son. With his education, he'd always been an outsider in that world, but Cynthia could also see

18

that over the last few years, her older son had begun to use that trained brain and to recognise that he could help Carl in other ways. He'd always been an affectionate and dutiful son to her. Hard to know which way he would go. He was thirty-one now. Cynthia had been over a decade younger when she'd had him.

She drifted off. By 5am, as dawn broke, she was wide awake again, staring at the ceiling.

Cynthia reached a decision suddenly, took her mobile from its charge lead and sent a short text. The reply came within a minute, despite the earliness of the hour. She rose swiftly from her bed.

It took her only five minutes to dress and another ten to pack two cases: clothes, jewellery, bathroom things.

By 5.45am the white Audi was heading down the drive. She left no note.

CHAPTER THREE

John finished tapping on his mobile and looked critically at the result. Third attempt and not much better than the others.

'Pathetic. How old are you?' he muttered to himself. 'Seventeen?'

He changed from text to voice and made the call quickly, before he could change his mind. Cathy had been happy (very happy) to give him the number. Maybe she'd told Sarah he'd asked for it, he thought in a flash of panic. Maybe they'd laughed together about it…

'Hello?'

Sarah answered after a couple of rings, sounding cheerful. John had begun half hoping that it would go to voicemail.

'Er – Sarah,' John said. 'It's John Gault.' He paused.

'Hello, John.' She sounded surprised but not displeased. 'Yes?'

'I hope you don't mind me calling…'

'Not at all. Why should I?'

Get on with it, thought John. 'I was wondering…'

'What were you wondering?' said Sarah, deadpan.

It's a hell of a long time since I've done this, thought John. 'Well, the thing is, if you're not doing anything else on Saturday, I wondered if you'd like a spot of lunch?'

There, he'd said it.

'That would be lovely.' He'd dreaded a feeble excuse, but she sounded pleased. His heart jumped.

'Where?' Fair question. Don't act dumbstruck.

'Oh – here. Forecast's good.'

'Al fresco, then. Just us?'

'Yes, I thought so.' John gritted his teeth and waited for the response. Moment of truth.

'Can you cook?' No backtracking. She sounded almost playful.

'I manage,' he replied.

'I'm sure you do. When?'

'Oh, er – say about twelve-thirty,' said John. Dead casual.

'Twelve-thirty it is,' said Sarah. 'I look forward to it.'

'Me too.' said John. That'll do for now, don't over-egg it.

'OK – see you then. Thanks. Bye.'

She sounded completely natural. John had never felt more inarticulate in his life.

'Bye.'

She rang off. Turning to Barney, John blew out his cheeks in relief.

Who'd want to be young again? Much too stressful.

* * *

Why the hell had he told her he could cook? That had been John's second thought, about two seconds after his initial elation.

He was by no means hopeless, but nor was he a culinary master because he'd never needed to be – Jenny had covered that aspect of their lives very well, and unlike him she had been genuinely interested in food. John had just been the beneficiary. He had survived well enough since her death but knew that there had been too many ready meals.

Several menu plans were made, and just as quickly discarded, over the few days before Saturday, but the weather came to his rescue: it would stay fine, as forecast.

So, he'd got away with a salad. He cheated a bit, with a quick foray to Waitrose to make it appear a little more sophisticated than it actually was, but it didn't look bad, he thought. He'd laid a table in the garden and would serve the meal from the kitchen, after a glass of Pimms or something soft, if she wasn't going to drink at all. He hoped she would. The house was as tidy as an outdoors man like John could make it; he knew that he'd let things slip a bit over the last two months.

He felt nervous, an unfamiliar sensation for such a level-headed man. It was anticipation, like the end of term at school. Saturday arrived just about as slowly.

But now it was here, and the weather was beautiful.

He was ready far too early and treated himself to a large Pimms whilst he waited. She didn't fall through the door at 12.30pm but then nobody arrives dead on time except Americans, he told himself, so his momentary concern that she'd forgotten was unmerited.

Barney sensed John's odd mood and watched warily from his basket by the Aga.

The spaniel had better hearing than John and was on his feet with a protective bark before his master had heard the car at all. Then the obvious scrunch of gravel through the open window. Better beat her to the door, thought John.

Sarah was casually chic, but John knew that such a look involved a lot of preparation; Jenny had been good at it too. Her smile was open and genuine as she emerged from the Golf. He felt flattered that she had made such an effort, and Sarah offered herself easily for a peck on the cheek. Barney fussed around her bare legs, welcoming her, and she ruffled his ears.

It was going to be fine, thought John.

* * *

And it was. She took a glass of Pimms before moving on to lemonade and complimented John's salad, even helping herself to seconds. Conversation was light-hearted, easy and general: John steered clear of Peter, and Sarah didn't bring up Jenny. Those things could wait.

He learnt that she was freelancing as an interior designer and that it was going well after a slow start. She'd bought a little cottage outside Ingatestone, practised on that first and was pleased with the result. He should come and see it sometime. Yes please, he thought.

After the meal he fetched them both coffees, and they sat in the sun in companionable silence.

'Any progress on the great novel?' Sarah's tone was slightly teasing.

'No, of course not,' John grinned, slightly embarrassed. 'It's just a pipe dream I mentioned to James once when I was in my cups.'

'No reason it should be,' said Sarah. 'Seriously. You just have to be disciplined.'

'Ah yes – "a writer is someone who writes", as the saying goes,' said John. 'I wonder how many abandoned novels there are in the world?'

Sarah smiled but stuck to her guns. 'You also need an idea.'

John made no comment. She looked at him expectantly. 'Have you got one?'

'Not really,' said John defensively. 'Perhaps… sort of.'

'And?'

Her enquiring eyes were very big and very grey, he thought.

'It would be a murder mystery…' John began lamely when the pause became unnatural. Sarah said nothing, waiting for more. 'The perfect murder.'

'Is that as far as you've got?' she said.

'Sorry,' John replied, feeling rather inadequate.

Sarah shook her head impatiently and pursed her lips in thought. She looked delightful, thought John.

'Tell you what,' she said after a few seconds.

John looked at her quizzically.

'Next Sunday: return match. Have lunch with me.'

His heart leapt. 'Well – great—'

'On one condition.' She looked at him, challenge in her gaze.

'Which is?'

'You think it through before then. Outline the story to me when you come.'

'Really?' John replied humorously, thinking she was teasing. The gaze never faltered. She wasn't teasing.

'OK,' he said helplessly. 'You win.'

They were out by Sarah's car, saying their goodbyes, when a battered Land Rover swept through the gate. It was John's old one.

'Tom and Emma,' John said quietly.

John's only child was smiling broadly, Emma prim as ever by his side. He couldn't quite disguise his surprise when he saw Sarah, but the smile stayed in place.

'Hi, Dad,' he said cheerfully, as he stepped out of the vehicle, tall and strong. He looked enquiringly at Sarah. Emma followed, blonde and petite in her jeans, giving a little wave.

'Tom – you remember Sarah Hall?' he said. 'Used to live in the village till a few years ago.'

With her husband, he thought and hoped Tom wouldn't put his foot in it.

'Of course. What brings you over here, Sarah?' he said, offering his hand.

'Oh – just lunch,' Sarah smiled. 'Such a lovely day.' There was a slight pause.

'Great.'

Tom was still smiling but with a hint of uncertainty. John sensed it and wondered if Sarah had too. Emma looked like a schoolgirl; she shook hands shyly with Sarah.

'Well, I'm just off,' said Sarah. 'Thank you so much again, John.'

She didn't make any reference to next week. Probably just as well, thought John.

She kissed him lightly on the cheek and got into the car. The others waved after she had reversed the Golf round and started towards the gate. Sarah gave a little flutter of her hand and a happy grin in response.

John looked expectantly at the young couple. They'd obviously come for a reason.

'Well,' said Tom after a moment. 'Emma…'

His wife dived back into the Land Rover and produced a bottle of champagne.

'We've got some news,' Tom announced proudly. Emma blushed and dropped her gaze, smiling.

John waited. 'The thing is…' began Tom.

'I'm pregnant,' interrupted Emma. Her delight was obvious; she paused for John's reaction as she reached for Tom's hand. He was touched that she cared so much what it would be.

'Well, that's wonderful news, really wonderful,' said John and meant it. He clapped his son on the shoulder and opened his arms to his daughter-in-law.

'Come here.'

Emma allowed herself to be enveloped by him. Such a tiny, pretty little thing, John thought, not for the first time. She'd seemed so diffident when Tom first brought her home early on in his university days, and neither he nor Jenny had expected it to last, Tom being such an extrovert. But it had. They'd married a year ago. He sometimes wondered whether they'd brought it forward so that Jenny could attend.

John had grown to appreciate Emma's calming influence on his sometimes-headstrong son. She had no country background but was proving to be a surprisingly adept farmer's wife. John still found her shy manner hard to penetrate, but he'd become genuinely fond of his son's choice. She'd been a quiet pillar of strength and sympathy in Jenny's last days.

'Break it up,' said Tom happily. 'The bottle's getting warm.'

They went through the house out to the garden, where the remains of John's lunch with Sarah had yet to be cleared away. John cleared it on a tray and saw them whispering together conspiratorially as he returned with three glasses. They went quiet as he appeared.

He might have imagined it, but the last thing he thought he heard was "too soon".

CHAPTER FOUR

Frank got out of his Jaguar resignedly. He wasn't used to being back at Carl's beck and call. The man who paid him so well had been locked up on remand for well over a month before the trial. People charged with offences like Carl's didn't get bail, especially if they were considered a flight risk.

He ascended the steps under the outsize portico and looked carefully through the upper half glass panes of the expensive panelled white door. Nothing.

'Come straight in,' Carl had said on the phone, but Frank had a healthy respect for Cynthia's territory. He couldn't see a bell. The door opened when he tried the gold handle after a tentative knock.

'Hello,' Frank called cautiously.

'In here, mate,' shouted Carl's muffled voice from the kitchen.

Frank went through the swing door, across the hall and down the stairs. The kitchen was a mess. Carl had just finished a fry up. Frank knew he wasn't used to self-cooking and raised his eyebrows slightly in surprise.

'Cynthia?' he asked.

Carl was pouring them both big mugs of coffee – instant, Frank noticed, though there was an expensive filter machine on the sideboard.

'Not here,' said Carl, handing over one of the mugs. Frank said nothing but looked at him. 'Come on through.'

He led Frank down the side passage to the big drawing room, with its French windows onto the gravel outside, and indicated that the lawyer should take a seat. Then he settled back himself on the sofa.

'Well – she's gone,' Carl continued. He paused to see how Frank reacted. 'Just for a bit.'

'Where?' said Frank. He was at a loss. Carl and Cynthia had had a few ups and downs, certainly, but at heart he'd always thought their marriage rock solid.

'God knows,' shrugged the man opposite, seemingly dismissively, though Frank wasn't altogether fooled. 'She'll be back.'

Carl clearly didn't want to talk about it. Frank sipped his coffee and waited to see what he did want to talk about. It wasn't long in coming.

'Where are we?' said Carl. 'I want to know.'

Frank knew that Carl meant legally; if money had been the issue, he'd be talking to his long-term bookkeeper Paul Liles or, increasingly these days, to his accountant son David. He had fingers in a lot of pies (or "many interests"), and some of those businesses had more trouble with the law than others.

They spoke for over an hour. On balance, Frank thought that things were broadly under control, though one of the clubs was facing a prostitution charge. No big deal.

'But,' said Carl. Nothing else was necessary.

'Yes – *Panorama*,' Frank replied. 'That could change things.'

Carl was calm. He finished his third coffee.

'We'll just have to watch it then, won't we?' he said.

After he had showed Frank out, Carl went back to the kitchen and checked his mobile phone again. Nothing.

He called Cynthia, and there was still no answer. He sent a text, the third since she'd left. No reply.

A grimace and a sigh, no need to keep up a pretence when he was by himself.

Carl missed his wife.

* * *

Cynthia heard the text arrive and looked at it briefly before returning the phone to her handbag and lighting a cigarette. He was certainly persistent, but she'd known that since the first time he'd clapped eyes on her.

She was at her older sister Marnie's, in deepest East Sussex, a long way from Hertfordshire. Carl well knew that she wouldn't go to her younger one, who was much nearer.

Marnie had been fine and told her to come straight down when she texted, as Cynthia knew she would. She'd arrived by mid-morning and been given a comfortable room in the Old Rectory, overlooking the back lawn and its well-manicured flower beds. She was resting on the bed now, shoes kicked off, whilst Marnie went shopping for more food. The problem, she thought grimly, would be Marnie's husband Clive, who wasn't back yet.

Clive had the sort of ingrained self-importance that comes of a minor public-school education, coupled with a mid-level role in the City which wasn't quite as senior as he implied. Marnie had supposedly "bettered" herself when she'd married him, or so he always seemed to infer.

Cynthia thought that being the insipid prat he was, Clive had got a pretty good deal in Marnie: a sweet, kind nature and overly deferential to his many whims. She'd even assented to calling their boys Tarquin and Cassius, which was probably why both of them had emigrated. Plus, Marnie had a figure not much less impressive than her own, mused Cynthia, though she had never made the same good use of it.

The thought of Clive's pomposity still riled Cynthia: married to her sister for all of two years when she had first got involved with Carl, and warning her about "chaps like that". As if he'd ever seen anything of real life. Besides, she'd been pregnant with David by then.

Clive had got back in his box pretty quickly when he met Carl face to face. Cynthia smiled briefly at the memory and the contrast in raw masculinity.

But he'd been right, albeit for the wrong reasons, and now he was going to gloat about it.

People like him always did. What a tosser, she thought.

* * *

'OK, Dad, OK. I'll do it.'

David put the phone down and paused for thought. After a few seconds he thumped the desk in frustration, spilling his coffee. He swore crudely and automatically. One of those days.

His father was asking financially illiterate questions and insisting on answers. All he cared about was cash. If one business generated £10,000 a month and another £20,000, then Carl would give whoever ran the second one more credit, even if he (it was never a she) had used four times the resources to generate the money.

David knew that the secret to good business performance was profit relative to cost: margin. In the weeks that Carl had been away on remand he'd made good progress in putting his father's business interests on a more professional financial footing and had looked forward to explaining the benefits of that approach. But he knew he'd need parental backing to bring round some of the dinosaurs. There were plenty of those.

The trouble was, Carl was the biggest dinosaur of all, David reflected ruefully. If he would only listen it would be so easy to become more profitable.

He stood up with a sigh of frustration and looked out of the window of his anonymous Chelmsford office into the drizzle. His reflection stared back at him. He was much less heavily built than his father; that was from Cynthia, as were the delicate good looks and the blond hair. He decided glumly that it was probably time for the thin moustache to go.

He'd never make his mark in the firm as muscle, David knew that now, and though he admired the machismo of some of the toughs, he wasn't one of them. It would be a waste of his education anyway.

No: finance was where he'd make his contribution. If Carl ever allowed him to.

* * *

Carl was restless, worried and lonely, though he'd never admit that to anyone but himself. He poured himself another stiff Scotch and reflected on his day.

His business empire seemed to have got along fine without him, which was galling. He'd visited a couple of places, just to make sure they knew who was boss, and they wouldn't forget it; few people did when Carl came in looking serious with Woody and Bill the Boatman.

He wondered idly where Bill's nickname came from. Best not to know.

He'd sharpened up Davey too. The boy had all sorts of ideas, but cash was king, and that simple belief had got Carl to where he was. His people understood it. Maybe there was a place in time for all those new ideas, but for now Davey had to learn how the business worked, show a little humility and respect.

But most of all, his thoughts drifted mournfully to Cynthia. She'd been eighteen when he first saw her in an amateur beauty contest in Southend, whilst on a weekend trip with his two brothers. He was twenty-three. She'd been on a school leavers trip and had entered for a dare. In the far off 1980s, a beauty contest was all bikinis, no politically correct rubbish preventing you from getting a good eyeful. Cynthia and bikinis were a match made in heaven. What he'd liked almost as much was the shy schoolgirl smile topping the spectacular body. Girl hadn't known what she'd got.

Carl had been instantly smitten. He'd learnt a phrase since – "coup de foudre". It was like that. Those Frogs know a bit about love, don't they? he'd thought when he heard it.

Terry and Jack had teased him mercilessly, but he'd never wavered. He'd sent an astonished Terry off to buy flowers immediately and done the stage door Johnny act, as if it was the West End. Cynthia had been surprised and a bit intimidated by this flash wide boy but clearly flattered. By the time he went back to the East End on Sunday night he had her phone number. Cynthia lived with her parents in Enfield – it wasn't far.

When Carl made a decision, he was absolutely single-minded; his courtship of Cynthia was an early demonstration of the trait which would bring him so much success. She had a boyfriend of sorts from her school days, but he'd taken one look at Carl and decided not to make an issue of it. If Cynthia had been disappointed, then she'd hidden it well. And Carl had charm, lots of it. He could make her laugh.

When he'd finally coaxed her into bed – and she'd taken some coaxing – it was even better than Carl had dreamed of, and after that she'd been as enthusiastic as he was. She was the one.

It hadn't been easy. Cynthia's parents were both schoolteachers and suspicious of this cocky young man who had no obvious source of income but seemed increasingly prosperous. The eldest of their three daughters, Marnie, had married someone respectable in the City. They wanted no less for their second.

Carl had always been confident that he'd win them round, but he hadn't had to – the pregnancy had seen to that. Respectability was indeed their watchword. Once Cynthia's parents knew, they couldn't get their middle daughter up the aisle fast enough. Carl had been as surprised as they were, as he and Cynthia were being careful. He sometimes wondered whether she'd let it happen deliberately, just to break the logjam. She could be pretty tough when she felt she had to be, as he well knew.

After their marriage it had been plain sailing: Cynthia had become a traditional wife, who kept a good home, and brought up their three children. She didn't involve herself in his business, and he didn't tell her, though she must surely have wondered where all the money for the house, the private education, the cars and the holidays came from.

He'd treated her like a queen and been entirely faithful, apart from that one time at the opening of a new club. The girl had even looked like Cynthia. He'd been drunk, and it hadn't been satisfactory – plus he'd felt guilty for weeks, which was not an emotion Carl was used to. He'd given Cynthia a mink coat and still worried about who knew, but nothing had ever come of it.

Now, after nearly thirty-two years of marriage, his loyal Cynthia had frozen him out completely after that unfortunate business about fifteen months ago.

Following his time on remand, Carl had convinced himself that they would make a fresh start and put it all behind them. Instead, she'd just left.

Never normally uncertain when there was a decision to be made, now he was.

Carl had no idea how to get her back.

CHAPTER FIVE

Thursday was a difficult day.

John prevaricated as long as he could: he did some shopping, which could perfectly well have waited; booked a service for his car; walked Barney; and then went round to the farm to see if there was anything he could do to help.

Tom was out somewhere, and though Emma gave him a cup of coffee, and was welcoming enough, it was perfectly obvious that she had things to be getting on with. After an unnecessarily protracted lunch at home, he was flat out of excuses.

He had until Saturday to come up with a plan for his novel, or he would have to face Sarah the next day without one. She would regard that as a pretty feeble effort. So, no option.

John sighed resignedly and opened his laptop, which seemed to be the right thing to do. Now what?

He sat back and gave it some serious thought for the first time: a perfect murder. What would that entail? He started tapping away but soon gave up in favour of a notebook.

It took John a couple of hours, and a lot of false starts, to come up with what was actually quite a short list. He sat back and looked at it critically. Then he typed it up and printed it. In principle at least, that was "how".

As to who and why, the gory details and the rest of it, after venturing down a few blind alleys over the rest of the week, he still didn't really know. However, he thought he'd done enough by Friday to convince Sarah that he wasn't winging it – that was the main thing.

Maybe she could even help.

* * *

Tom's trip had been to see his accountant. He was tired and flat when he got home.

Emma asked how it had all gone, and he summarised, without detail or enthusiasm.

"OK" seemed to be the gist of it, she thought, though they'd have to keep a tight watch on spending. The mantra of farmers everywhere: perennially glass half empty.

'And how was your day, darling?' said Tom once she'd got him settled with some tea and toast. 'Nothing too strenuous, I hope?'

Emma was getting rather irked by Tom's excessive concern but reminded herself that this was his first pregnancy too. It was actually rather sweet.

'Nothing special,' she replied. 'John came over this morning.'

'What for?' asked Tom, surprised.

Emma shrugged. 'Nothing really. Wanted to know if you needed a hand. I think he's at a bit of a loose end. He just had a coffee and went once he found out you weren't here.'

Tom pursed his lips. He loved his father but wanted to run the farm his way; they'd had that discussion when John had handed it over. He hoped that they wouldn't have to revisit it.

'No mention of you-know-who?' he said. John's unexpected lunch guest had become a bit of a topic between them in the few days since.

'No,' said Emma. 'I think it was just that: lunch.'

Tom had nothing against Sarah but hadn't liked seeing John with another woman so soon after his mother's death – especially such an attractive one.

He chewed on his toast glumly and said nothing.

* * *

There was no contact from Sarah all week, other than a brief postcard of thanks. It didn't mention the lunch invitation, so on Friday John thought that he'd better check.

After much deliberation, he sent her a simple text: "Sunday: 12.30 OK?".

She replied within a minute: "Sure".

John responded: "Looking forward to it". He left it at that – don't appear too keen, he thought.

Though he was keen, he admitted to himself. The timing wasn't great, as Tom's reaction had shown, but how many more chances would he get at fifty-five? Sarah was here; she was apparently single; she was definitely attractive; and they liked each other. One step at a time, definitely, but he intended to see where those steps led.

John took considerable care with his appearance before he left on Sunday, much more than he'd done in Jenny's days but then she'd always been there as the style police when necessary, and he'd never argued. He'd even had a haircut mid-week.

He looked at the result critically in the mirror: he was still slim, fit and ruddily tanned from his active life on the farm; only the increasingly dappled brown hair betrayed his middle age, and at least he still had it. His off-white chinos were clean and pressed, the blue shirt was properly ironed and he was wearing the smart new loafers which Jenny had bought him on their final holiday instead of his battered old favourites.

He hoped that she would have wished him luck, nodded approvingly to himself and headed out to her little blue Fiat 500. He hadn't been able to bring himself to sell it and used it most of the time these days. Even that had been through the car wash.

Satnav did its thing, and John got there as he intended at about 12.40pm – the polite ten minutes late. It was a sweet little thatched white cottage, just outside the village, seemingly very old but in excellent repair. He pulled up behind Sarah's Golf on the short gravel drive, and she appeared smiling in the doorway as he got out of his car.

She'd also clearly made an effort. The result was sufficiently distracting that John nearly forgot his box of chocolates and had to dive back into the Fiat to get it. It was another fine day, and Sarah wore knee-length shorts, which showed off her brown legs to advantage. Her curly, shoulder-length auburn hair was newly tinted, if John wasn't mistaken.

'Hi,' said John, as Sarah leaned in for a peck.

'Hi,' she smiled. 'Snap!'

She indicated their clothes with a wave of her hands: the same colour scheme exactly.

John grinned as he handed over the chocolates and followed her inside. Good omen.

'Welcome to my lair,' said Sarah, indicating around expressively. 'I'll fix us a drink.'

John looked approvingly around the small entrance hall as Sarah headed off into the kitchen. The cottage was a lot bigger inside than it seemed. Nice minimalist style, pale colours, a few small but high-quality paintings. Tasteful.

'Come on through,' Sarah called.

The kitchen was modern and open-plan, again with pale colours. Sarah was pouring champagne on the other side of the central island – proper stuff too, John noted. Lanson.

'Thanks,' he said, accepting a glass. He gestured around. 'This is great.'

Sarah looked pleased, even a bit proud.

'Well, it's taken a while,' she said modestly. 'But I think I'm about there now. I must think of something else to keep busy.'

They had a couple of glasses apiece and chatted away easily as Sarah fussed around her final preparations for the meal: roast chicken. She carved easily, and very capably, before ushering John through to the small glass-roofed lounge off the kitchen, where she'd laid a table for two. Again, John could see that'd she'd spent some time preparing for his visit.

Conversation was free-flowing and light-hearted: no awkward pauses, which John was relieved about. He'd never thought of himself as particularly articulate.

They'd finished the chicken, and were settling down to apple tart, when Sarah paused.

'Now,' she said meaningfully. John raised a wary eyebrow.

'You know,' she said. 'Don't be a tease.'

John sighed good humouredly. 'It may surprise you to know that I've made quite a bit of progress,' he said.

Sarah waited. 'Go on.'

'Well, I can tell you how to commit a perfect murder. I've thought that through. Around that I've got to build a plot.'

'OK,' said Sarah, cautiously.

John thought her gaze was most distracting. He made a meal out of retrieving the typed list from his pocket. She raised her eyes to the heavens.

'First thing.' The cool gaze was back on him. John looked at his list.

'Kill someone you don't know.'

'Why would anyone do that?' Sarah said.

'Leave that for the moment. Most murders are domestics. They aren't difficult to solve. If you kill someone you've never been in touch with – no emails; no texts; no letters – then you've got a much better chance of getting away with a clean kill.'

'But no motive.' Sarah spread her hands wide; she seemed genuinely interested.

'Sure, got to solve that,' said John. 'Maybe someone with a lot of known enemies.'

Sarah thought for a moment and nodded. 'Next.'

'Forensic awareness: shoes, tyres, fingerprints, DNA, blood, ballistics.' John counted them off on his fingers.

'How do you get round all that?' Sarah said.

'Well again, I've got to think it through,' replied John. 'Maybe pick a spot likely to have DNA from lots of people. Don't use a method that is going to get you covered in blood.'

He paused and shrugged.

'Plenty to think about,' mused Sarah. 'Electronics, I think that would be a big thing.'

John looked at her enquiringly. 'So, say.'

Sarah sized him up to see if he was being serious. He was.

'Well,' she said, 'mobile phones for instance.'

John waited for her to elaborate.

'You can't call your victim because it can be traced. Same with a landline.'

Sarah looked at him for approval.

'And your location can be pinpointed from your mobile too,' she added.

'Right,' nodded John. 'So, for everything you need to do, use a pay-as-you-go phone. And get rid of it.'

'Or a phone box,' added Sarah. 'If you can find one.'

'You've been thinking about this,' said John, both amused and pleased. 'What else?'

Sarah was reassured now she knew he wasn't going to tease her.

'Cash,' she said. 'For anything to do with money. If you use plastic, again, you'll reveal where and when you spent it and what you bought.'

John smiled. 'That was on my list too,' he said. 'Here's something else.'

Sarah looked at him expectantly – they were getting into the swing of it now.

'Cars,' said John. 'Lots of problems there.'

Sarah waited for him to elaborate.

'Cameras,' said John. 'They'll pick up your number plates. You don't want your car seen somewhere you can't explain.'

Sarah was quick on the uptake. 'Or to put anything in its satnav which might be a giveaway, either.'

They both paused.

'Cameras can get you on foot, too,' John added.

Their discussion went on for another half hour, becoming increasingly animated and less self-conscious. John had thought of most of what came up, but some new points emerged as he talked through the details with Sarah. It gave him a second perspective. He jotted them down.

It was almost 5pm by the time he left. They were both happy and relaxed.

'One more thing about this,' said John, as he kissed Sarah on the cheek after thanking her.

Sarah looked at him enquiringly.

'I've got to decide who gets killed,' said John.

'And by whom,' added Sarah.

* * *

John was buzzing when he got home. He felt he'd established a real empathy with Sarah, much more so than he'd dared hope. It was a long time since he'd felt such euphoria.

He recognised the symptoms; it had been just like that in his early twenties when he'd first met Jenny. He simply hadn't expected to feel it again as a mature middle-aged man.

The ever-hungry Barney received his supper, after which John wandered aimlessly around his kitchen with a glass of wine, grinning to himself. After pouring himself a second, he pulled himself together with an effort: grow up, he thought.

Scrambled eggs later, he decided. Meanwhile, he'd scan the *Sunday Times* he hadn't had time to read that morning.

He skimmed most of the news section – economic gloom, bankruptcies, political snakes and ladders, some soap actress he'd never heard of whose third marriage had just ended after four months, another statue that had caused offence and would have to go – pretty standard fare, he thought.

Then he reached the *Insight* section. He always enjoyed those in-depth investigations.

It was a double-page spread, with a bold headline across both pages: *The Strange Acquittal of Mr Big*. It carried the byline: *Joel Baxter, Simon Savage and the Insight team.*

John had heard about the case in passing on the car radio earlier in the week but hadn't taken much notice. The man at the centre of the investigation glared out of the paper angrily as he got into a car, with a blurred hand trying to block out the photo from the left.

Not a nice guy, thought John.

He didn't really feel much like reading two solid pages of worthy investigative journalism but then realised he wouldn't have to. At the end of the piece was a small box: Justice in Jeopardy – *a joint Sunday Times Insight/BBC Panorama Investigation: 8pm today.*

John looked at his watch, dropped his paper and made for the cooker. Twenty minutes' time. That would do for his TV supper.

CHAPTER SIX

Carl hadn't been out at all that Sunday and hadn't bothered to call anyone.

He'd packed poor old Woody off home three days after his acquittal; there was only so much time he could spend polishing the cars given that he had no driving duties, and Carl was bored of him hanging around listlessly. Usually, the chauffeur was constantly on the road with Carl to visit one or other of his businesses or, less frequently, taking him to the Chelmsford head office where Davey worked.

The sense of foreboding built up all day. The damn *Insight* article had been bad enough, but prime-time TV was far more of a concern.

Generally, Carl never worried about things much, as he was a man of instinct and then action. But there was nothing he could do about *Panorama*, and he didn't like the sense of powerlessness – especially when he saw that the programme had a five-star review and was strongly recommended in his *Sunday Mail.*

After the papers, he watched TV from mid-afternoon,

flicking restlessly between the channels. West Ham lost, to bloody Tottenham, which didn't help his mood. At 6pm (not before, he was disciplined about that), he started on the whisky. He had two strong ones and then opened a bottle of red to go with the pizza he'd found in the deep freeze and heated up. By 8pm he was installed in front of the widescreen TV in his den, with the rest of the bottle. He pressed the record button on his remote and sat back.

Carl bridled at the BBC announcer's spiel:

And now Justice in Jeopardy*: sit back as* Panorama *takes a close look at someone believed by many to be one of Britain's biggest underworld figures and probes why he is still walking our streets.*

He swore quietly to himself as the well-known introductory music came to an end – a single, foul expletive.

The programme started with the media scrum on the courtroom steps after his acquittal earlier in the week: Frank leading him through the shouting journalists towards the waiting Bentley, repeating mechanically:

No comment... no comment.

Carl himself said nothing in the clip, and the screen froze when he was staring grimly into a TV camera as he got into the car. It was the same image as used by the *Sunday Times*. A female voiceover said:

This man is Carl Barrow.
This week he was acquitted at the Old Bailey of

money laundering. He has alleged links to racketeering, drug trafficking, murder, extortion, bribery, corruption, prostitution, bookmaking, smuggling, fraud, arms trafficking and theft. In the view of many, he is the biggest organised crime boss in Britain.

The shot cut to the female journalist, with the caption *Tina Downs.* Probably late thirties, thought Carl. Normal lefty BBC media type. Quite attractive if you like that scruffy look. Carl didn't. He jotted down the name in his phone. The voiceover continued:

Tonight we ask: who is this man, what is the scale of his activities and how is it that tonight he is sitting at home freely with his family?

That's your first error, you silly cow, thought Carl.

There followed ten minutes of background, this time with a male voiceover.

It wasn't inaccurate: born in Hackney in 1965, one of seven children in a family already on the edge of the criminal world. Carl's father, now dead, had been to prison for burglary and aggravated assault but had never been big time. Carl was the youngest of the four boys, one of whom had been killed as a teenager on a stolen motorbike. Boxing, scaffolding, scrap metal, car and lorry theft had taken him through the eighties.

However, although he'd been arrested six times, Carl had largely avoided being charged with anything or, when he was, being prosecuted. He was clever; he was careful; he was intimidating; he was tough; and he was a leader. He was a man going places.

That clean record had ended in 1991, when he had been charged with handling stolen goods. He was sentenced to nine months imprisonment, suspended for two years. It was his only ever conviction. One of the witnesses who testified against him had disappeared shortly thereafter. The reporter left the implication hanging.

Carl swore again in disgust. That toerag definitely had it coming and from several different directions. He had a pretty fair idea what had happened, but it was none of his doing.

There was a short, 1993 clip of him being interviewed, looking very young. Suit, tie, respectable, smart.

Carl had forgotten it and what it was about. He saw himself complaining, and sounding reasonable:

> *My good name is being abused by the police. I am yet again being falsely accused of criminality on no factual basis.*

The reporter replied:

> *Your reputation is that of a hard man.*

The younger Carl then said, meaningfully:

> *I have a reputation in my area as a man of my word, and as a businessman I expect others to stand by theirs, that is all. Ask anybody.*

The menace in his gaze was clear. It needed no comment from *Panorama*.

Frank was watching too, away from his wife Esme, in his study, which she knew was sacrosanct. He'd appeared in the opening *Panorama* sequence, which was once too many, and hoped he wouldn't again.

The programme continued its summary of Carl's past: involvement on the edges of a prostitution ring in the mid-nineties (he was just providing security at some clubs and knew nothing about it) and then the alleged brains behind an armed robbery, for which some of his known associates had been convicted. Again, Carl had not been charged. His growing prosperity was credited to his scrap metal business.

Frank grunted. It was all broadly true. He braced himself for what he knew was coming next.

In 1997 Carl had been arrested for brutally beating up a young reporter from *The Sun*, Tim Heath. Tim had been either brave or foolhardy enough to doorstep him about a recent knife assault, after which the victim (a known criminal) had refused to testify.

After an introductory voice piece by Tina Downs, explaining the background over a photo of the smiling Tim, there was another clip of Carl. This time, he was in a T-shirt outside a pub, apparently calm but clearly irritated by the reporters around him. He said, mildly:

I did not assault Mr Heath in any way. He was making house-to-house enquiries regarding a matter I know nothing about. I asked him to leave, and he did so. He made an untruthful complaint to the police about me. I have no idea why. It was all nonsense.

The clip led straight into *The Sun's* front page the next day.

I did not assault Mr Heath in any way! screamed the headline.

Beside it was a close-up of Tim's face, staring up from a hospital bed. He was not smiling this time. One eye was closed and the other blackened; there was a badly split lip and heavy bruising of his cheekbones. Tina Downs spoke to camera:

Tim Heath reported this assault to the police, who arrested Carl Barrow. They were confident of a conviction. However, Mr Heath decided not to testify.

The film cut to Tim Heath at home, older and heavier. A new interview for the programme, thought Frank. He hadn't seen it before. The former reporter was apologetic:

I withdrew the complaint, and declined to testify, because I'm not a hero.

Tina Downs responded with a short question, bringing an immediate reply:

Would you explain that further?

I discussed it with my wife, who was pregnant with our first child, and decided not to. I knew enough about Carl Barrow from my investigations up to that point to know that he was not a man to cross. Frankly, I was a bloody idiot to confront him like that. But when you're a young journalist, trying to make your name...

He tailed off with a shrug. Tina, in her "concerned" voice, then said:

So, it was definitely Carl Barrow who attacked you?

The response was definitive:

Oh yes. It was all over in about fifteen seconds. As soon as he opened the door, and I said I was from The Sun, he headbutted me straightaway – within a second, I should think – and knocked me down. Then he kicked me five or six times and told me it would be a lot worse if I ever came near his house again. Except he put it stronger than that.

Tim gave a rueful laugh.

There's not a day I don't think about it.

Frank sighed. He'd just begun getting involved around then. Carl was generally good at keeping a low profile, but he'd been careless that time, and the episode had been a worry.

But the boy Heath had seen sense. He hadn't even had to be asked.

* * *

The *Panorama* programme hadn't been mentioned in Marnie's household. Cynthia had cried off supper, pleading a headache, and gone to her room rather than face the possible embarrassment of seeing it with her hosts.

She knew that they'd watch it (or certainly Clive would), and the unspoken disapproval would hang around the house like a bad smell tomorrow.

Meanwhile, she had her iPad and her headphones. She was bathed and in bed in good time.

Cynthia was shaken by the Tim Heath clip but not entirely surprised. She hadn't been at home that evening and had accepted Carl's explanation that it was all a storm in a teacup at the time, but she had learnt more about the sort of man her husband was since then.

The programme was now focusing on Carl's rise, both personal and professional. Tina intoned:

Before the confrontation with Tim Heath, Carl Barrow seemed to be settling down. In 1988, he married Cynthia Taylor, swimwear-model daughter of respectable schoolteachers.

Nasty little inference, thought Cynthia. In fact, she'd only done two amateur swimwear shoots after the beauty contest in Southend, but *Panorama* had managed to dig up a picture from one of them. It left very little to the imagination. After that, Carl had persuaded her to stop. She did, however, occasionally still admit to being a "former model".

A second picture of her and Carl, surrounded by their ushers, flashed up as Tina spoke: the two remaining Barrow brothers (Terry as best man) and four others, all looking well oiled but happy. They were in traditional wedding attire. The one caught by the camera staring down her cleavage was long dead, and another had been in jail for over eight years now, with a fair stretch to go. That aside, it wasn't a bad photo. Her younger sister Bim was off to one side, smiling shyly; she was then only fourteen. Tina announced, archly:

Their first child, David, was born seven months later.

Cow, thought Cynthia.

They went on to have two more children. The marriage is reported to be stable, though Mrs Barrow is seldom seen in public.

Cynthia didn't react. Tina continued:

In 1998, shortly after the Heath episode, the Barrows moved from East London to their current house near Bishop's Stortford, in Hertfordshire, which Carl Barrow had built to a design of his own.

The aerial shot of the house was a recent one: it showed the landscaped gardens; the pool; the tennis court; the long gravel drive; and as luck would have it, Carl's red Ferrari, which was parked out in front of the house on the big gravel turning circle.

To this day, he has never explained how he paid for it.

Again, no accusation from the journalist, just inference.

Cynthia didn't know, either. She did know that a lot of hard work by her had gone into it.

The *Panorama* reporter continued to camera. Cynthia was startled to see that she was filming from outside the house gates.

One clue came in 2002, after the unexpected discovery of nearly fifty containers packed with high-value stolen goods, mainly, it seems, the proceeds of lorry thefts. Contents included whisky, electronic goods and washing machines. Another twenty containers contained counterfeit products from Asia. The police launched Operation Caligula to probe how such significant crimes had gone undetected, with the individuals behind them unprosecuted. It concluded that the answer was a mixture of corrupt police contacts and witness intimidation. There were strong suspected links back to Carl Barrow, but again, nobody could be found to testify against him.

A couple of unflattering black-and-white pictures of Carl scowling followed.

The film shifted to another interview. The interviewee's face was opaque and his voice disguised. *Former Detective*, said the caption. The unidentified man was replying to an unspoken question:

Well, it was extremely difficult. It was plain that Barrow and his associates – and we were sure it was them – were being tipped off about our investigation from within the Met, but even so, we were getting close. We had a criminal informant, and we kept the identity of that individual very secure.

Tina then asked:

So, what happened?

The man laughed mirthlessly.

He disappeared.

Tina leaned forward.

Can you say who he was?

The reply came:

It's common knowledge now who he was. It wasn't then, of course.

Tina waited for him to continue. The man spread his hands expressively.

He was a man called Martin Hart. Career criminal. Commonly known as Mart the Fart.

And... he was providing you and your colleagues with information?
Intelligence – yes. Very valuable criminal intelligence, in return for leniency regarding other matters.

Tina looked at him. Again, the man shrugged.

That's just the way it is sometimes. The world of informants and what motivates them is pretty murky.

The obvious question followed:

What do you think happened to him?

The former policeman replied:

I have no idea. But I am quite certain that he is dead.

After a suitably reflective pause, Tina continued:

What happened then?

We still reckoned we had the goods on Barrow. Then I was myself the subject of a corruption complaint.

Tina asked:

Were you corrupt?

The man replied firmly:

No. But the investigation took two years. It found that I had no case to answer, but it stopped the Barrow case in its tracks. As it was intended to. Those on the investigation who defended me against all this feared that they would be framed too.

Who made that allegation against you?

A former Police Officer, quite a senior one. He was investigated and allowed to resign.

Do you feel bitter about that?

Well, it cost me my career. I was tarnished goods after that. What do you think?

After a pause, Tina said:

So, you resigned.

It was a statement of fact, not a question. The man replied:

Eventually. I spoke to a journalist, off the record I thought. He published it. I told him that I was quite sure Carl Barrow was ultimately responsible for the disappearance of Hart and for the allegations against me.

Tina said nothing.

Well, as you can imagine, that didn't go down well, and I was hauled over the coals. Then another police informant let it be known that Carl Barrow had put a contract out on me.

A contract – on your life?

If she was acting appalled, then Tina was doing a good job. The man said:

Yes – £200,000. Lot of money. Someone would try it for that amount. That's when I decided it wasn't worth the candle. And why you can't show my face or where I live. I have a new identity now.

Cynthia hadn't heard all this before, though she'd known all about the probe into Carl at the time. It had just seemed to go away, as most of them did.

She gave a small noise of disapproval.

* * *

David watched the programme alone, at home in his flat. He didn't have a girlfriend. Or even many friends really – not proper ones, just people who knew whose son he was. He knew it.

The background up until the last ten years or so was interesting up to a point, because although he'd heard most of it anecdotally, David hadn't been personally involved then. His attention shifted up a gear when the story reached 2010 and beyond.

There was still plenty of the old stuff of course: a mass brawl involving a rival gang involved in drug distribution; a huge warehouse fire of uncertain origin followed by a dubious insurance claim; more witness intimidation; involvement in two alleged gangland murders. But nothing had stuck, and increasingly (David credited himself with this; bookkeeper Paul Liles was a dinosaur), there was altogether more financial sophistication about Carl's activities.

'Make money quietly.' That was David's mantra.

It had started with loans secured on very favourable terms from a successful former pornographer, who now aspired to a knighthood for his charitable activities. Carl had got involved in property development, and that was expensive. That the pornographer would lend to someone such as him hardly fitted the aspirational knight's new "respectable" image. It was alleged by the programme, with due circumspection (its lawyers had clearly vetted the commentary), that Carl had exercised some sort of hold over his lender. But again, nothing had ever been proved. David smiled.

And so, the Channel Islands. In 2015, a man called Freddie Pyper had been convicted under the 2002 Proceeds of Crime Act of running a money laundering service for criminals from Jersey, via a company called LAX. LAX specialised in receiving money from its clients and then paying it out via the bank accounts of Jersey companies set up on behalf of these same clients or sometimes buying property on their behalf. Of course, it took a generous cut for this service. The beneficial ownership of these Jersey companies was concealed via a complex legal network of trusts. Even more carefully concealed, in similar fashion, was the ownership of LAX itself. It was money laundering, pure and simple, but conducted in a highly sophisticated fashion.

Freddie Pyper was not as clever as he thought, and despite his expensive lawyers, he was unable to explain why LAX was structured as it was; nor where its income came from; nor significant irregularities in his own tax affairs.

He was convicted and had gone to prison for six years.

The programme then showed a picture of Freddie dining with Carl and others, whose faces were pixelated out. The two men were in good humour and laughing together. David had not seen it before and swore under his breath. Tina's voiceover resumed:

LAX has now closed. Its ownership remains unclear, but those individuals made millions. Freddie Pyper would certainly have been treated more leniently by the courts

had he provided investigators with information on this.
He chose not to.

Again, the inference was clear.

David got up and replenished his Scotch. He had devised that scheme, which had worked well for four years, even though Carl had never really understood it. It would still be operating today had Freddie been a little more discreet. Getting caught drink driving in a Lamborghini on Jersey with a nightclub hostess in the car hardly qualified. The damn speed limit there is only 40mph for one thing, reflected David. Ridiculous human foibles undermined the best-laid plans.

But at least Freddie had kept quiet. His now ex-wife plus child would be looked after. He knew the game.

There was more in the same vein, including the takeover of onshore companies and the alleged washing of illegal funds through their books.

It was this that had led to Carl's recent brush with the law.

David conceded to himself that after its initial success, he'd probably pushed this scheme too far. However, what happened was just as much Carl's fault. They'd previously agreed on always bringing in management of their own when taking over a company, after some nastiness with an existing executive in one of the early cases. Often, they used people to whom they had family links and could thus be easily manipulated.

However, in this latest situation, Carl had thought that the current management was "respectable", which reassured people. He was also sure that the individuals were soft and could be leaned on to do the right thing. A little gentle arm twisting was all it would take.

Unfortunately, they'd run into a young Managing Director who was both honest and brave: a decorated former army officer, the bastard. He had gone straight to the police as soon as the nature of "the right thing" had become apparent, and thereafter he'd worn a wire. Very cleverly, he'd led Carl into spelling out exactly what was expected of him.

Clever but unwise – Carl wouldn't forget.

The evidence at the trial had appeared clear cut, yet the jury had not brought in a conviction.

That result had taken a lot of work, and it wasn't clear how Frank had managed it, but there hadn't been much time for subtlety.

It was attracting a lot of unwelcome attention, thought David. Like this programme.

CHAPTER SEVEN

John watched the programme in his little TV den with growing incredulity. It was amazing what different worlds people moved in, he thought. The man lived less than fifteen miles away, just across the M11! How could someone like that possibly be walking free?

He went back to his *Sunday Times* and read the *Insight* expose in full. It contained a lot more detail than *Panorama* had been able to cover. He shook his head, had a bath and went to bed. There were more pleasant things to dream about than Carl Barrow.

The next day he wrote to thank Sarah (only three drafts), then spent the morning doing various chores and walking Barney. After lunch he found himself at a loose end and without any excuse for avoiding his novel. Sarah would expect developments.

He sat down at his grandfather's Georgian writing desk with a sigh and started thinking through some of the practical details they had discussed together. It was colourless work, and after an hour, he had made little headway. He made a coffee, sat back and thought.

Who would want to kill a stranger? He realised there was little point in working through the practicalities involved until he had that fundamental plot issue clear. And what sort of a stranger might someone want to kill?

Suddenly, he jumped up from his chair, startling Barney, who followed him downstairs.

The *Sunday Times* was still in the den from last night. He picked it up and read the *Insight* article again, more carefully than before. Then he headed back upstairs with it.

Carl Barrow: that was the sort of stranger someone might want to kill.

John immediately felt more motivated, and he stayed like that all week. With a target for his perfect murder, albeit a theoretical one, it all began to feel much more real. By Friday, he was pleased by how much he'd got done, which included another viewing of the *Panorama* programme on iPlayer. He recorded it.

He'd begun thinking about how to follow up with Sarah without blowing it by appearing too keen, and he was still prevaricating – good old English reticence. However, suddenly that decision was taken out of his hands.

His mobile rang at about midday; he could tell at a glance that it was Sarah, as he'd put her number in his contacts. His heart leapt.

'Hello, John Gault,' he said, pretending he didn't know the caller. God knows why, he thought to himself.

'Hi, it's me,' Sarah said breezily.

'Oh, hello, Sarah,' replied John. 'What a pleasant surprise.' That sounded pompous, he thought.

'Yes – well,' said Sarah, more hesitantly. 'Look, I'm at a college reunion in Cambridge on Saturday and spending the night there. I'll be passing by on my way back on Sunday morning. Thought we might have a drink or something.'

'Delighted,' said John, trying not to show it an excessive amount. 'Here?'

'No, I can't impose on you again,' said Sarah. 'Let's just meet at The Swan at around midday.'

John thought quickly.

'Well, only if you let me buy you lunch. I've got a lot to tell you.'

Sarah giggled, sounding delightful to John's ear. 'You're on. It's a date. See you on Sunday.'

* * *

John got to The Swan just before they'd agreed to meet. Sarah was already there; he recognised her silver Golf in the car park.

He heard her laughter as soon as he entered the pub, before he'd even made it into the bar; the pang of jealousy caught him unawares.

She was standing with her back to the door; James and Cathy Venning faced him. It looked like James had just cracked one of his endless jokes. He waved cheerily over Sarah's shoulder, and as she turned, John caught her smile of pleasure. Just friendliness, John told himself, don't get ahead of yourself.

'Hi,' he said, kissing Sarah's proffered cheek.

He kissed Cathy too, of course, who smiled at him knowingly. She looked pleased.

'Drink?' said James. It looked like he'd already bought Sarah one.

'Well – thanks,' said John. 'Don't mind if I do. Pint of bitter, please.'

Churlish to refuse, he thought. God, he hoped they didn't want to team up for lunch.

'Don't mind us,' said Cathy.

She must be a mind reader, thought John.

'We're meeting my parents.'

John knew them vaguely, a cheery old couple. James sneaked him a quick wink and raised his eyebrows expressively: the brotherhood of sons-in-law (and former sons-in-law) everywhere.

They made small talk over their drinks until Cathy's parents arrived, late but radiating goodwill to one and all, and then there were the inevitable introductions.

'Daddy, Mummy, you remember John Gault?' Cathy waved vaguely at him.

'And this is his friend Sarah Hall.'

Blimey, not pulling her punches, thought John, as he went through the greetings ritual. He shared a mutual glance with Sarah; she smiled shyly.

Then the waiter was shepherding the whole extended family away to their table, before the poor parents had even had a drink. John and Sarah were left alone at the bar together.

'I thought for a moment we were going to have to join them,' whispered Sarah under her breath. John loved her conspiratorial glance. He laughed.

'Me too. They're nice, but...'

He smiled at her; no need to say more.

Before long, they were seated at their own table in the corner. John had reserved it straight after Sarah's call on Friday.

It was a great meal. They talked about family, Sarah's time at Cambridge and all manner of things – conversation just flowed. John had seldom felt wittier, or more at ease, and enjoyed himself immensely. They didn't stray into the difficult territory of Jenny or Peter, nor even the novel till they were well into their pudding course. Sarah brought it up.

'So, you promised me an update,' she said. 'You said you had a lot to tell me. Only reason I'm here.'

John smiled happily back at her.

'Well, I've definitely made one big decision,' he said.

Sarah waited, her big eyes intent on him.

John sighed. 'After our discussion at lunch the other day, I sat down to try and work out some of the detailed practicalities. And I just couldn't. Very sterile work.'

'What do you mean?'

'You can't plan a murder in isolation.'

A woman at the next-door table looked across sharply. John and Sarah ignored her.

'You have to have a victim. To visualise somebody.'

'Who?' said Sarah, with frank curiosity. She wasn't teasing him.

John looked at her. A thought had just occurred to him; it wouldn't have done had the lunch not gone so well.

'Are you busy after this?' he said.

'Not particularly, no,' replied Sarah. 'Why?'

'I'll show you,' said John.

* * *

Sarah followed John's car the short distance back to his house, and they drew up there just after 3pm.

'So, what's to see?' she said once they were inside.

John showed her into his TV room, off the kitchen.

'All in good time,' he replied. 'Coffee?'

Sarah nodded, and John bustled around the kitchen for a couple of minutes before returning with two mugs. He already knew that she didn't take sugar.

He turned on his TV with the remote and went straight to the *Panorama* recording. Sarah gave him a querying look.

'You'll see,' said John. 'Watch this.'

He started the programme. Sarah made no comment but settled back with her coffee to view it.

It was an hour long; John noticed bits and pieces he hadn't appreciated before. Sarah never said a word throughout. John glanced at her from time to time to gauge her reaction but thought it best to let her take it in without interruption. He could see that she was concentrating.

When it was over, he looked across to her. She was stock still, deep in thought.

'I think that's the sort of stranger someone might want to kill,' he said, keen to hear Sarah's reaction to his discovery. 'Don't you agree?'

She turned to face him, and his shock was immediate. Her eyes glistened with tears.

'God – what is it?'

Sarah waved him away, trying and failing to stave off full-blown weeping. It was only a couple of feet to her chair, and John was there in a second, on his knees and reaching for her hands.

'What?'

She made an effort to pull herself together, and gave him a small smile, but her eyes still brimmed.

'I'm OK,' she said. 'Really, I'm OK.'

John waited. Her eyes dropped, but she didn't pull away.

'Tell me,' he said gently. 'Please.'

Sarah sniffed and smiled weakly at him again. She broke his grip to reach into her handbag for some tissues and wiped her eyes. With a long sigh, she looked at John again, as if sizing him up.

'Alright.' She had come to a decision. 'Can I have another coffee, please?'

John went out to the kitchen and could sense Sarah hastily applying her make up whilst he made the two coffees.

She looked more composed when he returned, took the mug with a nod of thanks and waited for John to get seated. He gave her a worried look as soon as he was ready.

'Well, whatever it is, I promise I'll help if I possibly can,' he said.

Sarah flashed a grateful smile at him. 'That's very sweet.'

She paused to gather her thoughts; John waited.

'I've never told you about Peter, have I?' she began.

'No,' replied John. 'I thought, in your own good time, if you choose to.'

'Well, Peter was a Finance Director. A good one.' Sarah hesitated, gauging his reaction.

John nodded. 'Yes. I knew he was something like that.'

'It gave us a very comfortable life and allowed me to dabble in whatever I wanted to, without any pressing need to make money – especially as there were no children.'

John wondered why: choice or maybe infertility? Not the time to ask.

'OK.' His tone encouraged her to continue.

'About four and a half years ago, he was approached by someone. It happened fairly often, and he usually ignored them, but this opportunity paid nearly twice as much as his salary at the time. And it was via someone quite close. A newly taken over company, whose owners were looking for fresh management.'

She paused again, to check if John was following.

'I'm guessing he took the job,' said John.

'Yes. I pressed him to, to my eternal regret. And at first it was fine, though it was hard work; the company had a lot of problems. That's why we moved away from here, to shorten his commute,' said Sarah.

'Understood,' said John and waited for her to continue.

'Then the problems began. As I understand it, the owners began transferring large sums of money into the company and then paying them out to all sorts of people as dividends. Peter had no idea where this money was coming from, wasn't satisfied with the paperwork supporting the reasons for the payments and started asking questions.'

'Which probably weren't welcome.' John could sense where this was going.

'It got worse.' Sarah pursed her lips. 'You see, they compromised him when his questions got awkward.'

'Compromised? Financially you mean?' John asked.

'No. Peter was honest as the day. That wasn't the immediate problem.' John could see her lips puckering again. He made no comment.

'Well, there's no way round this – he had an affair.' She looked at him defiantly.

'It happens,' said John, non-committally. Dangerous ground.

'No – a gay affair. They set him up. And then they blackmailed him.'

John nodded cautiously. 'OK. That's certainly trickier,' he said.

'You see, he thought I didn't know,' said Sarah. 'I did – not that particular case, but I'd had my suspicions for ages. He'd stopped being… eager, if that's the right word.'

John nodded again but said nothing.

'Almost to nothing,' Sarah continued without embarrassment. 'I didn't really mind. We were friends more than anything else for the last few years. Best friends.'

'And so, they threatened to tell you, these owners?' John said. 'Threatened Peter, I mean?'

'They did, I think, and he couldn't face that. So, he did as they asked for at least a year: it was money laundering. I sensed something was badly wrong, but he wouldn't tell me. And then the fraud was uncovered.'

'What fraud?' John asked. That sounded alarming.

'Something to do with an audit,' said Sarah. 'I never quite understood it all. But he was hung out to dry by the owners, and with the blackmail too… it was all too much for him.' She gestured helplessly.

'Who were these owners?' John asked her.

Sarah's eyes flashed bitterly at him. Her accusing finger pointed at the TV.

'Ultimately, the owner was Carl Barrow. That bloody man we've just been watching.'

* * *

They talked for two hours afterwards, and at 6pm or so, John got out the whisky. He couldn't believe that Peter hadn't left some sort of suicide note which would incriminate his former employers.

'If he did, I've never seen it,' said Sarah.

There was a moment of hesitation. 'I'll show you what he did leave, though.'

She rummaged in her handbag.

'No – that's too personal,' John began to protest, stopping as Sarah pulled out her mobile phone.

She ignored him and began to search it. It took her only a few seconds to find what she was looking for.

'Here.' She handed him the phone. John took it reluctantly.

'Go on, look,' urged Sarah, forcefully.

John lowered his eyes. It was a text – the most recent of a sequence of many, as between any married couple.

"Sorry, darling – can't go on. Life ruined. Slough station 10.45", it read.

He looked at it in horror and then at Sarah.

'So, he—' he began.

Sarah interrupted him. 'Yes. It was a fast train, which didn't stop at Slough, but it was due through at ten-forty-eight. He'd planned it.'

'Christ, how bloody awful.' John was shocked. 'And that was all?'

Sarah nodded. They lapsed into a sombre silence, sipping their drinks. After a minute or two, John got up and poured them both another. Sarah accepted hers without demur.

'But why? What do you think?' John said, once he was settled again.

Sarah shook her head. 'Loss of professional respect. Pending criminal investigation. On top of that, he probably thought I'd leave him once the gay aspect came out. I wouldn't have,' she said, looking at John defensively. He didn't rise to it.

'And no clue?' asked John.

'Not that I recognised at the time. In hindsight, probably yes. Obviously, he was stressed.'

'Inquest?' suggested John. 'Surely there had to be one?'

'Suicide, whilst the balance of his mind was disturbed,' said Sarah, sarcastically.

'They put it all down to being caught out in the fraud. No interest in probing any deeper. I didn't understand a lot of what went on in the business till afterwards anyway, when someone in the firm wrote to me in confidence. Peter was trying to protect me from all that.'

She stared sadly into her whisky.

By 7 o'clock they were on their third; the conversation had moved on to Jenny and the awful inevitability of a terminal cancer diagnosis.

'I couldn't have stood what you had to,' said Sarah. 'Just couldn't.'

'No option,' said John. 'That's the hand I was dealt. Had to try to stay strong for her and for Tom. And look what you had to go through.'

'Probably easier,' replied Sarah, taking another sip. 'Completely out of the blue. No need to keep up any pretences.'

She contemplated her third depleted whisky.

'I'm supposed to be driving home,' she said mournfully, raising her gaze to John.

He didn't feel like laughing under that cool stare but did so uneasily and raised his own glass. 'Well, I can't drive you.'

Then a thought occurred to him. 'Look – you've got your things in the car, haven't you?'

Sarah nodded. 'Sure.'

'Well, stay here tonight,' said John. 'Plenty of room. I'm not saying...' he added hastily and then tailed off.

They both knew what he was referring to. Sarah frowned for a moment.

'OK,' she said. 'I'll fix us supper.'

She beetled around the kitchen, rustling up scrambled eggs on toast, and they ate it there. John offered wine, but Sarah declined with a rueful smile – 'better not.'

After they had loaded the dishwasher together it was still not much after 8.30pm. Sarah went and got her overnight things out of her car. They looked at each other uncertainly, both very slightly drunk. It was the moment, and they both sensed it.

'You know,' said Sarah, eventually, 'I really think I should go to bed.'

'Of course,' said John, his heart beginning to sink. 'I'll show you your room.'

Sarah smiled, almost with relief it seemed to John, and leaned into him. 'No – show me yours.'

* * *

Later, John found himself staring at the ceiling, wide awake. To his left, Sarah was fast asleep.

He tried to analyse his feelings: elation, certainly. Guilt, too. Logically, he knew he couldn't be unfaithful to his dead wife, but the memory of her was still very much alive and recent. He'd have to manage that and convince himself that Jenny would have wanted him to find someone else. Certainly, she had said so, but did she envisage him doing so in two months? Was it respectful? That was an internal psychological issue, which to some extent he could control. External reaction was down to other people. That would be harder.

He looked across at Sarah, barely able to believe she was there, and his mind turned to earlier. He'd been nervous – it had been over thirty years since he'd made love to a woman other than Jenny. Sarah had seemed similarly shy at first; he hadn't asked, but the thought had occurred to him that she might be in a similar situation, especially if Peter hadn't been "eager" in their last few years.

So, it had been a slow, and rather awkward, start after they had clumsily and shyly undressed each other; not a passionate one. But passion there had definitely been once they got into their stride; the sexual tension between them, which had been slowly building for days, had demanded release.

It had been both thrilling and satisfying for John and, from her reaction, he thought for Sarah, too. Afterwards they had giggled contentedly together, as much with relief as anything else, Sarah increasingly drowsily. She had dropped off a couple of hours ago, spooned backwards into him. John had slept deeply for some time too, her hair next to his face, until he had opened his eyes, remembered it wasn't a dream and rolled onto his back.

Suddenly, he sensed Sarah awake next to him and turning over onto his bare shoulder.

'Penny for them,' she said, sensing that he was deep in thought. 'No regrets?'

John kissed the top of her head briefly. 'None at all.'

He could sense Sarah smiling. Then she moved a little, and he felt the sudden shock of her touch. For an instant he thought it was accidental and was caught by surprise when it became gently, but insistently, rhythmic.

'Don't you want to make absolutely sure?' she breathed thickly into John's ear after a few moments more, when his reaction had become very evident to both of them.

Then she stopped with a little gasp because he already was.

* * *

Tom was up early, as ever, and he passed his father's gateway well before 6am. It was impossible to miss the silver Golf parked a few yards beyond, and he knew who it belonged to.

So, it was happening, he told himself. And not discreetly.

CHAPTER EIGHT

The Monday after the *Panorama* programme, Carl called Frank and David to the house at 10am. He was still miserable and lonely without Cynthia but hid it beneath his normal granite exterior.

David had not realised that his mother had left and wanted to talk about it. Since he'd arrived after Frank, he was waved away by Carl; that was a discussion for family only, and the very suggestion irritated him further. The meeting therefore started with father and son already at loggerheads. Frank's spirits sank. It was going to be a tricky one.

They sat down in the drawing room, and the East European maid was in for once, so she provided coffee and biscuits. Nobody said anything until she had withdrawn to the kitchen. She wasn't thanked. Once the door had closed behind her, Frank and David looked to Carl for a lead.

'Well,' he said brusquely. 'Several things to discuss.'

The others had a fair idea what was coming but waited to see Carl's take on it all.

'First – that bastard whose evidence got me charged. The ex-army guy,' he said coolly.

'Patrick Mills,' Frank reminded him. 'What about him?'

'Wore a wire on me! Can't let that go.'

'He won't scare easily,' said Frank. 'We know that.'

'I don't intend to scare him,' replied Carl. 'I intend to teach him a lesson he won't bloody forget.'

David interjected softly with his mantra. 'Make money quietly, Dad, remember?'

Carl turned angrily to his son.

'I don't give a shit about that,' he said. 'He disrespected me, and people know it. Thin end of the wedge if they start seeing that's possible.'

David pursed his lips and glanced at Frank.

'So, what do you suggest?' said Frank. 'Davey's right. Anything obvious is going to rebound on us and make things worse.'

'Then what do *you* suggest?' replied Carl savagely, turning the tables.

Frank was taken aback and paused before replying. Eventually, he shrugged. 'Do nothing. Bide our time till all this publicity is over. Watch him. Revenge is a dish best served cold,' he said.

Carl looked at him blankly – he'd never heard the old proverb.

'Bollocks,' he said succinctly. Then he reflected for a moment. 'OK – I'll think about it,' he said, with finality. Topic closed.

'What else, Dad?' said David.

'Bloody *Panorama*,' replied Carl. 'And the *Sunday Times*, too.'

Frank and David looked at each other.

'Look, Dad,' explained David, cautiously. 'Those are

77

big media hitters. Take them on, and we're going to get a bucketload more PR shit. Make money quietly.'

His frustration was plain to the other two men as he repeated his philosophy; it was common sense, surely. Carl glowered defiantly.

'What do you want? To sue them?' asked Frank patiently. 'I would not recommend that.'

The reasons why were left unsaid; they all knew them.

'Look – they're just individuals, aren't they?' said Carl. 'We know who they are. They bleed, like anybody else. They have secrets.'

'They're not just any old individuals,' said Frank bluntly. 'They'll be given security after this.'

'Oh, will they?' asked Carl, sarcastically. 'Oooh!'

His voice oozed contempt.

'But OK,' he said after a pause. 'Nothing hasty. As I said, I'll think about it.'

Frank and David exchanged a quick glance of satisfaction. They didn't like each other much, but they were on the same team over this, and though he would never admit it, Frank had a growing respect for David's financial acumen.

The rest of the morning was taken up with discussion of the many and varied legal and financial challenges Carl's empire was facing. None of these was immediate, but many of them were delicate, and careful contingency planning was needed. By and large, David and Frank believed they had kept Carl on the straight and narrow and obtained authorisation for most of the proactive actions they wished to take.

They left about midday. Carl didn't offer lunch, not even to his son, who clearly wanted to discuss his parents' domestic situation.

From the drawing room's French windows, Carl watched the two expensive cars heading down the drive, until they disappeared over the crest towards the electric gates. He knew those would open automatically. As soon as they were out of sight, he pulled out his mobile and stabbed at a number stored in it. His foul temper badly needed an outlet.

'Bill,' he said. 'Be here at five tonight. Got a job for you. Two, in fact.'

He rang off without waiting for an answer.

* * *

It had been predictably excruciating for Cynthia after the *Panorama* coverage; Marnie was worried, and almost tearful, making inane small talk, whilst all the while casting fearful glances at her ghastly husband. Clive sat there in his sanctimonious pomp, looking as if someone had placed a rotten fish under the nose he looked down whenever he was in the same room as Cynthia. He said the bare minimum and radiated hostility.

Nobody mentioned the programme, though everyone knew that they had all seen it. The original elephant in the room, thought Cynthia. Well, she wouldn't be the one to crack.

But after a couple more nights, she knew she had to go, if only to release Marnie from her conflicted loyalties – she'd been there over a week already. The question was – where? After much consideration of pros and cons, she decided on a high-risk solution. On the third morning, she picked up her mobile and punched one of her contact "favourites".

'David,' she said quietly, as the call was answered. 'It's Mum.'

There was a moment's pause, then a babble of questions. David had been trying to reach his mother ever since learning that she had left the family home.

'Well, I'll explain everything,' she said. 'Face to face.'

More queries. Cynthia cut them short firmly.

'I was wondering,' she said calmly. 'You're still alone in your flat, aren't you?'

She supposed she had better check that there was no girlfriend in residence these days, though it would have been an immense (indeed pleasing) surprise to her if there had. And it was a big flat.

The reply was brief and as expected.

'Then could I possibly come and stay for a few days?' she said.

The reaction on the other end of the line sounded astonished, the response (after due pause) cautiously positive.

'Good,' Cynthia replied. 'And thank you. One thing, though.'

The obvious query followed.

'Don't tell your dad. At least not yet. Promise me that. And I mean promise.'

Cynthia listened patiently but eventually got the undertaking from her eldest son that she wanted. Despite David's close relationship with Carl, she knew that he would honour it.

'OK, darling. We'll talk when I get to you. About six-thirty.' She knew that he'd be home by then.

After that it was simply a matter of packing, saying goodbye to Marnie against her faint, but obviously relieved, protestations (not to Clive fortunately, who was in London) and hitting the road in her Audi.

Cynthia had plenty of time in hand, even though she had to get round London on the wretched M25. She thought she would treat herself to a late lunch in a nice little Italian bistro she knew of in Great Dunmow. There, she could ponder the future.

It was a little close to home, but she knew that Carl would never go there.

* * *

Tina Downs was peeved and looked up briefly from striking her laptop's keys unnecessarily hard to steal a flinty glance at the man sitting quietly at the other end of her living room. He didn't appear to notice.

The endless questioning by the BBC's lawyers before they had given her *Panorama* programme the green light was a phase she had expected and was used to. She knew she had dealt with that well, convincing them of the fundamental truth of her story without compromising her sources.

But now, management was insisting on round-the-clock security for her, to which there seemed no end. She didn't like that, and more importantly, neither would her new lover, a high-profile media figure in his own right, who was separated but not yet divorced. The relationship was thus at a delicate stage – indeed, it was not yet public. And he was due to visit tonight, in an hour. The presence of Jez, or the other one, Andy, was hardly going to be conducive to romance. Even if Tina went out for a meal with her paramour, she knew that one or other of the pair would be close by, cramping their style.

So, she had not made them welcome, to which they seemed annoyingly indifferent. When Tina was told that her protectors would be former special forces soldiers, she had imagined macho, gung-ho types. Jez and Andy looked disappointingly ordinary, not people you'd notice in a crowd. Though that was probably the idea, she mused. Apparently, there was a female one too, but she had yet to put in an appearance. God knows what she'll be like, thought Tina gloomily.

Jez's phone rang quietly, its volume set low. Tina glanced up briefly as he answered it, mumbling inaudibly and turning his back on her. The surprise in his voice when he replied to the caller was unmistakable.

'What – now?' Tina heard him say. Then simply, 'OK.'

He stood and picked up his small day sack. 'Bye,' he said to Tina.

She gaped at him as he headed off in unhurried style, slinging the day sack over one shoulder. 'When will you be back?'

'We won't,' said Jez through the narrowing gap as he closed the door.

Tina was astonished but consoled herself with the thought that at least she now had her privacy back. She'd sort out whatever glitch it was with the BBC tomorrow, and meanwhile, her evening (or rather her night) could go ahead as planned. She was looking forward to it. A great deal, in fact.

She caught her reflection in the mirror, smirking, and knew what that smirk meant. Naughty girl, she thought happily and poured herself a drink to get in the mood.

However, Tina's much anticipated night of passion was not to be. Thirty minutes later, her lover called to say that there were half a dozen photographers outside her flat. He accused her of setting him up to give herself a publicity boost. The exchange was brief and angry, her denials disbelieved.

So, that's probably the end of that, thought Tina, as she stared miserably at her phone after he cut her off.

It rang suddenly in her hand. The number was withheld, but being a media pro, she answered instinctively.

'Hello,' she said. 'Tina Downs.'

'Hello, Tina,' said a calm, middle-aged male voice. 'Having a good evening?'

Tina was shocked into silence for a second but recovered fast. She'd had threatening calls before, all investigative reporters had. It was a rough trade.

'Who is this?' she demanded angrily.

'You don't need to know,' said the voice, still very calm.

Tina was still thinking of a suitable reply when the voice continued.

'But know this. You have made a friend of mine very angry. You fucked around with his life, so now he's fucked around with yours. Don't do it again, or it'll be worse. And don't expect those James Bond types to be back, or anybody else. They know what's good for them. So, learn it too, you silly bitch.'

He paused for a second. 'Nice flat, by the way.'

* * *

Simon Strange was concerned but not unduly worried.

His editor had called him and his Insight colleague Joel Baxter in that morning. He'd announced that the security firm which had been retained to look after them following the Carl Barrow expose had unaccountably resigned from the

83

job. Nor had their paper, the *Sunday Times*, as yet identified any willing replacements. Apparently, the BBC was having the same trouble covering its *Panorama* team, with whom they'd cooperated.

Concerned but also angry. Did these bastards think they could intimidate everyone? Were they really "just too big to take on", as one of his police sources had told him?

Simon was a tough, veteran journalist – he had covered crime in the capital on and off for years, plus he'd done stints in the Balkans and Northern Ireland in his early days, back in the nineties, and in Iraq since then. None of these places provided an easy working environment for a reporter, who could be put off the scent by a few mild threats when they sensed a story.

And Simon sensed one here. Indeed, he thought that "Too Big to Take On?" would make a pretty decent headline.

So, he wouldn't take that "short, paid sabbatical abroad" which his editor had proposed. He knew that Joel wouldn't either; they'd discussed it afterwards. Instead, they would run their new "intimidation" story past him in the coming days. Meanwhile, they'd hide in plain sight and dare the thugs to do their worst. Though they might be despicable men, he didn't think that they were stupid enough to attack senior journalists who had a national profile.

Scaring off their security was just that, thought Simon: a scare.

This was his mistake. Carl Barrow and his senior subordinates might well be capable of that sort of sophisticated analysis and to delay taking revenge or to do it with subtlety. But his foot soldiers – the muscle – were not, and they had their orders from Bill. They saw things in black-and-white terms.

Which was why Simon was beaten and kicked so badly on the tube platform by three of them that evening that he ended up in hospital with three cracked ribs, a fractured eye socket and a badly broken nose.

Plus proof for the editor, who visited his bedside later that night with Joel Baxter, that their new story definitely had legs.

* * *

Patrick Mills had been annoyed by the outcome of the trial because he'd done his civic duty (and more) in first reporting the original offences to the appropriate authorities and then by wearing a wire to provide the police with evidence against Carl Barrow.

The man was obviously guilty, as he knew from first-hand experience and the unsuccessful attempts to intimidate him from testifying.

But that's life, he thought. Move on. He had learnt during his eight years as an officer in the Parachute Regiment that even the best-laid plans often went awry, and there was no point in crying over spilt milk. Above all, he needed to find a new job, after resigning from his previous employers for obvious reasons. Though he had been warned by the police to take his personal security seriously in the aftermath of the trial, he assumed that Carl Barrow et al would also want to put the whole episode behind them after such negative publicity.

So, Patrick thought nothing of it that evening, when a big Japanese 4x4 with darkened windows came up fast behind him whilst he was out on his racing bike, training for his next Iron Man event. He simply cursed as he heard it, shot a quick glance behind and waved it impatiently past.

The nudge from Bill the Boatman's vehicle was deliberate, but it wasn't intended to do more than knock Patrick's bike into the ditch to teach him a painful lesson, as Carl had demanded.

Unfortunately, there was a one-foot-tall concrete BT cable marker in exactly the wrong place on the verge. Patrick Mills struck it at nearly 20mph as he fell from his bike.

He was killed instantly.

CHAPTER NINE

John was a little bemused in the aftermath of his night with Sarah, unsure what he was embarking upon. Was it just one-off sex or regular sex, or was it a full-blown relationship, and if so, how deep did he (and she) want it to become?

The first question was answered when Sarah texted him on the following Tuesday to thank him for "lunch – and everything". She also asked if she'd left a wrap behind. When John had looked around and found it, she texted: "bring it on over" with a winking emoji.

He had nothing specific on that day (bar more work on his embryonic novel, but he could always find a reason to defer that) so needed no second bidding. He was there within the hour, just before lunch. Barney came for the ride.

Sarah met John at the door, wearing a white skirt and a floral blouse, with a wide smile but said nothing. She said nothing, but simply took him by the hand and led him upstairs. On the landing, she turned quickly to him. They didn't make it into her bed, and barely onto it – she was astride John straightaway. It was vigorous, ecstatic and brief.

Afterwards, Sarah lay on her side – chin in hand, propped up on her elbow – and looked solemnly at John, whose gaze wandered further than her face. Her skirt was rucked up almost to her hip, her blouse open nearly to the navel and her bra undone at the front, hanging loosely from her shoulders – he had managed rather deftly to undo it as she pushed him down.

'Hello,' she said.

'Do you always say hello like that?' John replied. 'I must come here more often.'

Sarah laughed, happily. 'Only to you. And only if you're good.'

'What are you looking at?' she asked self-consciously after a few moments, feeling his eyes still on her.

'What do you think? It was dark last time, remember. Déshabillé, it's called,' John said. 'All the rage in Paris this year. The wanton look.'

He smiled at her tenderly. The fading flush on her chest still showed the imprint of his fingers, which he was unaccountably delighted by.

Sarah smiled back lazily and dropped her head onto the pillow beneath the ruffled bedspread.

'I definitely remember,' she said and paused. 'Anyway, what are you doing here?'

'You asked me,' said John.

Sarah thought for a moment, pouted and raised her eyes to his. 'Must have had a reason.'

And so, their gentle banter continued, laced with mild innuendo, like new lovers everywhere, till eventually they roused themselves. Sarah fixed a light lunch. John had no particular reason to leave afterwards and so hung around, happy simply to be in her company.

Later, they took Barney out together: Sarah knew her way around the lanes and footpaths. They met a few locals similarly dog walking, and though Sarah greeted them in friendly fashion, she pointedly didn't introduce John, despite their manifest curiosity. She didn't talk much, but whenever nobody was around, John was thrilled to feel her reach for his hand. Once, he caught her glancing at him thoughtfully after he broke away to call Barney back from pursuit of a hare he had no hope of catching. Her expression became a sunny smile as soon as she saw him watching.

Camouflage. She's as uncertain where this is going as I am, thought John.

* * *

John spent the whole of the following weekend from Friday night at Sarah's house. They both recognised that for her to stay with him would flaunt their developing affair unnecessarily before Tom.

It was a strange, delicate period. They coupled "like rabbits", as Sarah put it, and that particular hurdle in any developing relationship was very satisfactorily cleared. Yet, as personalities they were still in the early stages of getting to know each other. They were both very private people. John sensed himself looking for an emerging character flaw in Sarah or an irritating personal trait. Indeed, he almost felt that one or the other was inevitable. At the same time, he felt her quiet and guarded reciprocal scrutiny. However, by the time he left on Sunday evening, everything seemed better than ever between them. It was too good to be true, surely, he thought. Sarah had flung her arms around John when he left on Sunday night and hugged him fiercely. He thought there might even have been a tear in her eye when she closed the door hurriedly afterwards.

On Monday, John had agreed to see the accountant with Tom, who'd been worried by their previous meeting. He'd sent the invitation to John by email, who wasn't sure how things were going to be between them, especially as his absence over the weekend was sure to have been noticed.

Tom picked John up promptly at 9am, as agreed. He was cheerful enough, and though John was braced for probing questions about the last few days, they never came. Instead, Tom stuck strictly to his concerns about the forthcoming meeting as they drove into Saffron Walden, and John was happy to keep the discussion firmly on a professional basis, whilst providing paternal reassurance. He'd seen the cash flow situation that was concerning Tom before, and more than once. All experienced farmers had.

The meeting went well enough, and John was able to reassure Henry Hodge; his father Andrew had similarly tried to daunt John during his own early farming days. In both generations, the Hodges were about fifteen years senior to the Gaults, and the pessimism latent in all accountants had certainly come down from father to son. Well-meant their advice may have been, but farming was simply not viable if one took the pessimistic view on every yield and price projection. John could see that the accountant was simply trying to establish a professional dominance over his son and took mild pleasure in letting some air out of his tyres based on recounting the precedents of previous years.

Tom had looked at him with gratifying respect. However, the discussion in the car on the way back stayed on farming matters, and Tom had declined John's offer of a working lunch in The Swan, pleading pressure of work.

John was just back from his afternoon walk with Barney when he heard a knock on the door. To his surprise it was Emma, with her terrier Pip.

'Just passing,' she said. 'I wondered if you had time for a cup of tea?'

'Of course,' said John, sensing immediately that there was an agenda. 'Come on in.'

He got on increasingly well with Emma, whose own father had died when she was barely twelve. He knew that she would speak frankly to him. She waited quietly whilst he produced their tea, contenting herself with gentle scolding of the dogs, who were chasing each other around the kitchen.

'Well…?' said John, as he handed Emma her mug.

She sighed and looked at him quizzically.

'I don't really know where to start,' she said, awkwardly.

'I generally find that the beginning is a good place,' said John lightly, trying to put her at ease.

'Well, Tom is a bit worried,' Emma began cautiously and hesitated to see his reaction.

'About the farm?' replied John. 'We went through all that with Hodge this morning.'

Emma shook her head impatiently. 'No, not the farm. You.'

John thought quickly, whilst he downed half his mug. 'Why didn't he raise it with me?'

'Oh, father-son stuff,' said Emma. 'He doesn't want to. He's got no idea I'm here now. I'm just trying to help everyone.'

She gave a helpless little shrug and waited for John's reaction.

'OK,' he said calmly. 'Just between us, what's the issue?'

Emma paused. 'Well, you must know…' she began and hesitated again.

John did know. Time to put Emma out of her misery; none of this was her fault.

'Sarah,' he said.

'Yes,' she replied simply. 'Tom saw her car here early one morning last week. And apparently you were away all weekend. I've no idea if he's putting two and two together and coming up with five, but—'

John raised his hand. 'No, fair point. There is something happening. Early days, of course.'

Emma looked at him with her disconcertingly blue eyes. 'Very early, Tom thinks, after Jenny.'

'Yes, it is,' replied John. 'Nobody is more aware of that than me. But consider – we are both people who have lost someone in tragic circumstances over the last year. When might this chance come again? For either of us? It may come to nothing, but we must at least give it a try.'

Emma said nothing and looked reflective.

'What do you think?'

His daughter-in-law marshalled her thoughts for a moment. 'You know what?' she said. 'If someone nice had come along for Mum just after Dad died, I hope I'd have had the guts to encourage it. I wouldn't have, probably, because at twelve one fears change. And he never has come along.'

'So, what are you saying?' asked John.

'I'm saying take your chance but carefully, because I don't want to see you hurt,' said Emma.

'And Tom?'

'I'll talk to Tom. He's never said it, but I think he's a little worried. You know, inheritance…'

She tailed off.

'He should have no fears on that score,' said John firmly.

'I know,' replied Emma and drained her cup. 'Well, Pip and I must be off.'

Just before she got to the door, John took her gently by the arm.

'Thanks, Emma,' he said gently. 'You didn't have to do that.'

She turned and gave him a little peck on the cheek.

'Really hope it works out.'

* * *

The next day, Tuesday, John did some spreadsheet work on a revised farm budget which he'd promised Tom. He'd emailed it off by 11am and knew Sarah was visiting a prospective new client near Thaxted that day, so there was nothing doing there. He was footloose and fancy free for the rest of the day and plain out of excuses. The novel it would have to be.

He started with a long dog walk to think about it, convincing himself that this counted as work, and then dawdled over lunch. But thereafter, he was at his desk.

Carl Barrow: if someone wanted to kill him, how would he (or she) actually do it? And get away with it?

Not easy. Tough, vigilant, secretive, probably armed or with armed people around. How would anybody know his whereabouts?

John fired up his computer as he began to think all this through. But then he remembered that lunch at Sarah's house when they'd discussed what would be necessary – avoiding any planning on electronic media was fundamental.

Paper only. And get rid of it.

Might as well do it properly, thought John. He pulled a new pad of A4 out from his desk.

* * *

By Thursday, John had made some progress.

After much thought, he had decided that there was only one viable way of killing a man like Carl Barrow with any prospect of avoiding detection, and even that would be very difficult. He'd begun tentatively sketching out a scenario whereby his imaginary central character might want to take that risk with an imaginary Carl Barrow. As yet, it wasn't very convincing.

In tandem, he also decided to take the bull by the horns and ask Sarah to stay for the weekend, relying on his conversation with Emma to defuse any tension with Tom.

The first step was to clear his tracks. He texted Emma: "If S stays this w/e will you stand by to calm things if nec?".

The reply came within a few minutes: a simple thumbs up emoji.

He thought he'd better call Sarah to discuss the various sensitivities involved. They hadn't spoken since Sunday though had exchanged the occasional brief text.

She picked up as soon as he called, sounding pleased: 'Hi.'

'Hi,' replied John, so thrilled by her voice that he immediately lost his train of thought.

Silence. Sarah was obviously waiting for him to continue.

'Look – er, I wondered if you would like to come over

here this weekend,' John continued rather hesitantly. 'I mean, for the whole weekend. If you're not doing anything else, obviously.'

Better give her a let-out.

'Well, that would be lovely,' replied Sarah after a pause, to John's great relief, though she sounded a bit dubious. 'But didn't you say that Tom might not like me being around?'

'I think we're OK,' John said. 'Emma and I had a good chat. She'll handle him.'

They spent a few more minutes flirting mildly, neither wanting to put down the phone, but eventually the call ended, with both of them saying "bye" about three times like teenagers.

John snorted derisively at himself afterwards but grinned happily nonetheless. He'd never been a lovey-dovey type but couldn't help enjoying the experience. Sarah would be with him by 6pm tomorrow and wasn't going to leave until Monday morning. He looked forward to it immensely.

He sat down with a cup of tea and turned on his TV. It was tuned to BBC, and they were broadcasting a trailer for a programme showing tomorrow night at 9pm.

John gaped at it.

Panorama Special: Justice in Jeopardy – What Happened Next.

CHAPTER TEN

Bill the Boatman had been arrested under his real name, William Palfreyman, initially just for careless driving and leaving the scene of an accident. He'd been in his own car, with genuine plates. The registration number had been noted by a following van driver, and the police had collared him at home with the vehicle within a couple of hours.

Bill had been amateurish and overconfident. He didn't even have an MOT.

Then the police had begun piecing things together in more depth. The role of Patrick Mills as a prosecution witness in the recent trial was noted, as were Bill's well-developed links to Carl Barrow, whose penchant for revenge against those who crossed him was well known, if never proven. His car even had a scratch on it which could be linked to the paint on Patrick's bike.

The charge against William Palfreyman was now likely to be murder, or at the very least manslaughter. Bill the Boatman had been caught bang to rights.

Carl was shaken when Frank called to tell him on Friday

morning. If Bill started talking, there was no telling where it might lead. Furthermore, he was disconcerted by the accusatory tone in Frank's voice.

'Did you put him up to this?' Frank had asked pointedly during their call.

'Don't you bloody well use that tone with me—' Carl had begun replying, before Frank cut him off.

'Did you?'

Carl hesitated uncertainly for a second before replying.

'He was only supposed to give him a little scare—' he began.

'Thought so,' said Frank. 'You're a fucking arrogant dickhead. We told you, Davey and me. You've dropped us all in it. And it's going to get a lot worse after the *Panorama* follow-up tonight.'

He slammed the phone down. Carl was left looking at his handset in astonishment. Nobody ever spoke to him like that. It was usually the other way round, like telling the bloody TV people where to go when they'd asked for an interview a couple of days previously.

A wave of self-pity swept over him when he glimpsed himself in the mirror: unshaven, scruffy and bleary eyed from lack of sleep. That wasn't the real Carl Barrow. He'd hardly left the house since Cynthia had gone, and the troops were getting uppity.

He'd need to make an example of someone. Frank probably, insolent bastard. Nobody was irreplaceable. He'd find that out soon enough.

But above all, he knew he needed Cynthia back; then he could get his life back on track.

Carl texted her again and called. As ever, he got no response.

Neither David nor Cynthia had mentioned the forthcoming *Panorama* follow-up, but there was a tacit understanding between them that they would watch it together in his flat.

It was only a half-hour programme. After a light supper, they were settled somewhat nervously in front of the TV well before the 9pm start time, a bottle of red on the table between them.

And so, it began. First came the BBC continuity announcer:

> *Last Sunday, here on BBC Two, we showed a hard-hitting Panorama documentary on organised crime: Justice in Jeopardy. Now, in a special half-hour follow-up programme, we tell you – What Happened Next.*

Then it was into the theme music before an abrupt cutaway to a strained-looking Tina Downs. She was in a nondescript room, which could have been anywhere.

Tina's introductory pitch was brief and factual, fading halfway through into an unflattering picture of Carl.

> *Our programme last week, made in conjunction with the Sunday Times's Insight team, introduced you to Carl Barrow, reputedly one of the most prolific criminals in Britain. Mr Barrow was acquitted of money laundering shortly before we broadcast that programme, most surprisingly in the view of many legal commentators.*

David swore sharply. His mother stilled him quickly with her hand as the picture transitioned to somebody else. Tina's voiceover continued:

> *This man is Patrick Mills, a decorated former army officer and, more recently, Managing Director of Cursham, a company ultimately controlled via various shell organisations by Carl Barrow.*
>
> *Last week, Mr Mills testified in court under oath that Carl Barrow and his associates were laundering money through the books of that company.*
>
> *Patrick Mills is now dead. He was married, with two children under eight.*

Cynthia sat silently with her knuckles to her mouth, wine glass in her other hand. David glanced at her non-committally, then back at the TV. He took a reflective sip of his wine.

And so, the story unfolded, outlining the role of William Palfreyman, generally known as Bill the Boatman. Tina asked a silhouetted figure:

> *What's the story on the nickname?*

In a disguised, robotic voice, with his back to camera the figure said:

> *A few people took one-way boat trips with him, if you know what I mean.*
>
> *Though they weren't in much of a state to resist.*

Tina leaned forward:

Does that mean dead? He disposed of bodies?

The figure shuffled uneasily.

Well, you hear these things.

Tina let him dangle for a few seconds before continuing.

And this Mr Boatman – I mean, Mr Palfreyman – he is an associate of Carl Barrow?

The shadowy figure said:

Sure – common knowledge. Enforcer. Good at it, too. He enforced me once.

Tina asked:

That was after you fell out with Carl Barrow?

The figure shrugged apologetically.

Yes, but I don't hold it against him. No hard feelings – just business.

He gave a feeble attempt at a laugh. Tina pressed the point in a quickfire exchange.

And this is the man now under arrest after the death of Patrick Mills?

So it appears.

Do you think it was a coincidence that Mr Mills was knocked off his bike by Mr Palfreyman?

No, I do not. Definitely not.

And he would not have acted without the authority of Carl Barrow?

The man paused before replying.

Most unlikely, or highly improbable – take your pick.

As the interview ended, Cynthia turned accusingly to David.

'Bill had that bloody Boatman nickname before he ever started working for Dad,' said David defensively. 'Not in our time. I never even knew what it meant.'

'Did Dad tell him to kill that poor man?'

David was still on the back foot. 'We told him to let it be. Me and Frank.'

Cynthia stared at him grimly.

'It was probably an accident,' David added lamely, then tried to change the subject. 'Dunno who that fuzzed out bloke was—'

'He is out of control,' interrupted Cynthia calmly. 'You know that. Your father. He must be stopped. Or he will take us all down with him.'

* * *

Frank was watching in his study again as he had done the previous week.

He was still livid with Carl, and only marginally less so with Bill; if the enforcer was going to do something (which he had little choice about having been ordered to by Carl), then at the very least he should have taken elementary precautions. The man was supposed to be a pro.

Now he was whining like a little girl in police custody, a bully who had been caught, leaving Frank to pick up the pieces legally. He was tempted to let Bill stew in his own juice. But he knew stuff, and that was dangerous.

The programme continued, with Tina saying blandly:

We asked Carl Barrow to comment on his relationship with William Palfreyman and on the death of Mr Mills after collision with his vehicle.

There was no introductory comment to Carl's taped response on the phone – it was brutal and brief.

Yes, I know Mr Palfreyman. No, I don't know why he collided with soldier boy, but I'm not sorry he did. Now fuck off, and leave me alone.

The phone slammed down.

Frank sat bolt upright, shocked. Carl was always controlled and professional. He sounded anything but, and possibly a little drunk, too. Any queries from the press should have been politely referred to him; it was a basic discipline they had agreed on long before, and Carl had always adhered to it.

This was bad. It was about to get worse. Tina turned to the next part of her report. She said:

Last week's programme was produced in conjunction with the Sunday Times's Insight investigative team, and many viewers will have read the report which appeared in that newspaper two days later. The two award-winning journalists responsible were Joel Baxter and Simon Strange.

A picture followed of the newspapermen, grinning proudly together at an awards ceremony. It cut swiftly to another picture, to which Tina provided a voiceover.

This is Simon Strange today.

The veteran reporter was trying to do his best to grin bravely up from his hospital bed, but the extent of his injuries was obvious. Tina continued over the photo:

The Sunday Times was advised by the Metropolitan Police to provide private security for its Insight journalists after the appearance of their article last week.

It did so, but after two days, those private security contractors unaccountably resigned. Nor could the Sunday Times recruit any more, despite their best efforts. You see here the result.

After lingering on Simon for a moment, the film cut back to Tina herself, who gave a weary sigh.

The same police advice was given to the BBC with regards to those journalists who worked on the Panorama programme. The result was much the same. Our security contractors walked off the job too, and we could find no others. It is clear they had been warned off or threatened; indeed, informally they confirmed as much. I received a threatening phone call myself, and it is plain that the person who made it knows where I live. Which is why I am presenting this programme to you tonight from hiding.

She faded out with a brave attempt at a smile, but simply looked tense and tired.

Is this really the sort of country we want to live in? Goodnight.

She faded out with a brave attempt at a smile but simply looked tense and tired.

All this was news to Frank.

'Jesus Christ,' he murmured tiredly. He'd never been an original man, in oaths as in much else.

The text pinged in from David less than a minute later.

"Need to talk".

* * *

Cynthia lay wide awake on her bed in the flat, fully dressed, thinking. She'd gone straight to her room after the programme, and David had barely raised an eyebrow, too busy texting.

She felt both sick and ashamed, always the loyal wife to

Carl, who on the surface had been a loving, faithful husband and had provided all she had ever dreamed of materially. As a result, she'd simply blocked out everything that underpinned all that success, until confronted by the unavoidable in the year leading up to the trial. It was a simple matter of her choosing not to know, she realised. There had been plenty of clues.

She wasn't proud of herself, and after the two *Panorama* programmes, the scale of her self-deception was clear – she had simply chosen to avert her eyes. Furthermore, though he had once been so methodical and careful, now her estranged husband was fast becoming unstable and erratic.

Though she disapproved of Carl's methods, Cynthia's new-found morality did not extend to wanting to give up everything they had provided her with. Above all, she would do anything to protect her children.

Cynthia was perceptive enough to recognise the underlying reason for Carl's changed behaviour. The first flush of love had never wilted for him, and he'd always parked his business worries at the door every night of their long marriage. Her unquestioning loyalty, support and absolute lack of interest in his business affairs had provided him with a happy refuge from the daily pressures he had to confront.

His secure home life had been Carl's greatest psychological support. It was fundamental to who he was, and now it had gone. His increasingly desperate attempts to contact his wife reflected his growing distress, and the result of that was unpredictability.

Cynthia missed what had once been between them too but knew that it was all based on a false premise. Carl wasn't just a well-meaning wide boy with a heart of gold but a few rough edges, as she had always fondly imagined. He was a man prepared to deal with anyone who crossed him ruthlessly. And now it seemed, recklessly too.

She realised with a start that if she scorned her husband, and he saw no way back, then love might very quickly turn to hate, stronger in her case than with anyone else. There was danger there.

Cynthia hadn't spoken to her younger sister Bim for ages: Bim had "issues" with Carl. Now, however, she needed an ally, a confidante and a sympathetic ear.

She reached for her phone and sent a short text: "Bim – I've left. Would love to meet, C x".

It went with a swoosh. Though she waited hopefully for a while, there was no reply.

Cynthia promised herself that she'd call Bim in the morning if there was no response by then, had a shower and went to bed. She'd done all the thinking necessary and went straight to sleep.

CHAPTER ELEVEN

Sarah arrived at around 6.15pm, and although she looked pleased to be there and greeted John fondly with a kiss, she was clearly tired. John moved her car to the yard behind the house; though Emma would probably have told Tom about the weekend, there was no point in being deliberately provocative.

'Long day?' he said, as he carried her bags inside.

'Very,' said Sarah. 'Clients. Or one client in particular. Changing goalposts.'

She gave him a rueful smile. 'Sorry,' she said. 'I'll be fine after a drink, promise.'

John fixed her a decent-sized whisky and poured one for himself.

'So, how have you got on this week?' said Sarah as she flopped down.

'OK, but better if you had been here,' said John. 'You know what's on TV tonight, don't you?'

Sarah smiled at the compliment, nodded and sipped her drink. 'I do.'

'Look – I'm recording it,' said John, unsure of her feelings. 'We don't have to watch it tonight if you're not in the mood.'

'No,' said Sarah firmly. 'I want to watch it. Definitely.'

So, that being decided, they chatted on, Sarah gradually mellowing, and shared some chilli con carne which John had rustled up, plus a bottle of wine. She was happily relaxed by the time they sat down in front of the TV, to John's relief, but he sensed her tense up again as the *Panorama* theme tune began.

They watched the short programme in silence, hearing about Patrick Mills, Simon Strange and Tina Downs and wincing at Carl's coarse phone call. After it was over, John looked across quietly to gauge Sarah's reaction. She was reflective and silent. Eventually, she turned to him and paused. He waited.

'That man is a fucking bastard,' she said quietly. 'How can he get away with it all?'

'I don't think he will this time,' said John. 'He's overstepped the mark.'

Sarah gave him a cynical look; he hadn't seen it before and didn't like it.

'That sort always gets away with it,' she said decisively and lapsed into silence.

After a minute or so she looked up, sadly. 'I've been so looking forward to this weekend,' she said, 'but I'm not myself tonight. It's not that wretched man. I'm just very tired.'

John nodded. 'That's OK.'

'Would you mind if I just had a bath and went to bed?' she asked anxiously.

John was buoyed that she cared.

'No – of course not,' he said. 'You go on up.'

'You really don't mind?' Sarah asked.

'I don't mind,' said John, with a smile.

Sarah smiled gratefully and headed up the stairs.

'I'll be fine tomorrow,' she said over her shoulder and even tried a little wink, which didn't quite come off.

John sighed gloomily and poured himself a final whisky as he heard the bath start to run. He watched a rather dull documentary for an hour, cleared up the kitchen, gave Barney his final run out and then went upstairs himself.

At least Sarah was in his bed; she hadn't decamped to the spare room, which he'd feared. She was fast asleep. He climbed gently in beside her, realising this was the first time they had got into bed together and just slept.

Though they hadn't yet got out of it, he thought.

* * *

Indeed, they hadn't. On Saturday morning it was languid, gentle and much less frantic than the times before but rather lovely. Afterwards, Sarah lay thoughtfully in John's arms for a long time.

'Shall I tell you something?' she murmured, looking up at him.

'Sure,' said John quietly.

'You won't laugh or run a mile or anything?' Sarah said. 'Seriously?'

'Don't know what it is yet,' said John with a smile. 'But no, of course not.'

'That's the first time it's felt like making love,' Sarah said. 'You know, properly. Not just bonking.'

She pulled away and waited for his reaction, worried she

had overstepped the mark. John kissed her gently on the lips.

'That's a lovely thing to say,' he said. 'But I think I've been making love to you from the beginning.'

Sarah smiled, and her eyes brimmed. 'Not just bonking then?'

'No, definitely not,' said John gently. 'Sounds like that was just you.'

Sarah laughed, hit out playfully and kissed him, settling back into his arms with a sigh of contentment.

'What are we going to do today?' she asked, eventually.

'Don't know,' said John. Sarah looked at him and raised her eyebrows.

'That's the great thing about weekends,' he explained. 'You don't have to do anything.'

'I'd quite like to do some more bonking at some point,' said Sarah, with a mischievous grin. 'I mean, making love.'

John laughed. 'I'm sure we'll manage that.'

They dozed together until John remembered Barney and got up to feed him, let him out and make them both a coffee. They were lazing back in bed when a knock came at the door.

'Hell,' said John, glancing at his watch. 'Ten-forty-five…'

He grabbed his dressing gown from the back of the door and headed downstairs two at a time as Sarah waited helplessly. He could see immediately as he descended through the frosted glass panel on the front door who it was.

Tom.

John wondered wildly for a moment if he had seen Sarah's car and whether it was worth trying to bluff but dismissed it in an instant. He'd have to face the music.

He opened the door, for the first time in his life genuinely fearful of his son's reaction.

Tom stood there gravely, eyeing his father in his dressing gown, a faintly ridiculous sight. Then he looked at his watch, very deliberately.

'Late morning?' he said non-committally, after a long pause.

John was struck dumb. Upstairs, he could hear noises from the bedroom: Sarah hurriedly dressing. Tom could hear them too and glanced meaningfully up the stairs.

And then he smiled. 'It's OK, Dad,' he said.

'What?' said John, astounded.

'It's OK,' Tom said. 'Emma talked to me.'

He waited expectantly. John was still off-balance.

'You definitely owe her a drink,' Tom continued, eventually. 'May I come in?'

'Yes – of course. Of course,' said John, beginning to recover his equilibrium. 'Coffee?'

They went through to the kitchen, and John fumbled clumsily with the kettle. Tom looked at him in amused fashion.

'Well, at least this makes up for that time you caught Emma and me,' he smiled.

'Did we?' replied John, flustered. 'I don't recall.'

'You came back at an inconvenient moment the first time I brought her home,' said Tom. 'Maybe you never realised. Mum definitely did. I threw something on and pretended Emma was in the shower.'

John grinned, but it felt false and he feared must look it. He was still uneasy and embarrassed.

'Bring her down,' said Tom gently. 'Seriously. Nothing to worry about.'

He nodded briefly as John first looked at him for reassurance and then went up the stairs.

Tom was sitting quietly on his stool with his coffee when John and Sarah came down. She was leading and perfectly dressed; there was no sign of haste.

'Hello, Tom,' she said, without embarrassment.

'Hello,' he replied with a smile. 'Sorry to disturb you.'

'It's OK,' Sarah said. 'We needed to get up anyway.'

It seemed to John that they were both amused by the situation, and it was only him in his dressing gown who felt caught up in a bedroom farce. He made Sarah a coffee too.

The three of them looked at each other from their kitchen stools, wondering how to start the conversation. Sarah did so.

'Well,' she said. 'This is a turn up for the books, isn't it?'

Tom sipped his coffee. 'Yes,' he said. 'It is.' There was a long pause.

'You know,' he continued 'Every generation thinks it invented sex. Which is pretty illogical, when you think about it.'

Sarah and John waited for him to continue. He took another sip.

'The thing is, I understand,' said Tom. 'Really I do. It's not ideal coming so soon after Mum's death, and that worried me – surprised me really. But you've both lost people…'

He shrugged.

'Serendipity,' said Sarah quietly.

'I'm not sure I understand what that means,' said Tom. 'But I want Dad to have another chance of happiness, and if it comes sooner rather than later then so be it. Emma and I had a long talk about it. Or rather she talked, and I listened. I really hope it goes well for you both.'

John felt a great burden which he'd hardly realised was there lifting from him. Tom stayed for another twenty minutes and was charming and gracious to Sarah; that they liked each other was soon very obvious. John looked from one to the other with quiet delight as they bantered away.

Eventually, Tom made to go; he and Emma were going out to lunch with friends. John walked him to the door. Outside, and out of sight of Sarah, he grasped his son's hands.

'Thanks,' he whispered. 'It took a big man to do that.'

'Thank Emma,' smiled Tom and then turned serious for a moment.

'Sarah's lovely, but be careful.'

It sounded more like father to son rather than the other way round, thought John.

'I will be.'

* * *

That afternoon, John and Sarah went for a long walk with Barney, right up to the spinney at the far end of the farm. They met a few neighbours en route, and of course some of them remembered Sarah from the time when she'd lived in the village, so they aroused some curiosity together, especially with Sarah clinging so tightly to John's arm.

Nothing intrusive, very mild, but John could sense the situation being quietly noted. It wouldn't take long for the news to spread.

But he didn't care. He was walking on air. They wandered on slowly, in contented silence.

'You know, I've never imagined this,' said John after a while. 'Being with someone else, I mean. Even after Jenny died.'

Sarah smiled. 'That's because you were happy together,' she said.

John nodded. 'Yes. We were. Very lucky.'

'What about you?' said John, after a minute or so. 'You've been by yourself for longer.'

Sarah considered the question. 'Not by long. And towards the end we weren't so happy because of the strain of it all. But since you ask, no, I've never imagined it either.'

There was a thoughtful pause, then, 'Is that what we are now – together?'

She looked across at him, and he sensed her anxiety as she waited for his answer.

'We are,' said John, decisively. 'At least I'd like us to be. I can't imagine things being much better, can you?'

'Well, it's early days,' said Sarah. 'They're certainly energetic! Let's just take it slowly and see how things go.'

She was still clinging tightly to his arm and turned to look up at him.

'I'm very happy, John,' she said, simply. 'And I think Tom is a sweetheart.'

John smiled down at her, appearing calm, he hoped, but every nerve in his body was telling him to move faster, not slower. He wanted this woman with him always, even after just a month or so.

The raw strength of that unexpected emotion left him feeling suddenly scared and vulnerable. He was in thrall to her. Be careful, he told himself, as Tom had.

But he knew he was probably already beyond that.

* * *

John and Sarah went to bed early that night and eventually had a good night's sleep.

Sunday morning. They both luxuriated in the need to do nothing in particular that day, rose late again and agreed on a division of labour: Sarah would rustle up some brunch, and John would head out to get the papers. It was about half a mile to the village shop, the weather was fine and so he walked it with Barney.

As usual, he bought the *Sunday Times* and the *Sunday Mail*, which he'd always called "the comic" in Jenny's day, but she'd enjoyed the fashion coverage, and over the years he'd learned to aim off for the particular editorial slant of the paper. He'd continued with it after Jenny's death, largely out of habit.

Brunch smelled delicious when he got back – scrambled eggs and something, it seemed.

'Very right on!' Sarah laughed, as she saw the *Mail*. 'After you…'

They read the magazines in companionable silence as they ate. John was glad to see that Sarah wasn't so insecure as to insist on constant conversation. His brother Michael had served in the Army for a few years and once told him that silence at breakfast over the papers was sacrosanct in the Officers' Mess, which he thought was an excellent custom.

Afterwards, they adjourned to the TV room, where Sarah was quick to purloin the main *Sunday Times* paper. John didn't mind; he started with the sports section and then finished another supplement before glancing across to her. She was still in the middle of the paper, stretched out on the sofa, looking very studious and rather sexy in her reading glasses, he thought.

'Must be fascinating, whatever it is,' he said, lightly. Sarah looked up at him over her glasses.

'*Insight*,' she said. 'Much more detailed than the *Panorama* follow-up.'

John hadn't realised that the newspaper would be pursuing the story again.

'Anything in particular?' he asked.

'Read it later,' said Sarah impatiently, with an offhand wave of her hand. 'But here's one thing. His wife's left him.'

'Well, she's probably seen the light after all these years,' said John.

'He's apparently living alone in that big house,' continued Sarah. 'Not seeing anybody. People are a bit worried about him.'

'My heart bleeds,' replied John, without much interest.

Sarah folded the paper away, sat up on the sofa and looked at him directly.

'How are you getting on with the great novel?' she said.

John was surprised. He hadn't given it enough thought lately as his relationship with Sarah had begun to blossom.

'Well, I told you I think that there's only one way to do it—' he began.

'No,' said Sarah. 'You didn't. What's that?'

'Shoot him. The only possibility with someone like that,' said John. 'Consider the alternatives. Knife – not likely, very risky. Poison – I'm not trying to be Agatha Christie. Run him over – bound to get caught. Realistically, it would have to be a gun.'

'OK,' replied Sarah. 'Tell me how you would do it.'

'Well, obviously my character needs a gun—' began John.

'Not your character. You. How would you do it?' said Sarah.

John looked sharply at her. 'Seriously?'

'Seriously,' she replied. There was no hint of a smile on her lips. John decided to go along with it; it might even prove to be a useful exercise.

'OK, Lady Macbeth,' he said. 'What do you know about guns?'

'Absolutely nothing,' said Sarah.

'Right, to shoot someone, ideally you need a rifle, which you fire from the shoulder, or a handgun, which can be either a revolver or an automatic pistol. You see all of those on TV all the time. They're designed for the job. Follow me so far?'

'Yes,' said Sarah.

'They come in many different calibres, which means size of bullet, but rifles are more powerful, more accurate and have a much longer range. You've got to be close with a handgun,' he said.

Sarah nodded. 'So, which would you use?'

'Neither,' said John. Sarah looked at him in bafflement.

'I don't have either of them,' shrugged John. 'Handguns have been illegal in this country anyway since that terrible school massacre at Dunblane in the nineties. That was a legally held weapon.'

'And a rifle?' Sarah asked.

'I could get one if I was interested in deer stalking, say, or target shooting, but I'm not. And if I wanted a rifle I'd need to apply for a firearms certificate, which means very careful police vetting. They'd have all the details of that weapon.'

'So, what?' said Sarah.

'Ballistics,' said John. 'If I shoot someone with it, there are going to be bullet fragments in the victim, or maybe even a whole bullet. And that can be traced because of unique rifling in the barrel. The police may come looking.'

'What's rifling?' said Sarah. 'And anyway, how do you know all this?'

'It's the twist inside the barrel, which spins the bullet to give it accuracy,' explained John. 'It makes identifiable marks on the bullet traceable to an individual weapon. And I'm a farmer. Most of us have handled a few guns in our time and know the legal requirements.'

'Well, if the rifle makes a unique mark on the bullet, get rid of it afterwards,' said Sarah.

'No,' said John. 'I'd have to declare that disposal to the police or explain if the rifle went missing. Potentially a criminal offence if I don't.'

'Hmm,' said Sarah, doubtfully.

'So, if I was to use either a handgun or a rifle, it would have to be an illegally acquired one, which I then got rid of immediately,' said John. 'I don't think that's a very risk-free start to my perfect murder, do you?'

'OK,' said Sarah, puzzled. 'So, you say it has to be by shooting, but you've just said that's impossible.'

'Patience,' said John. 'Do you know what a shotgun is?'

'Not really,' replied Sarah, uncertainly.

'A shotgun is designed to shoot either vermin – such as crows, pigeons or rabbits – or game birds, such as pheasants and partridges,' explained John. 'Most farmers have them.'

He could see the beginning of understanding in Sarah's eyes.

'But the firearms certificate—' she began.

'Different certificate,' said John. 'Shotgun certificate.'

'And you've got one?' Sarah leaned forward.

'Sure,' John nodded.

'And a shotgun – here?'

'Sure,' said John again, amused by her eagerness.

'Can I see it?' Sarah said.

John was surprised. This was getting slightly beyond a joke.

'Well, yes, if you really want to. It's locked up in my gun cabinet upstairs of course.'

John hoped that this inconvenience would make Sarah retract but soon realised that he was very much mistaken. She sat back on the sofa, crossed her arms and gave him a challenging stare. It was obvious what she was waiting for. John sighed heavily and got to his feet.

The keys to the secure gun cabinet were in John's safe, which was in his study, so he had to unlock that first before going upstairs. The cabinet was fixed to the wall in a cupboard in the spare room. It was a good five minutes before he returned.

He was holding a double-barrelled, "side by side" 12 bore shotgun. It was a fine old one, made by renowned gunsmiths Henry Atkin, which his father had bequeathed to him, very much the thing in its day and for quite some time beyond. John was aware that increasingly, people were turning to "over and unders" instead, but it was of no concern to him; he saw guns as tools, not fashion items.

'Here you are,' he said. He held it out to Sarah.

'I've never touched a gun before,' she said, looking at it cautiously. 'It's not loaded, is it?'

John chuckled. 'No. It's not loaded. Go on, hold it.'

Sarah reached out gingerly from her position on the sofa and took it.

'It's much lighter than I thought,' she said, turning it on

its side. 'Lovely engraving. Why's it got two triggers?'

'One for each barrel,' said John. 'Then you have to reload. Two shots only. That gun was made for my father's Godfather in 1928.'

Sarah looked up at him. 'So, this is what you would use?' she said. 'Something nearly a hundred years old?'

John grimaced. 'Well, if I personally have to do it, this is what I've got. And it works. But I agree, there are a few problems,' he said, as he took the gun back from her.

'What?' Sarah replied. He could see that her interest was genuine.

'One: it's pretty big,' said John. This one's got thirty-inch barrels. Add in the stock, and it's another fifteen inches or more – so, well over a yard.'

'Yes, but so's a rifle, surely?' protested Sarah.

'With a rifle, you shoot from a distance – say, a hundred or a hundred and fifty yards – and a professional sniper, much further,' said John. 'You conceal yourself beforehand and wait for your opportunity.'

'Why not with that, then?' asked Sarah, almost indignantly, indicating the shotgun.

'Because a shotgun doesn't fire bullets,' explained John. 'It fires a whole lot of pellets that spread out. Range about thirty yards if you're shooting a pigeon. Twenty yards maximum to do serious damage to a man, and even then, it would probably take more than one shot. So, you've got to be very close, and something this big is not easy to conceal.'

He placed the shotgun carefully on a chair.

'Here – have a look,' he said, handing Sarah a shotgun cartridge he'd bought downstairs with him in his pocket. Above its brass base it had an opaque orange plastic body, transparent enough for the scores of pellets it contained to be plainly visible. She held it up to her face, fascinated.

'The good thing about using that would be no ballistics,' John continued.

Sarah put the cartridge down and looked across at him.

'Go on. Explain,' she said, with mock patience.

'Smooth barrels: no rifling, and no bullet to impart unique markings to. Just a whole mass of pellets which couldn't be traced to any particular shotgun.'

'So even if you used that gun to kill Carl Barrow, nobody could prove it?' asked Sarah.

'Subject to precautions, yes,' said John. 'I'd need to make sure it hadn't obviously been recently fired, and I'd have to be pretty quick into the bath afterwards too, because forensic tests can tell if someone has recently fired a weapon. But that shouldn't be difficult.'

'But it's just too big,' said Sarah. 'He'd see you coming with it a mile off.'

John thought for a moment and then got to his feet.

'Wait here,' he said.

He was back in a minute or two with something solid, wrapped in an old orange blanket.

'This is what I'd use,' he said to Sarah.

CHAPTER TWELVE

The Saturday morning after the programme, Cynthia's phone rang, just after David had left to go out somewhere. She looked at it warily in case it was Carl. No: Mary. She had a fair idea how the conversation would go and took a deep breath.

'Hello, Mary darling,' she said, as cheerfully as she could muster.

'Mum – what the hell's going on?' her daughter replied. No preliminary pleasantries, Cynthia noted.

'What do you mean?' she said calmly. 'Explain.'

'With Dad. He's bloody miserable. Almost crying on the phone to me this morning,' said Mary indignantly. 'Says you've left him. Is it true?'

'I'm not living with him at the moment; that's true enough,' replied Cynthia.

'What? Why? Where are you?' Mary's tone was increasingly aggressive.

Cynthia thought fast. She wasn't going to say where she was, though it was quite possible Mary had been in touch with her brother and already knew.

'Well, you know about the trial. And what's happened since. Plus, he'd overstepped the line well before all that,' said Cynthia quietly. 'I've had enough.'

Silence on the other end of the line. Then Mary's tone became pleading.

'But he was found not guilty, Mum.'

Cynthia permitted herself a brief, cynical snort. 'Do you really believe that?'

Silence again.

'He needs you, you know. Can't you work it out? At least meet him or talk to him. You're driving him mad, behaving like this,' said Mary.

'I need to work a few things out myself first, darling,' Cynthia said, still very calm. 'Then perhaps we'll see.'

'Well, I think it's cruel,' replied Mary, ever her father's daughter. 'Shame on you.'

She rang off abruptly. Cynthia gave a long-suffering sigh. Mary's reaction was exactly what she had expected. She knew that Carl was behind it.

Hardly had she put her phone down than she heard a text arrive. Probably another from Carl, she thought wearily, as she picked it up again.

But it was a reply from Bim to her earlier text.

"Yes – let's meet" it said.

* * *

Frank Paton hadn't been to the organisation's small head office in Chelmsford very often. Usually, he met Carl either at his house or on neutral ground: the premises of one of the businesses perhaps, or a restaurant. The office was pretty humdrum, but he liked that. Flashy offices attracted attention, and attention meant scrutiny. Frank didn't like scrutiny.

There were just the two of them. David had a PA, Linda, but had made sure that she stayed away that day. He'd also made sure that there was no mention of his meeting with Frank in the online office diary he shared with her. She was loyal enough, he thought, but she'd been provided for him by Carl and had been grateful for the opportunity. David wasn't going to risk Linda having a higher loyalty.

He made Frank a mug of coffee as he got settled, refilled his own and sat down at his desk. The two of them looked at each other.

'So,' said David.

'So,' replied Frank, non-committally.

'Where are we legally? I suppose that's what I'm saying,' continued David. He took an unhurried sip of his coffee.

Frank sighed in frustration, took off his glasses and began to polish them with his handkerchief. David could see that he was tired and worried.

'It's a bloody mess,' Frank said eventually. 'A completely unnecessary, bloody mess.'

David knew that more was coming. He waited.

'First – Bill,' continued the lawyer. 'I don't entirely blame him, because your dad gave the orders. But he completely cocked up. Knocking that Mills guy off his bike in his own car was amateurish. It was clearly deliberate; the van driver behind will testify to that. Killing him was bad luck, but it's a manslaughter charge at best. We don't do plea bargaining here like they do in the States, but assuming he's charged, we'll probably ask for an indication from the judge of the likely maximum sentence if he pleads guilty. It's best that he does, both for him and us, so that's what I'll make sure he gets advised. Not by me, of course, as that'll just be another link to your dad. We don't want the Prosecution looking under all sorts of rocks in a contested trial.'

'No,' agreed David. 'We don't. So, Bill's going to prison?'

Frank nodded. 'Ten years, maybe. Less given a good brief and time off for good behaviour. Out in five or six, perhaps. He'll probably keep quiet in those circumstances. We'll need to worry, though, if he sees any advantage in telling the police what else he knows.'

'Let's make sure he understands the disadvantages, then,' said David evenly.

Frank accepted this with a nod.

'Next – those arseholes who beat up the reporter,' he continued. 'Lowlifes used by Bill. They haven't been caught yet, but chances are, they will be. And then they'll probably talk. Links to Bill mean links to Carl, who ordered the whole damn thing, of course. They were probably supposed to get the other hack, too. Baxter.'

'Christ, couldn't Bill see how bloody stupid all this was?' said David, with quiet vexation.

'Bill's just overpromoted muscle – he got where he is because he does exactly what Carl tells him, no questions asked,' replied Frank. 'He's not the sharpest knife in the box.'

'No,' said David, with an ironic smile. 'Dad has a bit of an aversion to people with brains. I suppose it was Bill who made the call to that TV presenter, too?'

'Probably,' replied Frank. 'She says the caller's number was withheld, but given the level of professionalism he's shown to date, I expect the police will find her number on his mobile.'

He grimaced in disgust. 'That'll be another link back to your dad.'

David thought long and hard. 'Ultimately, this is all down to Dad,' he said. 'It's got to stop.'

He looked across at Frank, who had his best lawyer's face on. Deadpan.

'What do you suggest?' Frank asked, mildly.

'Well, I'll say it again,' said David. 'One way or the other, it's got to stop. And it will. But let's talk to him first. We owe him that.'

Frank looked at David carefully, assessing whether he'd understood the implications of what he'd heard correctly. It would be dangerous to misjudge them.

Then he nodded again.

* * *

Cynthia had arranged to meet Bim at a little country pub near Braintree, where she was unlikely to be recognised. She arrived early and bought a diet coke to tide her over whilst she waited. Bar a few emails, they hadn't been in touch for over a year, and Cynthia was nervous. She was six years her sister's senior, quite a gap when they were growing up, and so they'd never been as close as she was with Marnie, who was less than two years older.

Bim was twenty minutes late. When she eventually turned up, Cynthia was surprised how well and happy her sister looked after the bitterness of their last meeting: tall (taller than Cynthia), slim, well dressed and blooming, with freshly styled hair. She offered herself easily for a peck on the cheek as Cynthia rose, asked what she would like to drink and cheerfully went to the bar to order for both of them. Gin and tonics. 'One won't hurt,' she said.

Once they were settled, Bim came straight to the point.

'So, you've finally left him?' she said airily, with just the slightest hint of "told you so".

'Well, I'm not there at the moment, put it that way,' replied Cynthia.

Bim was a widow; indeed, a merry widow, it seemed to Cynthia. 'I'm so pleased,' she said.

'That my marriage has broken down?' Cynthia tried and failed to conceal her annoyance at Bim's tone. Her sister realised that she'd overstepped the mark.

'Sorry – that came out wrong,' she said. 'I'm just glad you've finally seen him for what he is. You watched the TV programmes, I take it?'

'I did,' replied Cynthia. 'And read the newspaper articles. But it was over before that. You know why.'

There was an awkward silence. They both took a sip of their drinks. Thankfully the waiter arrived with the menus, and after much debate, they both ordered the same thing: scallops.

'How's life?' asked Cynthia, as the waiter retreated. 'You're looking good. Really.'

Bim flashed her a happy smile. 'Life is good, thanks. House is fine. Work's fine.'

Cynthia thought there might be more to it than that but let it pass.

They gossiped for some time, largely about her visit to Marnie and how awful Clive was. The previous frost between them thawed fast as they laughed about him, though they both admitted that Marnie seemed happy enough with her lot. Only as their food arrived did the conversation move onto the darker subject of Carl.

'I've got to stop him, Bim,' said Cynthia, after outlining the background. 'He's gone loco. That's what caused all that nonsense on the follow-up programme. He may have been a wide boy—'

Bim grimaced. 'A bit more than that, Cyn.'

Cynthia waved her away. 'OK. I may have been late to realise it, but he was always kind at home. Very kind. A good provider. And a logical thinker. He'd never act like that. I think it's because I've left. He can't handle it.'

Her sister looked at her evenly. 'So at least talk to him.'

Cynthia shook her head. 'If I do, he'll try to persuade me, and I'm not going back. Once he realises that I think he could be quite dangerous.'

'To you?' said Bim, concerned.

'I think so, yes. To himself, too. And also, to be honest, I'm afraid of losing everything,' confided Cynthia. 'For me and the children.'

'What do they think?' Bim asked. Cynthia sighed.

'Mary's a daddy's girl. Spoilt. She says I'm being unfair.'

'Hardly,' snorted Bim.

'Rob's not been in touch at all. Probably doesn't even know. Oblivious in his own academic world. And David… you know I'm living there, right?'

'No,' said Bim. 'I didn't.'

'He's as worried as I am. We're discussing what to do. I'm a bit stuck. It's not easy.'

'Anything I can do to help,' said Bim, 'you just ask.'

The sisters were happy to be reconciled and chatted easily as Bim settled up – 'my treat.'

'Why did we call you Bim when you were young anyway?' asked Cynthia, catching the full name on the credit card. 'Where did it come from?'

'No idea,' shrugged Sarah.

* * *

David had a dental appointment on Tuesday morning, and it ran late. It wasn't worth going into the office afterwards, so he rang Linda and told her he'd work from home in the afternoon. It was just spreadsheet stuff anyway.

He bought a sandwich from Pret on the way home, as he knew his mother was out having lunch with Aunt Bim. He hoped it went well; he'd always liked Aunt Bim, not that he knew her very well, and was sorry that there seemed to have been a sisterly falling out after what had happened to her husband.

Uncle Peter's suicide was the moment the scales had finally dropped from his mother's eyes, thought David, though she'd had have to be wilfully blind not to have sensed anything before. He didn't feel remotely guilty himself about devising the LAX offshore scheme, which had been the root cause of all the trouble.

David was deep in his beloved spreadsheets when a knock came at the door, firm and insistent. Cynthia wasn't yet back.

He rose from his desk, mystified but cautious. He looked through the peephole before slipping the latch. It was Carl.

'Hello, Dad,' he said, opening the door to his flat. What the hell did he want?

Carl said nothing as he entered, but he was well dressed and looked much more himself than when David had last seen him. That was good.

Or maybe not.

'So, she's not here?' Carl said quietly, returning from a brief look into the living room as his son closed the door.

David was nonplussed. He hadn't told anyone his mother was staying, but Carl had clearly found out and had dressed to impress her. He'd have to brazen it out.

'No,' said David, trying to make Cynthia's stay seem routine. 'She's out to lunch. With Aunt Bim, I think.'

'Aunt Bim,' sneered Carl. 'I might have guessed. And you never thought to tell me that my wife was holed up in this dump? Which I paid for.'

'She's my mother,' replied David, trying to keep things calm. 'She needs a bit of space.'

The explanation cut no ice. Carl was now very close to his slightly built eldest son and still moving forward.

'Let me make one thing very clear to you,' he said menacingly. 'People who work for me are loyal to me. Or else. And that includes you.'

David was slowly retreating. 'I am loyal to you, Dad,' he protested. 'But Mum asked – there's no harm in her staying here for a few nights. We're all one family, aren't we?'

Carl's eyes flashed dangerously. He pushed his son brusquely back onto a sofa and then leant over him. David cowered as a jewelled finger jabbed his chest unpleasantly hard.

'You tell her to call me once she gets back,' Carl said quietly. 'If she doesn't, I'm going to be disappointed. You've disappointed me once already today, Davey. Don't do it again.'

Carl pinched his son's cheek hard and then made to strike him. He laughed contemptuously as David flinched, then stood back and turned on his heel. At the door, he paused and looked over his shoulder.

'Understand?'

David nodded, speechless.

'You better.'

David was still sitting there fifteen minutes later, when Cynthia returned. She knew immediately from his ashen expression that something was wrong.

'Dad?' she demanded. 'What's he done?'

'Wants you to call him,' said David, cowed still. 'Said I was to pass it on, without fail.'

Cynthia was unmoved.

'Well, you've done that. Well done. Did he call, or was he here?'

'He was here. Knows you are too.'

'Did he threaten you?'

'Yes,' replied David miserably. 'Didn't hit me or anything. But you know him…'

'I know him alright,' said Cynthia grimly. 'Right. I will sort this out, once and for all.'

CHAPTER THIRTEEN

After Sarah had left on Monday morning, John reflected on the preceding day. It had been a rather surreal one after he'd produced what was under the orange blanket.

Sarah had looked at it in astonishment. 'But surely that's a toy?' she'd said.

'No,' said John, pleased at her reaction. 'It's a shotgun. A .410.' (He pronounced it four-ten.) 'A poacher's special, in fact.'

The little gun on the table had a single octagonal barrel, which was folded back almost parallel to the butt and trigger mechanism, protruding a little behind it. In that state it wasn't much more than fifteen inches long. John unfolded it so that the mechanism clicked home. There was a hammer at the rear, a trigger and a lever on the right-hand side with a flat top within reach of the thumb: this opened the gun. It was about thirty inches long fully extended and well weathered.

'See?' John demonstrated, folding it again. 'It fits into a pocket in a long coat. You just fish it out when the coast is clear, click the barrel into place and pot your pheasant.'

Sarah took the gun from him, fascinated, and closed it.

'Why have you got this?' she asked.

'We went to a house clearing sale once when Tom was about fourteen,' replied John. 'He was mad on shooting rabbits then, but my 12 bore was too heavy for him, and his air rifle wasn't up to the job. He persuaded me to bid for it, which I could because I've got a shotgun certificate. It's Belgian. Thirty-five quid, I think.'

Sarah was still handling the gun and cautiously pushed the side lever which opened it.

'It looks pretty ancient,' she said dubiously.

'Pre-war, probably. Of course, it was a bit of a flash in the pan,' continued John. 'He pretty soon lost interest. I doubt it's been fired for seven or eight years, just been sat in the gun cupboard.'

Sarah looked up from the gun. 'Have you got bullets for it?' she asked.

'Cartridges,' John corrected her. 'Shotguns have cartridges. I think there's a few around, yes.'

Sarah handed the gun back to him.

'You know we were wondering what to do today?' she asked.

'I thought you had some good ideas about that,' John reminded her.

Sarah waved him away impatiently. 'Later! I've never fired a gun. Could I have a go with it?'

She looked at him anxiously, like a little girl. 'It could double as research for you…'

John thought for a moment.

'Well, I don't see why not,' he said. 'We'll take a few tins up to the spinney so that nobody gets disturbed and see if

Annie Oakley has anything to worry about.'

Sarah flashed him a winning smile and went off to get her boots and coat whilst John headed back to the gun cabinet with the 12 bore. There was a plastic bag inside with about fifteen loose .410 cartridges, plus a sealed box of twenty-five. He took the plastic bag out before locking the cabinet and returning the keys to the safe in his study. That would be enough.

Barney came with them as they headed out to John's grey four-wheel drive Volvo estate: newish, but not often used these days. There were a few old paint tins in the garage, and John loaded them in the back with Barney before laying the little gun carefully across the back seat.

'This could do with a clean,' said Sarah, as she looked around inside the car.

'It's a farm vehicle,' replied John in a long-suffering tone. 'It's supposed to be dirty.'

'I see,' said Sarah, in her best ironic voice.

It was a mile or so to the spinney, which was a field's width away from the road, and John drove into the middle of it, where there was a small clearing. There he stopped and set up five of the old paint tins on a fallen tree trunk.

'Before you have a go, I'm going to demonstrate a few disadvantages of this as my murder weapon,' said John.

'You only get one shot,' suggested Sarah.

'True enough,' replied John. 'But I can reload. Watch this.'

He broke the gun open by operating the side lever with his thumb, inserted a cartridge and closed it again.

'Now,' he said. 'This gun is loaded, and when you have it, you must be very careful where you point it. Either down at the ground or up at the sky until you're ready to shoot.'

'Is there a safety catch?' asked Sarah. 'Don't guns have those?'

'Generally, yes, they do,' said John. 'But not this. Effectively, the safety catch is the hammer here, at the back of the barrel. See?'

He showed her. 'It's not going to fire until I thumb this back. Watch.'

He did so with his right thumb, until the spring-loaded hammer clicked into a locked back position.

'This is now completely ready to fire,' he said, with the gun carefully pointed at the ground. 'The trigger will release the hammer. I'll show you what it can do. There'll be a bang, but not a very loud one. Watch.'

John stood twenty yards from the tree trunk, took aim at the left-hand tin and fired. Sarah watched carefully. The tin wobbled but didn't topple. Before they went to look at it, John opened the gun, which was wreathed in smoke. The used cartridge stayed in the breach, though pushed out about half an inch by a U-shaped bracket gripping its brass base from beneath.

'See that?' he said. 'Non-ejector. I've got to take the used cartridge out by hand before I can reload. A more expensive gun would eject it automatically. Takes a couple of seconds. But that's good if it's my murder weapon.'

'Why?' asked Sarah.

'Because it means I won't lose the cartridge,' explained John. 'The pellets I've fired can't be traced to the gun. The cartridge can because it'll have unique marks on the brass base where it's been struck by the firing pin of this particular gun. So, I take it out and put it in my pocket before I reload. If the gun ejects the old cartridge automatically, I'll probably lose it in a bush or something.'

Sarah nodded. 'OK – what damage did it do? I saw you'd hit it.'

'Come and see,' said John. Sarah trailed after him, curious.

A few pellets had penetrated the tin, but most had just dented it, and the pattern of strikes wasn't very dense.

'That doesn't look like much,' said Sarah, sounding disappointed.

'It isn't,' said John. 'Remember I told you that a shotgun is only any good at short range? Well, this is a small shotgun, as small as they get. I wanted to show you. Now, let's see what happens from closer.'

They moved back but only about twelve yards. John turned to face the trunk and handed the gun to Sarah.

'Here, you load it,' he said.

She took the gun nervously, after a glance for reassurance, and opened it with the side lever. John gently kept the barrel pointing in the direction of the tree trunk and then handed her a cartridge.

'Go on,' he said, encouragingly. She put the cartridge into the breech and then closed the gun.

'So, that's loaded now but won't fire till I thumb back the hammer?' she asked uncertainly.

'Yes,' said John. 'That will cock the gun. Now give it back to me.'

Sarah did so awkwardly, and John thumbed the hammer till it clicked back again.

'Watch,' he said.

This time, the tin jumped into the air and was knocked off the trunk. John led Sarah forward and picked it up. The pattern of pellet strikes was much denser, and most of them had penetrated.

'What do you think?' he asked.

'Well, it looks painful—' began Sarah hesitantly.

'I know what you're going to say – but not fatal,' interrupted John. 'And you'd be right. You have to be really close.'

He led her back again and reloaded, this time standing only six feet back from the trunk. As the third shot rang out, the middle pint-sized tin was blasted back a good distance. John retrieved it and handed it to Sarah: the pellets had barely dispersed and had collectively punched a hole about two inches across right through, emerging the opposite side.

'Now, that looks nasty,' Sarah said.

'It is. That's about as close as I've got to get to commit murder with this gun. So now you know.'

Sarah looked pensive. 'Come on, your turn,' said John.

He handed her the gun, and they returned to where John had fired from, just a few feet back. Sarah managed the loading procedure very capably and then looked to John for guidance.

'What next?' he asked her gently. Sarah nodded and then thumbed back the hammer till it clicked into place.

'You're ready,' said John. 'Keep it pointed in the right direction, and put it into your shoulder. Pull it in hard.'

'Will it hurt?' asked Sarah, anxiously.

'You'll barely feel it if you pull it in tight,' said John. 'Now – look down the barrel, and line that little bead on the end of it up with the next can. No rear sights with a shotgun.'

Sarah did as she was told. It looked to John as if she was squinting, and she would probably flinch, but he thought it best just to get the ordeal of the first shot over.

'Go on, fire,' he urged her. 'Squeeze the trigger.'

Sarah did flinch, and she jerked the trigger rather than squeezed it, so the shot wasn't very accurate, but it was undoubtedly a hit. It clipped the bottom of the tin, knocking it off the trunk. As luck would have it, the paint residue inside was red, adding visual drama.

'Whoa,' Sarah exhaled, the gun flailing.

'You got it,' said John calmly. 'Keep the gun pointing in the right direction, remember.'

Sarah was thrilled with herself. After that, there was no stopping her. There were only ten cartridges left, but she fired all of them with rising confidence and from increasing distance.

'I could get used to this,' she grinned happily at John after her final shot.

'You've done very well,' said John, taking the gun from her. 'Not so difficult, is it?'

'No,' replied Sarah. 'Really it isn't.'

* * *

Once they were back, John cleaned the shotgun and returned it to the cabinet, watched all the while by Sarah, who chatted away happily. Afterwards, they settled down with a cup of tea.

'So, you've solved one problem,' said Sarah, firmly. 'That's what you'd use.'

'I suppose I could make sure my murderer had something similar,' replied John with a smile. 'But if it was genuinely me doing the job, there'd still be some critical difficulties to solve.'

'Such as?'

'Well, for one thing: I've got to decide where and when to do it,' replied John. 'Then I've got to be sure that he's there at the right time and that I can get access to wherever it is. And I must have a decent chance of getting away again. Plus, hopefully an alibi. These are pretty important considerations!'

'Otherwise, it's not a perfect murder,' agreed Sarah, reluctantly. 'Yes, I can see all that.'

She lapsed into silence, lost in thought. Then she looked up.

'Well, we know he's shacked up at home – alone,' she said. 'That's one question solved.'

'Yes, but how long will he be there, how can I guarantee he's by himself, and how do I get in?' said John.

Sarah thought. 'Got to do it soon. Whilst he's still there, rather than out and about again. It's been a month or so already.'

John nodded. 'Probably. But it doesn't solve the other problems.'

'No,' said Sarah. 'It doesn't. But I'm definitely going to think about it.'

She looked oddly determined. John appreciated her becoming so closely involved in his project. Indeed, she seemed rather more enthusiastic recently than he was, he thought ruefully.

But anything they were jointly involved in was fine by him.

* * *

Sarah decided to stay for Sunday night. It began predictably actively as a result of the wishes she had expressed earlier about

139

the weekend, which John did his best to satisfy. Afterwards, he slept soundly and contentedly.

Something disturbed him in the early hours, and he sensed Sarah wide awake on her back next to him. It was obvious that she was deep in thought. A sixth sense warned him it was best not to interrupt her, and after a few minutes he dozed off again. But he hadn't forgotten when morning came, and intuition told him she was not in the mood for another bout of lovemaking, much as she seemed to enjoy them.

At breakfast, Sarah was still strangely diffident, to the extent that John became concerned something had gone amiss between them. If it had, he wasn't aware why.

'Everything OK?' he said, as lightly as he could muster when she lapsed into a thoughtful silence.

'Yes.' She flashed him a strained smile. 'Don't worry. Nothing to do with you. It's just… I've been thinking.'

Sarah looked at him uncertainly. 'Go on,' John encouraged her evenly.

'Well, you know that little gun?' said Sarah, after a long and reflective pause.

'Of course,' replied John.

'I wondered – could I borrow it?'

John looked at her in astonishment. 'What on earth for?'

Sarah came around the table and kissed him gently on the lips.

'Come and sit down,' she said. John made no resistance as she led him by the hand from the breakfast table to the sofa.

Sarah turned to face him once they were seated. John thought she looked very serious and extremely attractive. Dangerously so, in fact.

'I want to kill him,' she said simply. 'Carl Barrow. After what he did to Peter.'

John had never been genuinely lost for words in his life, but there was always a first time.

'What? You cannot be serious?' he said, after a while. 'How? I mean, you'd never get away with it.'

'I think I would,' she said calmly. 'Or at least I could if it was carefully planned.'

'Talking about something like that in the abstract for a novel which'll probably never get written and actually doing it are poles apart,' John replied. 'It's ridiculous. I mean, how would you ever get near him?'

Sarah smoothed back her hair. 'I'm going to tell you something in confidence,' she said. 'Promise me you'll keep it to yourself?'

Despite himself, John nodded, still in shock from her earlier declaration. 'OK.'

'He's split up with his wife,' said Sarah.

'I know that,' said John, with rising impatience.

Sarah saw it and raised her hand to still John's protestations.

'She says he's become completely unpredictable and probably dangerous. She wants to stop him but doesn't know how. And she's my sister.'

* * *

Afterwards, they went for a long walk with Barney. John was silent and deep in thought. Sarah knew better than to interrupt him and waited patiently.

After a mile or so, he turned to her.

'You absolutely mean this?' he said.

141

Sarah nodded. 'I absolutely do.'

John walked on for another hundred yards or so, before turning to her again.

'What made you think I wouldn't just go to the police?' he demanded.

Sarah shrugged. 'Intuition. Plus, if you won't lend me the gun, I've got no plan; I'm finished.'

John turned to Sarah and gripped her by the shoulders, almost as if he wanted to shake her.

'This is a mad fantasy. Look, be realistic; I don't want you winding up in a prison cell. Or worse, like that chap they knocked off his bike. Or the journalist. Carl Barrow and his sort don't muck around.'

Sarah shook herself free and walked on.

'I think it could be done,' she said stubbornly.

'Nonsense. You've fired ten shots in your life, all of them at tins sitting on a tree. It's not the same, firing at something alive and moving,' John said urgently.

Sarah carried on walking. They lapsed into a frosty silence until they were back at the house, with John increasingly pensive.

When they got there, she turned to him decisively.

'I think I'd better go now,' she said.

John saw the tears beginning to well in her eyes and instinctively reached for her arm.

'I understand,' he said gently. 'Take some time to think. I will too. I think you'll conclude that it's just not feasible.'

Sarah shook her head. 'I'm sorry. Sure, I'll think about it. About how to do it.'

She was packed up and in her car in five minutes, with a very determined set to her jaw. John waved half-heartedly as the Golf nosed out of the gate and could sense the mood Sarah was in from the hard burst of acceleration which followed. He shook his head sadly and went back inside.

That was very probably that, he thought, and all over a hopeless pipe dream. What a waste.

CHAPTER FOURTEEN

Frank recognised David's number as he answered his phone.

'Dad's been called in for questioning.'

'What? Why didn't he tell me?' asked Frank, taken aback.

He'd drummed into Carl for years that any contact from the police was to be notified to him, without fail. Hitherto, his client had always done that scrupulously. It was a rule which had served them both well.

'Disrespect, he says. Apparently, you swore at him.'

'I did, and he bloody well deserved it,' replied Frank. 'Silly bugger. He hasn't gone alone, has he?'

'No – he's taking Jim Steiner, who got a lot of pleasure out of calling to tell me this morning. The meeting's in a couple of days' time.'

Frank swore. Jim Steiner had done some legal work for him in the early days, and he was definitely a competent lawyer, but he was also manifestly ambitious. He'd clearly had his eye on Frank's position as what the Mafia would have called "consigliere" to Carl. Too clearly.

So, Frank had got rid of him a couple of years ago – just

like that. When Carl learnt of it, he had jested clumsily about anti-semitism, but Frank had responded seriously.

'The reason I don't like Jim is not because he is Jewish but because he is a nasty, untrustworthy little worm,' he'd said.

Carl had accepted the reproach at the time without comment. He'd just nodded.

But clearly, he hadn't forgotten the man or his competence. Maybe he was just teaching Frank a lesson. Or perhaps this was a permanent shift to Steiner. Frank cursed.

'This is getting beyond a joke,' he said. 'I'll call him.'

'Good luck with that,' replied David. Then he revealed Carl's visit to the flat.

'What does your mum say about that?' asked Frank.

David was caught momentarily off balance; he hadn't revealed that Cynthia was staying with him. But the question didn't infer that Frank was actually aware of that, he decided.

'Didn't think she knew such language,' he replied with a chuckle. 'Hopping mad. She's had it with him.'

There was a pause on the line before Frank responded.

'I reckon that makes three of us then.'

* * *

That evening, Cynthia cooked David's favourite meal – it was in the oven when he got back from the office. She knew he could smell it from the look on his face, which he'd had since childhood when steak and kidney pie was in the offing, though he tried hard to conceal it.

'You called him, yeah?' he asked his mother anxiously, as she emerged from the kitchen and offered him a glass of red. She already had one herself.

'No,' Cynthia said forcefully. 'Most certainly I did not.'

'Mum…' began David in the small boy, whiny voice he'd never quite got out of when pleading with her.

'I texted to tell him I'd got the message,' said Cynthia. 'So, you're in the clear.'

She took a sip of her wine, awaiting his reply.

'And that's all?' said David.

'That's all,' replied Cynthia.

David gestured helplessly. 'OK.'

Once her son was busily guzzling down the meal, Cynthia got to the point. She'd been thinking about it all day.

'There are a couple of things I'd like to talk about,' she began carefully.

'Yeah?' said David, with apparent disinterest, reaching for a second helping.

'Number one: I'm moving out.'

David looked up sharply. 'Yeah?'

Cynthia reflected (not for the first time) on his limited vocabulary, strange, in someone so bright. It went in tandem with his social gaucheness. Maybe he was on the spectrum; she'd heard something about it on the car radio, whilst driving around the M25 on the way back from Marnie the other day.

'It's not fair on you. I'm not having your dad dragging you into the middle of this. It's for me to sort out.'

David hesitated for a moment and nodded his approval. 'Where are you going?'

'Never you mind,' said Cynthia. 'Close by. But you can't tell what don't know.'

'I wouldn't, Mum,' protested David.

'I know, darling,' she replied. 'But your father can be… persuasive, shall we say?'

David reflected unhappily on the truth of that statement. 'When?' he queried.

'Tomorrow.'

David's expression indicated acceptance, possibly with a hint of relief, Cynthia sensed. She'd arranged the flat that morning, sight unseen. Small, but sufficient for the moment. It was only a couple of miles away.

'What was the second thing?'

This was more delicate, Cynthia thought.

'I am very worried about how your father is behaving,' she began cautiously.

'You and me both,' said David, still chewing his food. Cynthia wished she'd done a better job on his table manners, but it was difficult with Carl as a role model. The difference was that Carl had trained himself to do it if he had to. She was less sure about David, despite his expensive schooling.

'He has threatened you; I think he is becoming a danger to me; and he is imperilling everything we have,' she continued. 'He's ruining the business.'

She knew that the potential commercial carnage would weigh heavily with David, which was why she ended with it.

'I'll tell you something else – he's sacked Frank,' David responded, after a moment's reflection.

Cynthia looked at him, appalled.

'Well, not exactly sacked,' he continued, 'but Dad's being interviewed under caution tomorrow. He's taking Jim Steiner instead of Frank.'

'Jim Steiner?' Cynthia's appalled tone made further comment superfluous, but she added it anyway. 'He's a horrible man.'

She remembered Jim's eyes wandering lasciviously and

blatantly over her the first time they'd met. Creepy. She'd sworn then and there never to have him in her house and stuck to it.

'Yes,' agreed David. 'Capable though. And I suppose better than Dad going alone.'

'We need to stop him, darling,' said Cynthia, quietly.

'How, Mum?' replied David with a helpless shrug. 'Can't you do something? You know why he's like this. It's all about you—'

'I'm never going back, so forget it,' Cynthia interrupted, with quiet determination. 'So, we need another plan.'

'What sort of plan?' David asked.

'I think probably a permanent one,' said Cynthia and awaited her son's reaction. He paused for several seconds, inscrutable, before giving it.

'Permanent as in a final solution?' David knew the unspoken connotations of that terrible term and used it as a code.

'Yes,' said Cynthia coolly. 'And I am beginning to think there might be a way.'

* * *

Jim Steiner had been surprised, but delighted, when Carl had called him.

Carl said he'd been asked by Bishop's Stortford police to attend a voluntary interview under caution regarding his possible involvement in the death of Patrick Mills. Should he go?

Jim's first thought, quickly discarded, was to ask, 'What about Frank?' But he knew that opportunity seldom knocked twice.

'Yes, but not without me,' he said quickly.

He explained that a voluntary interview was the same as any other sort, though he was pretty confident that given his long and colourful career, Carl was well aware of that. Anyone could still incriminate themselves. Carl was entitled to legal representation, and though the police might infer he was doing himself no favours by insisting on it, Jim knew that it was the only prudent course.

'It's a fishing expedition,' Jim assured Carl. 'They're looking for enough evidence to charge you, and they don't have it yet, or they'd have already done so.'

'What if I don't go?' asked Carl. 'It's voluntary, isn't it?'

'It is, but it's risky not to,' said Jim. 'Let's say you're tried and found guilty. The extent to which you cooperated with the investigation can be brought to the court's attention before sentence is passed. You don't want to trip over that hurdle.'

Carl stayed silent.

'Do it, but have a legal adviser present,' urged Jim. 'That'll put them on edge; they'll have to follow the letter of the law, and they won't be tempted to try anything oppressive.'

'Will they record it?' asked Carl. The Patrick Mills thing had definitely been a mistake. He didn't want to make another one on tape.

'You can refuse to allow it, but that carries the same risk as not turning up at all,' replied Jim.

'Non-cooperation,' reflected Carl. 'Fuck it – bring it on. You be there, Jim.'

* * *

On Thursday, the day after she'd moved into her new flat, Cynthia asked Sarah over. The invitation was intended partly

149

as a continuation of their earlier discussion at lunch, when they had mended a lot of fences, and partly to obtain her help in getting settled. And partly regarding something else.

Sarah had been pleased to be asked and was there by 10am. The rented, one-bedroom flat in Chelmsford was not big, but it was furnished and comfortable enough, given that Cynthia only expected to be there for a short time. Most of her belongings were still in the home she'd shared with Carl, which was becoming something of a problem. But that could wait.

The sisters had everything pretty much shipshape in the flat by lunchtime. They both instinctively knew that only then was the main business of their meeting about to start. They settled down with a strong gin and tonic apiece, and the verbal fencing began.

'So, how are things?' began Sarah, non-committally.

Cynthia grimaced. 'Worse than when we last met.'

Sarah took a sip of her drink and waited for the inevitable explanation. She knew her sister.

'I told you I thought he was becoming dangerous, right?' began Cynthia, knowing she had. Sarah nodded.

'Well, it's started. He threatened David. Just because I was living there. It's why I moved out.'

'Is he still texting and calling?' replied her sister.

'No, and that worries me,' said Cynthia. 'He told David in no uncertain terms to get me to call him. I didn't, but I texted to say he'd passed on the message, so he was in the clear. I didn't get a reply to that.'

Sarah digested this for a moment. 'He doesn't know you're here, does he?' she said.

Cynthia shook her head. 'No – I don't think so. But I didn't think he knew I was at David's, either.'

She looked up for reassurance.

'And you say he's acting irrationally?' asked Sarah.

'Completely. He's sacked his solicitor Frank, who in hindsight I think has been the only person between him and a jail cell for years. He's off to see the police next week with some smart-arse lawyer Frank got rid of ages ago.'

'What about?'

'Oh, links to that Boatman guy, the one who ran over the cyclist. Patrick Mills. Voluntary interview under caution, David says,' replied Cynthia. She took a long pull from her drink.

'He'll screw it up without Frank.' She shrugged apathetically.

'Isn't that what you want? To see him put away?' asked Sarah.

'Well, yes and no,' Cynthia replied. 'I'd have liked him to go down on the money laundering charge because he was guilty. And also because—'

'That led to Peter's suicide,' interrupted Sarah calmly.

Cynthia sensed the challenge in that cool stare. It was true. The death of her brother-in-law had finally opened her eyes to the sort of man she had married. She'd known it in her bones for a long time but had never had to confront the reality personally.

'Yes,' she said simply. 'And another thing, too.'

Sarah stayed silent again, waiting for the elaboration. Cynthia deliberated momentarily, then decided to tell her.

'If he was locked up, he wouldn't be in a position to jeopardise everything we have now – me and the children,' she explained. 'I know some of it is ill-gotten gains, but I'm afraid of being left with nothing. David was talking to me about

Unexplained Wealth Orders. A court can issue one ordering Carl to reveal the sources of his assets, even if he's not been charged with any offence. That could result in confiscation. The more he sticks his head above the parapet with silly stunts like intimidating the press, the more that's likely to happen. David's very worried. Frank too.'

'So, what are you going to do about it?'

Cynthia looked at Sarah long and hard, appraising the likely reaction to what she was about to say.

'I'm prepared to do anything,' she said. 'Within reason or not. And that's easier if he's not in jail.'

'May I ask how?' replied Sarah. Cynthia was amazed at her sister's cool reaction to what was being implied.

There was a long pause.

'I don't know yet,' said Cynthia. 'I think Frank and David might be persuaded, but one's been a friend for years, and the other's his son. So, as I said the other day, I'm a bit stuck.'

'You know how much I hate him, Cyn, don't you?' said Sarah simply.

'I've got a fair idea, yes,' her older sister replied. 'That's why we fell out.'

'I've been planning to do something about it. Something terminal. If you're prepared to help, I think it would work.'

Cynthia looked at her sibling in astonishment, and then recovered herself. She had been vaguely hoping for her sister's help but had hardly expected her to take the lead.

'What's your plan?' she said, intrigued. 'If it's any good, I'm probably in.'

Sarah shook her head and finished her gin. 'A few days yet. Some work still to do. But good to know you might help.'

CHAPTER FIFTEEN

John had thought long and hard since Sarah had left, and he sensed how guarded she was when he called to ask if he could come over that afternoon.

She allowed him to kiss her on the cheek when he arrived but was still fairly distant; he could have been any old acquaintance. Barney acted as a bit of an icebreaker, which was why John had bought him along. After making a fuss of the dog, she made them both a cup of tea, sat opposite him on a stool at the kitchen island and appraised him frankly. John sensed what was coming; no need for the little speech he'd prepared.

'Well,' she said. 'Will you lend it to me or not?'

So, no beating about the bush. That made it easier. John took a deep breath.

'I have reached a decision, yes,' he said. He paused, seeing the wariness in her gaze.

'The thing is,' he continued, 'I don't think you'd succeed, even if your sister helped.'

'You don't think I've got the nerve to shoot him?'

'I don't think you've got the experience to shoot him. Not the same thing.'

'So, it's a no, then,' said Sarah calmly.

'I didn't say that,' responded John carefully, seeing how deflated she was. 'Look, here's what I propose.'

He drained the remainder of his tea.

'I can't believe I'm saying this, but let's plan this thing together, just like the book. If I'm convinced it's feasible – and I mean really convinced that we can get away with it – then…'

He hesitated and grimaced.

'Then what?' said Sarah.

'Then I'll do it,' said John quietly. 'I'll do the shooting. He'd be no loss to the world.'

Sarah came quickly around the table and kissed him on the lips.

'Thank you,' she said, gratefully. 'I did have my doubts about the shooting.'

'Let's be quite clear about this, though,' said John, still sitting on his stool but with his arm around her waist. 'If I don't think it's possible to kill him cleanly, and get away with it, then I won't do it. And neither will you, at least not with my gun. Understood?'

Sarah stood back from him.

'Understood. As long as you do your best to make it happen and don't just look for reasons not to. Promise?'

John nodded. 'I promise,' he said, seriously.

He saw again the lazy, sexy smile he'd begun to adore, reappearing for the first time since their disagreement. Sarah reached for his hand and pulled him up from the stool.

'What are you doing?' he asked.

'Sealing our deal,' replied Sarah, pulling him gently towards the stairs.

* * *

That evening, Sarah poured them both a whisky, and they sat down for their first planning session. John protested that he was driving, but she quickly waved that away.

'Stay the night. Plenty of Peter's old stuff here.'

John thought briefly and then nodded his assent. He had Barney with him, so there was no need to return home.

'OK, that's settled,' she said, raising her glass. 'To partners in crime.'

John raised his whisky in response. 'Partners in crime.'

Sarah took a deep pull at her drink and looked up thoughtfully.

'I've been thinking a lot about this,' she began.

'I bet you have,' said John, with a sardonic smile. She smiled back and continued.

'Where, when, how – that's what it's all about.'

'And most important of all, how to get away with it,' John prompted her. 'I agree. It's a bit like war, though. Deciding what you want to do is pretty simple, but even the simplest thing is very difficult.'

Sarah smiled. 'Well, let's talk all that through for real, not as a book plot. First – where?'

'We can deal with all those questions straightaway in principle,' replied John.

'Where – it's got to be at his house if he's holed up there alone. When – soon. We don't know how long that situation's going to last. As for how I'd do it – we've already discussed that. The devil's in the detail.'

'I agree with you about the house,' said Sarah. 'But as you say, there are difficulties. We've got to be sure he's there. We've got to be able to get in – he's got electric gates and a surveillance system. And we've got to get out again.'

'Assuming you'll be there at all,' said John. 'Maybe it's best done by me alone?'

Sarah shook her head vigorously.

'That's a no, I take it?' said John. 'Well, that's one decision made.'

He paused for thought. 'We've got to think both earlier and later than that.'

'What do you mean?' asked Sarah.

John took another sip of his drink.

'I mean, we've got to get there without attracting suspicion or being seen. What is it, fifteen miles from me? Then we've got to do the same in reverse. And we'll need some sort of alibi.'

Sarah nodded slowly in agreement. 'Not easy.'

'To what extent will your sister help?' asked John. 'Does she know about me?'

'Not in so many words,' replied Sarah. 'She knows I've got an outline plan, and I think she's supportive in principle. She's worried about losing everything, and she'll do whatever it takes to stop that. I suppose it comes down to what we ask her to do.'

She paused and looked up, shyly.

'I also think she knows I've got a new man,' she said. 'We haven't discussed it, but she's pleased for me.'

'I'm pleased for you too,' said John, reaching for her hand. 'And for me as well. Very. But try and keep any details about me between us, eh?'

Sarah could see the sense in that. 'OK.'

'To get in, and to know he's there, I can't see that there's any other way than to have her arrange that,' continued John. 'So, you'll need to speak to her once we've firmed up some more details.'

'It'll mean some sort of reconciliation between them probably or at least a meeting to talk,' said Sarah. 'She's not going to like that.'

'Nevertheless,' said John 'If she wants it to happen, she's going to have to do quite a few things she doesn't like. As are we all.'

They continued their discussion for another hour, over a working supper. There was lots to think about. John jotted it all down in a notebook Sarah dug out for him.

'Remember – nothing in your phone,' she reminded him. 'Or your iPad. I'm going to sort all that out tomorrow.'

John wasn't sure exactly what she meant, but by then he was flagging and had had enough of plotting for one day. His co-conspirator realised it and that a lot of issues had arisen which he wanted to double-check.

She left him rewatching the *Panorama* programmes with his notebook, whilst she headed upstairs for a long bath. Afterwards, she fell immediately into a deep sleep.

John didn't bother to wake her when he slid into bed later; he was tired, and the deal had already been well sealed that afternoon.

* * *

The next day John headed home shortly after breakfast, as Sarah said she had to go shopping, after rather mysteriously asking for his foot size. She also said that she'd join him at his house by lunchtime. John spent a quiet morning thinking about what he'd let himself in for, and more specifically how to get to Carl's house and back without being identified. By the time Sarah arrived, he had the germ of an idea.

She was there shortly after midday, smiling at him broadly from her Golf as she drew up in his drive.

'You look like the cat that's got the cream,' said John from his doorway, as Sarah got out of the car.

She moved to the rear and opened its tailgate, pulling out two large, identical sports bags. John looked at her questioningly as she handed him one of them.

'Presents,' grinned Sarah, cheerfully. 'I'll show you inside.'

John followed her in, and she made her way to the kitchen, laying her bag on the table.

'Go on,' she said. 'Have a look at yours.'

John opened his bag whilst she watched expectantly. The first thing he pulled out was a mobile phone, still in its packaging. It didn't look like a very expensive one.

'Pay-As-You-Go,' said Sarah, triumphantly. 'Plus, twenty quids' worth of credit. I've got one too.'

She pulled an identical phone out of her bag, and then a third.

'Who's that one for?' asked John, looking concerned.

'It's for my sister, Cynthia; I'm sure I can persuade her,' replied Sarah, before moving on briskly.

'Now, listen. I paid cash for these; there's no credit card trace or anything about the purchase which identifies me. After this, we store each other's numbers in these phones, and I'll have Cynthia's too. Anything to do with our plan – anything at all, texts, calls or emails – we do it on these. Nothing from them to our normal numbers. Though obviously there must be a few calls between us on those – it would be suspicious if they just stopped.'

John digested this. 'What about CCTV cameras in the shop?'

'I don't think there were any,' Sarah replied. 'But I wore a wide-brimmed hat, a scarf and sunglasses. It wouldn't be easy to identify me, even if there were. And we're going to get rid of these phones straightaway afterwards anyway.'

'OK,' said John, after a moment's thought. 'Did you withdraw a large sum of cash?'

Sarah shook her head, pleased with herself. 'No. I've been taking enough out in dribs and drabs for some time. Nothing big enough to attract attention.'

'Good,' said John calmly. 'And when you say we're going to get rid of them—'

Sarah jumped in. 'Straightaway. Back in the bag. Look what else is in it.'

The next thing to come out was a pair of cheap white trainers in John's size, still in their packaging. He looked at Sarah for an explanation.

'That's what you wear when we do it. Never wear them at your house – we don't want any prints from them here or at mine. I've got a pair too, and we get rid of them afterwards as well. Back in the bag.'

John nodded his understanding, peered inside his bag again and pulled out a tablet, again still in its packaging – once more not expensive, certainly not an iPad. He didn't know the brand and thought it was probably Chinese.

'What's this for?' he asked.

'That's for any internet research you do, and you can also

set up a new email account on it,' said Sarah. 'As I will do on mine and my phone. We don't want any trace of stuff like that on our normal electronic gizmos in case they are ever examined.'

'Also bought with cash?' John queried.

Sarah nodded. 'Different place to the phones. And also to be got rid of ASAP afterwards. Back in the bag.'

'You have been busy,' said John. 'What other goodies have you got me?'

It was rather mundane after that: notebooks, a pack of four biros, batteries.

'For anything you write,' explained Sarah. 'And—'

'I know. Back in the bag,' John interjected.

He picked up all his new acquisitions and examined them carefully before looking up at Sarah.

'This is really happening, isn't it?' he asked simply.

'It's happening,' said Sarah, her eyes sparkling. 'Don't you feel excited?'

John was indeed excited, but more by being in a conspiracy with Sarah than by the conspiracy itself. He didn't think she would appreciate the distinction, and in his heart of hearts he wasn't convinced that their plot would go ahead anyway. But he would humour her and plan in good faith.

'Sure,' he replied. 'Well, let's get on with it, shall we?'

They spent the next forty-five minutes setting up their phones and tablets with new email accounts, fitting the PAYG SIMs and then testing the communications between them. Sarah seemed very capable in that respect, and John happily let her take the lead. Afterwards, he produced two bin bags from under the sink and handed one to her. She looked mystified.

'All your packaging,' John explained. 'We don't want that found anywhere near us. In the bag.'

Sarah could see the sense in that. She collected up her boxes, and everything that had been inside them other than the electronic purchases themselves and the shoes, whilst John did likewise.

'Well, I think that was a successful morning,' she said, zipping up her bag. 'Now what?'

'Lunch,' replied John. 'After which I want to try something out.'

* * *

After their meal, John asked Sarah to take Barney out for half an hour's walk whilst he did a bit of research on his new tablet. It was simple. The answer was as he thought. After that, he went off to the garage for five minutes to dig something out, and eventually succeeded in doing so.

'You're looking smug,' said Sarah on return, taking off her boots.

'I am,' John replied. 'You know that problem of getting there and back without detection?'

'You haven't solved it, surely?' said Sarah, in slight disbelief. 'I've been gone less than half an hour.'

John inclined his head modestly. 'Well, it's not perfect, but I think it'll do.'

'Go on then, I can see you're dying to show me how clever you are.'

'OK,' said John. 'What car do I have? Not the little Fiat, the other one?'

Sarah paused for a moment, puzzled. 'Er, some sort of

161

Volvo estate. A grey one. Four-wheel drive. The one we used when we went shooting.'

'Correct,' said John. 'And what sort of car did I have before that?'

'Search me,' shrugged Sarah. 'If it was the one you had when Peter and I were living here then I can't remember.'

'I'll tell you,' said John. 'A grey four-wheel drive Volvo estate.' He looked at her expectantly.

'How very unimaginative of you,' Sarah responded. 'And more to the point – so what?'

John produced a pair of car number plates from behind his chair, 2012 registration. The yellow one had a slight crack in it.

Sarah looked at him uncertainly. 'Again, so what?'

'Those are the number plates of my old car,' John said. 'You can see one of them is cracked. I got a new set three years ago and changed them before trading the car in so that it looked as good as it could do. These old ones have been knocking about in the garage ever since. Don't know why I never threw them out.'

He could see that she still didn't get it.

'I'll explain,' he said. 'My old car is still on the road, three years later – MOT'd, insured and taxed. No reason it shouldn't be, but I checked online to make sure whilst you were out.'

'You can do that?' replied Sarah, still mystified.

'Yes – easily,' said John. 'But here's the thing. In theory, nobody can order number plates for any car except the owner. You have to have the logbook, as I still did when I bought the ones that replaced these. Basically, so that crooks can't pass cars they've stolen off as similar ones. Ringers.'

'Yes – I see the logic of that,' said Sarah. 'But—'

'In practice, it's pretty easy to get plates made without all that bureaucracy; I've just checked online. There's a place in the Channel Islands. People call them show-plates, implying they'll never be used on the road. But I don't want to do that because there'll be a trace.'

Sarah was looking confused.

'I already have plates for that old Volvo,' John said patiently. 'Don't you see? And I own a near identical one.'

Sarah began to understand. 'Ah, so if you put those old plates on your new car…'

'Anybody doing a routine plate check would see exactly what they expected to see: a grey Volvo four-wheel drive estate. Just not the one currently registered to me.'

'That's brilliant,' said Sarah.

'Well, it's luck really,' said John, modestly. 'I happen to have bought the same type of car twice, in the same colour, and I happen still to have plates for the old one. And it's not perfect – the current one is a bit more swish: satnav and all that. But if you don't look too closely…'

It would work. Sarah could see immediately that it would, subject to a few basic precautions.

'But you mustn't let the car be seen here on that old registration,' she said urgently. 'And you must change it back as soon as you can afterwards. And—'

'In the bag,' John finished the sentence for her, picking up one of the plates. 'Yes, I get it. And we'll still try to avoid any cameras. But otherwise, it's a plan, isn't it?'

Sarah nodded gravely. 'It's a damn good plan.'

CHAPTER SIXTEEN

Carl met Jim Steiner in the car park at Bishop's Stortford police station just under half an hour before the 10am interview on Monday, as agreed. Jim had wanted an hour with his client, but Carl had refused impatiently. He was well dressed, as Jim had advised, although rather less so than if Cynthia had been at home to give him a once-over before he left.

He arrived noisily in his Ferrari, a few minutes late, and Jim winced to see it; he'd hardly thought to stress the need for Carl to be unprovocative. Frank would undoubtedly have done so; he knew Carl's exhibitionist, sometimes childlike streak.

Red rag to a bull, Jim thought, staring ruefully at the expensive scarlet sports car, its powerful engine still burbling. Carl beckoned him over, and Jim got awkwardly into the low-slung passenger seat. He was not a slim man. His client gave a final noisy blip of the throttle before switching off and turned to his lawyer with a grin.

'Love it!' he said. 'Morning, Jim.'

'Morning,' replied Jim. 'I'm not sure this was wise.'

'What?' replied Carl innocently, though he knew full well.

'This.' Jim indicated around the lavish leather interior of the Ferrari. 'They've got cameras. It'll be noticed.'

'Bollocks,' replied Carl. 'It's just a car. Anyway, make the bastards jealous. Sod 'em.'

It was going to be a long morning, thought Jim.

'Right, Carl,' he began. 'Interview under caution. We haven't got long. You've had one before?'

Carl nodded. 'Yep. I know the drill. They'll go through that "anything you say may be given in evidence" rigmarole.'

'They will,' replied Jim. 'Let's just remind ourselves why this is taking place.'

'OK – shoot,' replied Carl.

'Under the Police and Criminal Evidence Act of 1984, there's no absolute requirement for one of these to happen before any decision to prosecute a suspect,' began Jim. 'But they're a tool to gain further evidence or information, which may or may not lead to a prosecution and indeed to allow you to answer allegations and to give your own account.'

'Yep – got it,' said Carl. 'They want me to incriminate myself.'

'They're almost certainly short of evidence,' said Jim. 'So yes, that's about it.'

'But it's voluntary, so I can leave at any time, right?' replied Carl.

'Yes – just as long as you recognise that you may be immediately arrested if you try.'

'So just stay quiet if I don't like the question?'

'You have that right, certainly. But it can be drawn to the attention of any jury in a subsequent trial – what's called an adverse inference,' said Jim.

Carl paused. 'Well, you're the bloody lawyer. How do I play it?'

'They've provided me with some pre-interview disclosure material,' began Jim. 'In essence, they want to establish your links with Bill Palfreyman, and they will probe whether you asked him to rough up Patrick Mills, the cyclist. He's singing like a canary, it seems.'

'I didn't ask Bill to kill the bastard,' replied Carl. 'I just didn't, and they can't prove otherwise.'

'What did you do then?' asked Jim. 'Obviously under legal privilege.'

Carl spread his hands as wide as the cramped interior of the Ferrari would allow.

'I expressed some frustration about the evidence Mills gave at my trial,' he said eventually. 'And that's all. Anything Bill did after that was off his own bat.'

Jim had seen this scenario before: clients convincing themselves of a version of the truth which exonerated them. Carl was a classic case. It looked like he genuinely believed it. The question was, would the police? It would be sufficient to sow the seeds of doubt if Carl was to avoid being charged as an accessory.

'You mustn't explicitly lie in there, whatever they insinuate,' said Jim. 'We'll go with that line. I'll intervene whenever I think it's appropriate. And for God's sake, keep calm.'

Carl nodded and opened the car door confidently. 'OK, pardner, let's go.'

* * *

That same morning, Cynthia left her flat in Chelmsford and

walked to the multi-storey car park where she'd arranged to leave her distinctive white Audi so that it wasn't spotted in the street. Then she headed off to see her sister for lunch. It was her first visit to the new cottage, and she was impressed, sensing Sarah's quiet pride in showing her around.

They didn't wait till lunch to get down to business, Sarah's generous gin and tonics acting as the starting gun.

'So…?' began Cynthia once they were settled. They both knew what the querying tone in her voice referred to.

'It can be done,' said Sarah. 'But only with your help.'

'By who?' replied her sister. 'Some sort of hired killer?'

The hitherto unspoken reality of what they were talking about was out in the open now. Sarah took it coolly.

'Not a hired killer, no,' she said. 'I've no idea how to find one. But I've got somebody. He knows what he's doing. Best if you don't know who.'

Cynthia took a reflective sip of her drink. She could see the logic in that.

'What would I need to do?' she asked eventually.

'It has to be done at the house,' said Sarah, 'because that's where he seems to be spending most of his time. And there's no guarantee how long that will last, so it'll have to be soon. Which means getting in at a time he's definitely there.'

Cynthia digested this.

'I see. So that's my role.' It was stated as a matter of fact, not a question.

Sarah nodded. 'There are electric gates, aren't there? And a security camera?'

'Gates, yes,' replied Cynthia. 'I've got the fob in my handbag. You just press it on the way in, and the gates open automatically on the way out.'

'Who else has a gate fob?' asked Sarah.

'Aside from Carl, all three children have one. I'm sure his driver Woody does, too. And I'm pretty certain his lawyer Frank has as well.'

'Hasn't Carl fallen out with him?' said Sarah.

Cynthia paused. 'Supposedly. But I doubt he's sent anyone round to retrieve the fob.'

'OK,' said Sarah. 'And the camera?'

'Don't worry about that,' said Cynthia, with a wave of her hand. 'Bloody thing. It's always breaking down. Last time, Carl said just leave it. Nobody outside knows. Unless he's had it fixed since I left, it's just a visual deterrent now.'

'Do you think that's likely?' asked her sister.

Cynthia laughed ironically.

'What, had it mended? No, he never even understood it. It was always me who dealt with the contractor.'

'That's good. So—'

'I know what you're going to ask,' said Cynthia resignedly. 'I'll need to be there to make sure he is.'

'Yes,' nodded Sarah. 'I know that'll be unpleasant.'

She stood up, walked over to her desk and pulled something out of a drawer. It was in a bag. She handed it to her sister. Cynthia took it curiously.

'What's this?' she asked, without looking inside.

'Mobile phone,' replied Sarah. 'Pay-As-You-Go, and there's twenty quids' worth of credit on it. I've got one too, and the number's stored in yours under "X". Anything to do with all this, you do on that phone. I've set you up an email account on it too, and mine is in there. Never call my normal number from it, or anybody else. Afterwards, you hand it back to me.'

'There and then?'

Sarah nodded. 'Yes. Straightaway. I'll get rid of it, together with mine.'

Cynthia took the phone out of the bag and turned it on experimentally. 'What about you-know-who?'

Sarah looked at her in confusion.

'You know, your *Day of the Jackal* guy,' continued Cynthia.

'That's all covered,' said Sarah, with a shake of her head.

'He your new man?'

Sarah shook her head again and pursed her lips, colouring slightly.

'That'll be a yes, then,' said Cynthia smugly, pleased with her detective work. 'I hope you'll be a little less transparent with the cops.'

It was said light-heartedly, but Sarah didn't take it that way.

'This isn't a joke,' she retorted angrily.

'I'm well aware of that,' the older sister replied calmly. 'Just to remind you, we are plotting to kill my husband, the father of my children. I don't happen to think that's a laughing matter.'

Sarah was chastened. 'Sorry,' she said, near to tears. 'But I've spent so long thinking about this.'

Cynthia reached out to her. 'It's OK, Sis,' she said gently. 'And it's going to be OK.'

They adjourned for lunch and discussed two significant unknowns. When would Cynthia be in a position to guarantee Carl's presence at the house? That was the first. She hoped it would be within a week but would confirm.

And the second was how to keep her above suspicion. That was pretty important, Cynthia thought. Sarah would consult with the man they were now calling "Jackal".

On her way out afterwards, Cynthia reached into her handbag and pulled out the key fob. Sarah looked at her enquiringly.

'I'll tell Carl I lost it,' Cynthia explained, as she started to hand it over. Suddenly, she snatched it back, just as Sarah was reaching for it.

'Don't touch it,' she warned and hurried back into the cottage. When she returned, the fob was in a plastic bag from Sarah's kitchen drawer.

'Gloves only. And give it back to me afterwards.'

Sarah nodded. 'OK. Think it all through. I'll give you a call tomorrow.'

* * *

Carl blasted his Ferrari past a small car dawdling along as he approached his drive and then swung to the right aggressively ahead of it, pressing the gate fob as he did so. Some old codger in a flat cap. Bloody noodle.

He entered the house via the internal door to the garage, moody and downcast, and hung the Ferrari keys on their hook.

The place was a mess, even though he'd had the maid in on Friday. The remains of breakfast lay scattered around the kitchen, and that was unlike him, usually so fastidious. So was the half empty bottle of wine from last night and the stained sideboard.

He knew why. He was depressed, so standards were slipping in tidiness as in other things. And that was dangerous.

It had showed at the police interview, and he was angry

with himself. They'd been polite and measured, as Jim had said they would be, but they'd also been extremely persistent and shown a worrying amount of knowledge. Carl prided himself on his calmness under pressure, but he'd allowed himself to get rattled and (worse) to show it. He wasn't himself. And he knew who was to blame.

The first couple of times that he'd got angry, Jim had managed to calm him with a gentle squeeze of the arm. But on that last occasion, he'd lost control, challenging the police aggressively to prove their insinuations. He'd seen the quiet triumph in the detective inspector's eyes as he rose to the bait, and that had made it worse.

He'd doubled down. 'Well, charge me then if you're so fucking certain.'

'All in good time, Mr Barrow,' the policeman had replied. He looked disconcertingly confident.

Jim Steiner had got him out of there as soon as he decently could, but Carl had been able to sense his annoyance too. Jim didn't like to lose, and his client's uncontrolled behaviour, coupled with his refusal to prepare properly, had now made a prosecution much more likely. It would not be an easy one to defend.

'Don't you fucking start,' Carl had said as soon as they were out of the police station, sensing Jim's mood.

Jim had simply got into his own car without another word. Carl knew that was the right response, just as he knew that his aggression towards the lawyer had been unmerited.

'You prat,' he'd said to himself in disgust as he'd got into the Ferrari. To compound his foul mood, some truck had thrown up a stone and cracked his windscreen as he roared past on the way home, and on top of that, a text from Jim had arrived whilst he was driving, which the car infotainment system read out to him. It was short and business-like: he thought it best to resign from the case and wished Carl luck.

Carl didn't like feeling vulnerable but knew that increasingly, he was.

He also knew that in his line of business, vulnerability meant trouble, usually sooner rather than later.

* * *

Frank didn't have an office as such, visiting Carl's house or occasionally the Chelmsford HQ as necessary, but the meeting between him and David needed to be discreet, so for the first time, he'd invited the young accountant home.

He'd chosen a time when he knew Esme would be out playing bridge, which was often these days. She'd become a fanatic in recent years, and though Frank had no understanding of the game, he was pleased that she had an interest now that all the children were gone. It satisfied her social aspirations too, hobnobbing with the great and the good, albeit of a certain age.

David was impressed as he drove up the drive, just a few miles outside Chelmsford, on the edge of a prosperous looking village. The house was probably Edwardian, he thought, and handsome enough if you like that sort of thing, which personally, he did. Much classier in his view than his parents' brash new-build on the other side of the M11. A gardener mowing the already immaculate lawn; fresh paintwork; new gate. Frank clearly made a good living as Carl's lawyer.

David guessed that he wanted to keep it that way, hence the invitation.

Frank emerged from the house, looking quite the country squire as David parked on the gravel, and welcomed him into the hall with becoming modesty. However, his quiet pride was self-evident. God knows whose ancestors all those paintings on the wall were, David thought irreverently as he looked around. Certainly not Frank's, whose parents had run a fairly notorious pub in Peckham.

Esme had laid them out an extensive cold salad buffet in the dining room, which Frank had paired with a rather delicious Merlot (one of the indulgences he'd become accustomed to), and they helped themselves before settling down. A bit pretentious, thought David. The kitchen would have done equally well, but he knew that Frank liked to make an impression.

'Do you know how the interview went yesterday?' asked David, an opening gambit.

Frank nodded self-importantly. He had his sources.

'Not well. Underprepared and overconfident.'

David grimaced.

'And what is more,' continued Frank, 'thin-skinned. He got riled. Lost his temper.'

'Not like Dad.'

'In normal times, I'd agree,' said Frank. 'But these aren't normal times. He's been a loose cannon ever since your mother left.'

He sniffed portentously. 'Of course, taking legal advice from Steiner didn't help.'

David took a mouthful of the excellent rare beef.

'I tried to arrange a meeting between the three of us, as we agreed,' he said, having swallowed.

'He won't have it. Not with you. And telling him it was

173

a mistake to hire Steiner won't help. I'm sure he knows in his heart of hearts things would have gone better with you.'

Frank reflected as he topped up his glass. 'So, what are we to do?'

David wondered whether to confide in him. He took a sip from his own glass and came to a decision.

'Mum's got a plan.'

Frank's eyebrows rose. 'What sort of plan?'

David waved his fork helplessly. 'I don't know for sure. But the phrase "final solution" came up. Make of that what you will.'

'I see,' said Frank thoughtfully and took another mouthful. 'And what do you make of it, may I ask?'

'I think she means it. It's not just divorce – that wouldn't put an end to anything.'

'And you are content with that?'

David paused. 'He's destroying the business. And he'll destroy you and me too unless he's stopped.'

Frank liked a logical mind. There was no place for emotion where business was concerned, and in that respect, the two men were as one.

'And can we help?' he asked non-committally.

'I'm not sure,' said David. 'I don't know how realistic her plan is or what it involves. But I'll let her know as best I can that we're prepared to.'

Frank nodded. 'And meanwhile…'

'Meanwhile, I suggest we prepare our own plan in case it's all nonsense.'

Frank smiled. 'How very gratifying. My thoughts entirely.'

He didn't think the boy had it in him, though.

He'd make his own arrangements.

CHAPTER SEVENTEEN

If it was to happen soon, John knew he had some urgent preparations to make. He decided upon his priorities during an early morning walk with Barney, on the Monday after Sarah had left.

"Time spent in reconnaissance is seldom wasted". It was an old adage which he remembered from the military biographies he enjoyed, and he knew that the first necessity was to apply it, discreetly of course.

On return, he dug out his new tablet. He knew from press reports and the *Panorama* programmes that Carl lived just outside the village of Bury Green, a few miles west of Bishop's Stortford. He downloaded the Google Earth app and immediately homed in on the area. It took him a few minutes, but with the help of an aerial photo from the *Sunday Times* he soon identified the sprawling, isolated property and examined it both from above in 2D and obliquely in 3D, rotating the view to get as comprehensive an impression as possible.

The curved gravel drive was obvious, and John thought he could see the gates at the end. He estimated that it was at least three hundred yards long, leading into a small country road; it didn't look like there would be much passing traffic. It was a good half a mile in one direction to the village and probably two miles in the other till a T-junction with the first major road. Good. There were no immediate neighbours, and the rear of the property beyond the drive which circled it faced into dense woodland, which seemed to go back a long way. Even better.

Next, John went out to the little Fiat and brought in his AA Road Map, seldom used these days because of satnav, but nonetheless, he was a man of set habits and never travelled without it. Carefully, he plotted a back roads route from his own property, just outside White Roding, to Bury Green. The aim was to avoid likely traffic camera spots. He had to get across the M11, whilst avoiding Bishop's Stortford, and the smaller town of Sawbridgeworth to the south. It took him around fifteen minutes, but eventually, he was satisfied. Then he double-checked the route visually on Google Earth. Finally, he went to Google Maps on his new phone and checked the time it would take to drive it. Twenty-five minutes, via the most direct route. He'd allow ten minutes more on his rather less obvious one.

John then made his way back to the Fiat, which had no part to play in his intended plan on the day. With him, he took both his phones and the road map but not the tablet, which he concealed under a bed in the spare room. He wore a cap and pulled the car's sun visor down, even though it was an overcast day. Barney came too; a dog would always be a conversational distraction if need be.

He drove carefully, well within speed limits, and kept a wary eye out for cameras, plus any other location where he might be in danger of being noticed. He knew the country roads east of the M11 well. The motorway underpass near Hatfield Heath was a minor one, deliberately chosen as such, and he was glad to see so little traffic in the vicinity.

Thereafter, it was very much local lanes as he navigated cross-country between Sawbridgeworth and Bishop's Stortford. Twice he made errors, before stopping a couple of miles short of his destination. He turned around and went back to the underpass, before driving the route again without a mistake. There couldn't be any navigational mishaps when he executed his emerging plan.

A couple of miles short of Bury Green, he hit the A1184, which was effectively the ring road west of Bishop's Stortford. He turned left, seeking the spot he'd identified on Google Earth. It was exactly as he hoped: a section of old tarmac a couple of hundred yards long, which the ring road had rendered superfluous. Now it was just a lengthy lay-by in a dip, shrouded by trees. He pulled in and stopped there for fifteen minutes. Nobody passed through in that time, and he was virtually invisible from the main road.

John was now ready. It would be a simple drive past. There was no reason for him to be nervous at this prospect, but logic doesn't always apply in such situations, and his mouth was dry as he pulled back onto the A1184. After no more than a minute's travel, he spotted the lane the other side of it, leading off to Bury Green. He could feel his heart beating as he turned right onto it. The road was steeper than had been apparent on Google Earth, but thankfully otherwise much as he expected, and he passed only one car coming the opposite way in the two miles. As he approached the Barrow drive on the left, he slowed but did not stop. The forbidding electric gates were obvious, as was the prominent camera, but he hadn't appreciated the gradient of the drive from Google Earth: it went over a crest, and only the very top of the roof of the house within the grounds could be seen from the road.

John continued the half mile or so into the village and then parked briefly to take stock. He'd planned not to go back the same way, but what was the harm? He could easily be popping to the village shop for a pint of milk from somewhere, and he might have missed something first time around.

He convinced himself and then drove around the village green to return the way he'd come. Soon, the entrance to the drive was in sight again, on the right this time, and he slowed down to take in as much as he could whilst he drove past.

Then his heart leapt as a red Ferrari roared past, swinging sharply right into the driveway immediately after it had done so. John swore violently – what was the point? It would only have had to wait a few seconds for him to clear the entrance. Then the realisation hit him as he came opposite the drive and saw the gates beginning to open whilst the car waited. He could only see the back of the driver's head through the Ferrari's narrow rear window, but he'd caught a brief glimpse in profile as the car turned off the road ahead of him. There was no doubt who it was.

Carl Barrow. The man he was planning to kill.

* * *

Sarah looked in shock at the text on her new phone: "Saw CB yesterday. Explain later x".

She hadn't been in touch with John since leaving the day before, other than to send a brief email summary of her meeting with Cynthia couched in innocuous language. He'd simply replied "Understood".

Sarah responded to the text with a suitably astounded looking emoji and then continued with her shopping trip in Cambridge. It was a fair way from where she lived, but there were reasons for that: she was unlikely to bump into anyone she knew, and there was a wig shop there – Wiggit – which she remembered from her time at university. It still existed. She'd looked carefully at their website on her "murder" tablet the night before and knew exactly what she wanted. It could have been ordered online, but of course that would never do. She would visit personally and pay anonymously with cash.

The business was in a depressing industrial estate on the outskirts and looked as if it was primarily geared up for e-commerce these days, but Sarah knew from her internet research that it had a small factory shop attached. That was where she was heading. The reception desk was unmanned but had a button with a "press for attention" sign. When Sarah did so, a scruffy, bored-looking girl, who didn't look much more than twenty, emerged from the factory area.

Sarah had an explanation of why she wanted a black-haired wig all prepared: it revolved around an amateur dramatic production. However, she could tell at a glance that this particular individual wouldn't be remotely interested. Three minutes later, she had her wig, after a perfunctory fitting. It cost £105.99, and the only flicker of reaction Sarah got from the assistant was when she produced cash to pay for it, instead of the expected card. But it was momentary.

On the way back to the car park, Sarah passed a small branch of Boots and entered on impulse. She bought a cheap pair of sunglasses, with frames which were nothing like the brand she normally wore. Again, she paid cash and then grabbed a sandwich and a can of diet coke at a corner shop.

Once back in her Golf, she ate her late lunch and then phoned John before setting off. She hadn't linked the new phone via Bluetooth, as she didn't want any trace of it in her car, so she called using the handset.

'Hi, it's me. What do you mean you've seen him?'

'I was driving past doing my recce yesterday and he overtook me, going bloody fast. In his Ferrari.'

'Are you sure it was him?'

'I only caught a glimpse but ninety-five per cent. He turned into the driveway, and the gates opened. And I recognised the car – it appeared on the first *Panorama* programme.'

'He didn't notice you?'

'Well, he overtook, so obviously he saw the car. But no, I doubt he gave me a thought.'

Sarah paused. 'Sounds like no damage done. Just a fluke. Everything else go OK?'

'Sure,' replied John. 'I've found a good, out-of-the-way route and timed it both ways. No cameras. Also a concealed place nearby, where we can wait until your sister texts us – it's just under three miles to the house. Have you spoken to her again since yesterday?'

'I'm about to call her,' replied Sarah. 'She's had time to reflect now. What are you up to?'

'I'm working out how to dispose of those bags afterwards,' replied John. 'It's not as easy as it sounds.'

'No, I expect not,' replied Sarah. 'But I'm sure you'll work something out. See you later.'

She put the PAYG phone back in her bag and pulled out her normal one. "Be there about 4 I expect x", she texted.

Routine ongoing communication, as between any couple: nothing remotely specific or suspicious. All part of their agreed plan; they didn't want a noticeable void on their usual devices.

"Look forward to it x," replied John immediately from his own phone, playing the same game.

Sarah switched back to the PAYG and dialled Cynthia, who picked up immediately. She now had to find out once and for all if her sister was willing to carry out her assigned role.

Within moments, Sarah was convinced that unless Cynthia was an exceptionally good actress, she meant business. She was livid that Carl had apparently had a disastrous interview with the police the day before and that charges were now likely. She wanted to move against her husband as soon as possible and before that happened.

'How do you know it was so bad?'

'David had lunch with Frank.'

'The lawyer Carl sacked?'

'Correct. Wouldn't have happened if he'd been there. But Frank's got good contacts with the police; he knows.'

'Any further thoughts on our discussion yesterday?' asked Sarah.

'Right, here's what I'm going to do,' Cynthia replied firmly. 'I'm going to call him. Arrange a meeting.'

'Not text initially?' asked Sarah. 'Just to gauge reaction?'

'Too slow. He may not reply; he hasn't been in touch at all lately. But he'll pick up, and when he does, I can talk him round.'

'Sure?'

'I'm sure.'

'OK – what then?'

'It'll be at the house. I'll say I'll do lunch for him, and I only want the two of us there. To discuss the future.'

'Is that the best time? Maybe in the evening, when he might feel there's a chance of something more than dinner, if you get my drift?'

'Well, there bloody well isn't!' replied Cynthia savagely. 'No, lunch it is. Look, I've been thinking about this ever since yesterday.'

'OK. Understood.' Sarah waited tactfully for her sister to continue.

'When I'm there, I'll text you on these new phones. Be somewhere close with Jackal and then get there fast. I've given you the gate fob. I'll tell Carl someone's coming up the drive. He'll be out there fast enough. I'll make sure it's through the French windows: dead ahead across the gravel turning circle as you come up the drive; you can't miss them. Then it's over to you.'

'What about you – afterwards, I mean?'

'I'll say I was in the kitchen, making lunch. I heard Carl swearing about someone being outside and going out to investigate. Then I heard shooting and hid.'

'Doesn't explain how the gate was open.'

Cynthia paused thoughtfully. 'OK – I say I heard him talking on the intercom, couldn't tell who to. He buzzed the gate open and went outside to meet whoever it was. How about that?'

'Just about plausible. I suppose you definitely have to be there, don't you?'

'I think so,' replied Cynthia. 'We've got to be certain that there's nobody else about, and that he goes out to meet you through the French windows. Not possible unless I'm there, having a drink with him in the drawing room. I can't leave before you arrive, as there's no telling what he'll do, or where in the house he'll be. It'll be suspicious if I leave afterwards. No, I think the best thing is for me to make sure there's obvious evidence of the meeting having been agreed between us and then to play the terrified housewife hiding away when it happens.'

'Ideally, it'll look as if he invites you, rather than you instigating it.'

'Ideally. I'll think about that.'

'We'll have to meet briefly there of course,' said Sarah.

'Why?'

'As we discussed yesterday, I need to hand back your gate fob, and you need to give me your phone, the new one. So I can get rid of it.'

'How are you going to do that?'

'I don't know yet,' Sarah replied. 'John's working it out now.'

'John, eh?'

Sarah felt herself blush at her slip. 'Shouldn't have said that. Jackal. Anyway, when are you going to make this call?'

'Today. Straight after this.'

'OK. And when are you going to propose that this meeting takes place?'

'As soon as possible. Let's say at least three days' time, so you and John-call-me-Jackal can get your act together. Any time after that – probably Saturday. Is that long enough?'

Sarah pursed her lips. 'It'll have to be. I'll leave you to it. Good luck.'

She knew her sister was dreading the call, but Cynthia's reply was calm. 'I'll let you know when.'

John picked up his phone and looked at the screen as it rang.

'Tom,' he said brightly.

'Hi, Dad,' began Tom, slightly diffidently. 'Look, I've got a bit of a favour to ask, if you don't mind.'

'Depends what it is,' John replied, feeling apprehensive.

'Yes, well, you know I'm an usher at Percy Maitland's wedding this weekend?'

'I think you mentioned it, yes,' said John. 'Where is it?'

'That's the point – Leicestershire,' replied Tom. 'We're going up on Friday morning for the rehearsal and all that and staying in a pub with the other ushers. Only we've left it a bit late to book the kennels – they're full. I don't suppose you could have Pip till Sunday night?'

John knew that Emma's terrier got on well with Barney.

'Sure – no problem. I've got nothing planned, just a quiet weekend with Sarah. Bring him over on Thursday evening.'

He sensed the slight hesitation in Tom's voice before he replied. 'Great – thanks, Dad.'

'And give my regards to the happy couple.' John knew and liked Tom's old university flatmate, Percy.

'I will. And thanks again. See you about six on Thursday.'

Once Tom had rung off, John made himself a cup of coffee and sat at the kitchen table, thinking. The conundrum he'd been mulling over was how to get rid of the two murder bags after the deed was done. Throwing them on the tip was out of the question – too many scavengers. It would be hard to explain a bonfire, and he wasn't sure that everything would get completely burnt beyond recognition anyway. On balance, he thought that burying them somewhere obscure on the farm was probably easiest, but then there might be DNA traces if they were ever discovered and being on his land would constitute a personal link. He'd never rest easy in those circumstances.

So perhaps bury them somewhere else, where there was no personal connection? It would be harder to pre-prepare a disposal pit in those circumstances, and he'd need to be certain of not being spotted. Or maybe scatter their contents far and wide?

None of these options were satisfactory. Eventually, he concluded that there was only one safe answer.

Thomasina.

* * *

Sarah arrived just before 4pm, as planned. They settled down over a cup of tea to update each other.

'So, it could be in three days' time,' said John. 'Blimey.'

'No reason why not is there?' said Sarah. 'We're pretty well ready, aren't we?'

'I think so,' said John. 'We know it has to be soon. Tom and Emma being away will be a bonus if it's this weekend.'

Sarah looked at him. 'Why?'

'No chance of them dropping in. The story is that you're here for the weekend; people know we're newly together – who'd intrude?'

'So, we make sure your car and mine are obvious in the drive,' said Sarah. 'And let imagination do the rest.'

'Yes,' replied John. 'And just make sure nobody sees us leave in the Volvo. I'll change the plates after Tom's dropped Pip off and keep it in the garage. Once we're a mile away, you put on your wig, and I'll put on my hat – after that, nobody will connect us with this place. We can put our trainers on then too.'

'Have you thought about the actual shooting?' said Sarah. 'How you'll do it?'

John nodded briefly. 'You just drive and leave that to me.'

Sarah laughed. 'You could almost be him.'

'Who?'

'The Jackal. Like the film. That's what Cynthia calls you.'

John grimaced.

'I hope it ends better for me than it did for him.'

CHAPTER EIGHTEEN

Carl was surprised to hear the landline ring around lunchtime and very nearly didn't answer it. Like most people, he took more calls on his mobile these days and generally preferred it that way – he could see who was calling.

But he couldn't this time on his old landline handset, and it was Cynthia. He was caught completely off guard, after six weeks without speaking to her.

'Carl, it's me,' she said.

He was shocked by the powerful and unexpected rush of adrenalin as he heard her unmistakeable tones, followed by something like shyness. Carl didn't have a shy bone in his body, so it was an unfamiliar feeling to him. His instinctive reply was far from articulate and almost gruff.

'Hello. What do you want?' He winced as he said it. If it was on the cards, he wanted a reconciliation with his wife above all else.

'Well, I think we should talk.' She sounded hurt, Carl thought. And hesitant. Maybe regretful?

'So, talk.' Again, too brittle. 'I'm listening, doll.' He

hoped his familiar term for her would take the edge off it.

'Not like this. Face to face. An adult discussion.'

'What about?'

'Everything. The future. Where we go from here.'

'I'm not sure we're going anywhere, are we?'

Cynthia sensed the sadness and recognised that her husband was in a fragile state. Carl normally kept his emotions well concealed, even from her. She didn't feel sorry for him; she just felt that the situation gave her leverage.

'Well, all that's what we need to talk about. I've made no firm decisions.'

There – a little bait for him. Carl bit immediately, his eagerness badly hidden.

'That's good. Meet where?'

'I thought at the house. Just the two of us – no children. Then we can be completely frank with each other in privacy.'

'Like a married couple should be,' said Carl. He was on the hook now, Cynthia hoped.

'When?' he asked.

'Saturday lunch? Have a drink together in the drawing room, then I could cook us a nice meal. Whatever you want – one of your favourites.'

Cynthia could sense Carl thinking, or maybe he was just trying not to appear too keen. He failed.

'Great. Steak,' he said. Predictable as ever, thought Cynthia.

'Steak it is. Say if I come over about twelve, then?'

'Yep – great. No chance of you staying?'

Cynthia knew he'd try that on. Better not bolt the door completely, she thought.

'I don't think so,' she said, with faux uncertainty. 'Probably just a chat at this stage…'

Carl laughed. He'd always been confident of his persuasive powers, and usually rightly so.

'A chat it is, doll. See you at twelve on Saturday.'

'Yes. See you then. Bye.'

She thought for a moment and then texted a follow-up to Carl: "Thanks for asking me. See you on Saturday".

It was pretty rudimentary but implied that the lunch was at his instigation.

Cynthia put her mobile down and immediately picked up the PAYG alternative.

"Saturday", she texted Sarah. "I'll be there at midday".

* * *

Woody wasn't used to being called by Frank. He worked exclusively for Carl, if indeed "work" was the right term at the moment.

He'd only driven his boss twice in the last few weeks and knew for a fact (because it had been left dirty) that the last time he'd been out he'd taken the bloody Ferrari, which Woody wasn't allowed to drive. He wasn't needed around the big house (Carl had made that very clear) so had been skulking at home most of the time recently, "on call", bored and thoroughly under-employed.

So, when the lawyer called him early on Wednesday morning, Woody's first thought was that he was about to be notified of redundancy, no doubt with all the legalities neatly tied up. He'd been in Carl's employ for a long time, and though loyal, he understood his boss well enough to know that he was not a sentimental man. He wouldn't pay for anything – or anybody – he didn't use.

But either Frank was being very subtle, or he did not want to talk about redundancy – though maybe just not over the phone, thought Woody in a sudden panic.

Instead, he simply wanted to meet, away from the office. He was very calm and controlled. Woody tried to reassure himself that it didn't sound like bad news.

They agreed to meet for lunch at a slightly dingy pub, about two miles from where Woody lived, called The Black Rabbit. He was surprised Frank knew of it and even more surprised when he arrived to find that it had a private room, which he'd never known about. Frank had booked it and was waiting for him there. He was all geniality and "hail fellow well met". Surely not redundancy then?

Woody sat down, rather nervously. The trappings of the room certainly weren't the last word in elegance, but they were sufficiently so to make him uneasy. So was the white tablecloth and the place setting, with its confusing amounts of cutlery. What to use when always worried Woody, but he was shrewd enough to realise that he was being deliberately destabilised.

Frank had a gin and tonic ready for Woody, and they made small talk whilst surveying the menu. Frank ordered something foreign and unintelligible, but Woody stuck to tried-and-tested Steak & Ale pie. Once their orders had been taken, it was apparent that the main event was about to begin. Woody waited in silence whilst Frank pursed his fingers together.

'Now, Woody,' he began, 'remind me how long you have worked for Carl.'

Woody was certain Frank had access to the staff records but played along.

'Well,' he said. 'Let me see. Six years, I guess, this time.'

'This time?'

'Well, I'm sure you know this,' Woody began, reluctantly. 'There was a time when I was away for a bit…'

'In prison, I believe,' said Frank, imperturbably.

'Yes,' conceded Woody, discomfited. He didn't like talking about that time.

'Remind me what for,' replied Frank, perusing the wine list, and then indicating his choice to the hovering waiter.

'GBH.' Woody waited till the man was out of earshot. 'Four years, with remission.'

'With a pistol, wasn't it? You were lucky it wasn't attempted murder.'

'Well, it was only one shot from a piddling .22. And I wasn't shooting to kill, or he'd have been dead. Just a punishment. In the knee.'

'A punishment. I see. Good with guns, are you, Woody?' said the lawyer.

'Good enough. Four years in the Army when I was a lad. So, I've been trained.'

'Hmm, yes, dishonourably discharged,' said Frank, smoothly.

Woody bridled sullenly. 'Well, yeah. The guy I hit was a dickhead.'

"Hit" was a marginal understatement, as Frank well knew. Woody's Company Sergeant Major had been in hospital for a month, with a fractured skull. The man opposite him was clearly unafraid to use violence, and that was a trait which interested Frank.

'So, how did you first start working for Carl? Before prison, I mean?'

'I was at school with one of his brothers. He put a word in for me.'

'What sort of work?'

Woody shrugged. 'A bit of strong-arm stuff. Enforcer. Debt collector. You know.'

'Until the shooting.'

Frank noticed Woody hesitate at this.

'Look, I know,' he continued. 'I'm his lawyer. Carl asked you to do a job, and you did it. Then you kept quiet, which probably kept him out of jail. So, he looked after your family. Or rather, I did.'

Woody nodded briefly, and they both lapsed into silence as the waiter delivered their food.

'I know. I'm grateful,' he said, once they were alone again.

'And Carl was grateful, too. That's why he made you his driver. Cushy number.'

'If you say so,' said Woody, defensively. 'I'm a bloody good driver.'

'The trouble is,' said Frank, as he took his first mouthful, 'that role may be about to end.'

Here it comes, thought Woody. Stay calm. 'Oh?'

'There hasn't been much of it recently, has there?' asked Frank.

'Not much.'

'And that's been a worry. Normally in such circumstances, we'd have to let you go. But…'

He paused to take a sip of wine, leaving Woody on tenterhooks. He had a big mortgage and an expensive and temperamental wife. He needed his job.

'What if I said that there's a way to earn a lot of money

and to stay on the family payroll for the foreseeable future?' asked Frank.

'What sort of money?'

Frank shrugged, as though this was a minor detail. 'One hundred thousand, maybe.'

Frank tried, but failed, to suppress his astonishment. 'What?'

'And your current salary, inflation linked plus two percent, for, what shall we say, ten years?'

'What would I need to do?' Woody was agog.

'What you did before. Shoot someone. Properly, this time.'

Woody thought hard. 'And if I don't?'

Frank looked regretful. 'Well, as we've discussed, there hasn't been much for you to do lately…'

The threat was implicit. Woody sensed with a sinking heart that there was only one way out.

'I'm not going to jail again – especially not for murder,' he said.

'There's very little risk,' replied Frank calmly, pouring them both a second glass. 'Not if it's properly planned.'

'You have guns? I'm not going to try and source any. That's a mug's game.'

Frank nodded and took a sip of his wine. 'Whatever you need can be obtained. And got rid of.'

Woody took a rather less elegant sip, more of a gulp.

'Who? And when?'

Frank smiled. 'That can wait for now. As long as you're on board in principle.'

Woody nodded, his heart thumping. 'I suppose so.'

The rest of the meal passed in small talk; both men were

anxious to finish it quickly, and they were out of there in twenty minutes.

'One thing,' said Frank as they strolled towards their cars afterwards. Woody looked up, and Frank produced his mobile phone.

'Don't be tempted to talk to anybody about this, anybody at all. I've recorded every word. You've just agreed to commit murder.'

Woody looked at him open mouthed, as Frank got into his expensive Jaguar. The window whooshed down.

'Bye, Woody. I'll be in touch.'

* * *

David looked round the little flat critically.

'Bit small, Mum,' he said eventually.

Tiresomely obvious, thought Cynthia. 'Well, it's not for long, darling,' she replied patiently. She hadn't asked him to come round, and he hadn't warned her, which was fairly typical, though she knew that he meant well. She wasn't sure how he'd found out where it was.

'How long?' her son responded.

Cynthia knew what he meant well enough: how long till all this is resolved? And how's that going to happen?

She was set on keeping her son out of it all, confident that he didn't have the balls to address the situation himself, so his follow-up surprised her.

'If you're nowhere near, there's an alternative.'

Cynthia looked at him, astounded. 'What sort of alternative?'

David looked slightly shamefaced. 'Been talking to Frank.'

Cynthia exhaled gently. Frank was a great talker, and probably an astute plotter. She didn't think he was a man of action, not outside a courtroom, anyway. She wasn't going to put her own well-developed plans on hold for something that might never happen.

'Then keep talking to him. Don't do anything that's going to get in my way.'

'How long?' The same question again, calmly put. He was persistent at least, she thought.

Cynthia paused for a moment.

'I think the situation should resolve itself soon – within a week,' she said eventually. 'If it hasn't, make your move.'

* * *

Carl was increasingly concerned at the way his moods were so variable; it left him feeling out of control, and generally, he was a very controlled person.

One moment he was buzzing at the prospect of seeing Cynthia again on Saturday, the next he was raging inwardly at her disloyalty; then he was full of self-pity at the situation he found himself in, exacerbated by the underlying knowledge that his own actions had made things a lot worse than they need have been. He'd seen the respect draining away in the eyes of others, not least his son. It was both exhausting and depressing to be on such an emotional rollercoaster. It had to end.

He poured himself a glass of malt and forced himself to think calmly about the forthcoming meeting with his wife. That was the key.

What was his priority? To get Cyn back, of course; he was half the man he had been without her.

She'd given no indication in their brief call as to whether she was open to that possibility. He knew if he was to persuade her, he'd have to own up to the heavy-handedness that had led to that milksop brother-in-law of hers topping himself. That seemed to have been the catalyst for her, though if truth be told, he'd been surprised at the extent to which she'd been able to ignore his activities over the years and simply play the dutiful housewife, eyes averted. It meant he'd been able to leave all his work-related worries at the front door, and he was beginning to realise how important that pressure relief valve had been to him.

So, he was prepared to be conciliatory; change a few things; maybe adopt some of Davey's new ideas. Make money quietly. Carl grinned mirthlessly at the memory of his son's oft-repeated mantra. Maybe there was something in it.

What if Cynthia wasn't open to a reconciliation and wanted out? He felt sick at the possibility, engulfed by another wave of self-pity.

He'd never underestimated her shrewdness and expected that she would have taken legal advice in those circumstances. He definitely did not want a lot of busybody lawyers prying into the extent and origins of his assets. So that possibility had to be stopped somehow.

He knew that Cynthia was quite materialistic, despite any misgivings she might now be displaying about the source of the family's wealth. She was also always concerned about her children's prospects. So, the threat of changing his will was a lever he might use in extremis. But he had no enthusiasm for holding onto his wife through blackmail, nor did he want to penalise the children. He simply wanted his marriage back.

Carl poured himself another malt. Bloody Frank had sent

him a snooty email about his recent police interview, citing "people I know". "If only you'd listened to me" – that was the clear implication, albeit unstated. He was definitely getting too big for his boots, but he was a good lawyer who knew his client well.

Carl thought that on balance, he'd have to let Frank go, but only once he was through the current Patrick Mills issue. Flashy Jim Steiner wasn't the man to steer him through that, and anyway, he'd resigned.

So, get the wife back. Head off any prospect of separation or divorce, certainly in a legal sense. Get through the Mills issue, with Frank on board. And then make some changes.

He drained his drink decisively and headed off to bed without clearing up the kitchen. It was still well before 9pm, but it had been a long day.

For Carl, they all were nowadays.

CHAPTER NINETEEN

On Thursday morning, John gave Tom a call.

'When you bring Pip round tonight, do you think you could drop the boat keys off too?'

'Sure. Going sailing?'

'Well, the forecast's good. I thought we might do that over the weekend. Dogs can come too.'

'Fine, Dad – Pip loves going in the boat.'

'You left it tidy, I hope?'

He said it playfully. Tom was a meticulous sailor.

'Ha! Don't worry – she'll be impressed!'

'OK – see you later.'

After that, there wasn't much that John could do. He needed the house to himself after Tom had visited in the evening, and Sarah wasn't due till Friday morning. He topped the Volvo up with fuel, cleaned the inside that Sarah had previously commented upon and bought some green bin liners from the petrol station, paying normally – nothing suspicious about that; indeed, it would have attracted attention if he'd paid with cash.

The afternoon loomed ahead, as he had known it would do. John welcomed it. He specifically wanted time to reflect and to prepare himself psychologically.

After lunch, he drove to Hatfield Forest with Barney, where there were many trails. He'd walked them often enough with Jenny, but for some reason had never done so since her death. It was a sunny day, and there were plenty of people about, many also with dogs. John started walking, thinking hard as he did so. Barney stayed closer than usual, seemingly detecting his master's serious mood.

He couldn't quite believe the situation that had arisen. He, John Gault, pillar of the local community, respected local landowner and gentleman farmer, had agreed to commit murder. The most he'd ever transgressed against society before was in incurring a few points on his driving license. Was he mad?

The logical thing, indeed, the only sensible thing, was to withdraw now that the plan actually seemed likely to happen. He knew that this would mean going back on his word to Sarah, almost certainly striking a fatal blow to their blossoming relationship.

Yet who was this woman who had entered his life so unexpectedly over the last few weeks, at a time when he was probably more vulnerable than he knew due to the loss of his beloved Jenny? He didn't really know her very well, except in the biblical fashion. He did know that she seemed prepared to kill. That did not seem to commend her as a long-term future partner.

Even as he ran through these thoughts, John knew with a sinking sense of the inevitable that it was hopeless. He didn't think Sarah was a bad person – indeed quite the opposite. He admired her, quite as much as he despised the likes of Carl Barrow. Indeed, he was in thrall to her, and well beyond just sexually. He simply wasn't capable of deliberately disappointing her. In short, he'd fallen genuinely in love. And of course, love is blind, he thought ruefully.

That he recognised this made no difference. The guilt in being complicit with Sarah in this conspiracy felt secretly delicious. It would bind them together.

So, although he'd actively considered abandoning the plan, as he had promised himself he would reflect upon, John knew within a mile or so that he was definitely in and that he had consciously made that decision.

He felt a flood of relief. Now he could devote all his energies to making it work.

For another six miles, he mulled over detailed practicalities, visualising them from every angle. He was confident he had thought it all through by the time he was back at the car.

So, John was in a cheerful frame of mind when Tom dropped off Pip that evening. Being a red-blooded male himself, his son was confident that he knew why.

'Don't do anything I wouldn't do,' he said with a wink, as he handed over the boat keys.

'Wouldn't dream of it,' said John, with his best poker face.

* * *

Sarah arrived just after 10am the next day, Friday, in time to see John emerging from the garage. He smiled as he saw her.

'Plates changed,' he said, as she got out of her Golf. The two dogs scurried around, greeting her enthusiastically. John kissed her briefly on the lips, then Sarah returned to her car.

As she pulled her overnight bag from the boot, a big BMW pulled up opposite John's drive: James and Cathy Venning. The passenger window whirred down.

'Hi, just passing!' shouted Cathy. James smiled salaciously across her from the driving seat, realising that Sarah was obviously arriving for the weekend.

'How are you?' replied John. 'Come in for a coffee.'

He glimpsed Sarah's brief look of surprise but ignored it. The Vennings glanced at each other, and Cathy nodded almost imperceptibly, though John saw it clearly enough.

'OK,' she said. 'Just a quick one. We're off to a funeral.'

As James backed the car up before turning into the drive, John spoke briefly to Sarah.

'It'll be useful. Establishes we're here. Make it sound as if we're not going anywhere.'

'I'll imply just bed,' smiled Sarah. 'James will love that.'

'Some truth in it, too,' replied John, giving her bottom a gentle squeeze. He removed his hand quickly as the BMW nosed into the drive, but not quite quickly enough. The Vennings saw, as John had intended them too. Sarah seemed to play along, overreacting with a mock indignant jump.

'I hope we're not disturbing you two,' smiled James meaningfully, as he emerged from the car in his dark suit, complete with black tie.

'Not at all,' said John, giving the elegantly dressed Cathy a peck on the cheek. He could see her hat on the back seat. 'Who died?'

James pulled back, after kissing Sarah briefly. 'My Uncle Ted. You won't know him. Grand old boy. Eighty-seven.'

'Pretty good innings, I suppose,' John said, as he led them inside. 'Going far?'

'Far enough,' said Cathy. 'Amersham.'

It was said in a "I'm not sure we needed to go" tone, but James blithely ignored it. They made small talk for fifteen minutes before the Vennings rose to go, Sarah throughout being very tactile and sitting on the arm of John's chair. By the time their visitors left, she and John had clearly established the impression that they had only one thing on their minds that weekend and that this would be taking place upstairs.

'Good at charades, are you?' whispered John out of the corner of his mouth as they waved the BMW off.

She pinched his bottom in revenge for earlier. 'Well, as you said, there's some truth in it.'

'Worth doing, though,' smiled John, as he led her back inside.

Sarah nodded. 'Yes.'

They settled down with another cup of coffee.

'So, to work,' said John.

'The car's plates are changed. Your sister will be there at midday tomorrow; let's say she texts us fifteen minutes later. We don't want to be waiting in that lay-by for too long. I've allowed thirty-five minutes, and that's ample. Leave here at eleven-thirty to be on the safe side.'

'OK,' said Sarah. 'What else?'

'I think you need to establish some sort of code with your sister,' said John. He never seemed to call her Cynthia.

'What do you mean?'

'Well, let's say, text "A" for I'm going in; "B" for I'm there and he's here; "C" for I'm there and he's not here; "D" for come now; "E" for abort. I think that should just about cover it,' explained John.

'Hang on,' said Sarah, fishing in her handbag for her PAYG phone. 'Repeat that.'

John did so as she typed, then waited as she added a couple of lines of explanation. The text noise followed.

'Done,' said Sarah. 'We should leave our normal phones here, in case someone tries to track our position.'

John considered this. 'Yes, I suppose so. There's a vague chance that somebody may try to get hold of us on them, but we're going to be away less than two hours.'

'They'll just have to use their dirty imaginations when we don't answer then, won't they?' said Sarah lightly. John grinned.

'I'll drive as far as the lay-by. You take over then and give me the gate fob. I'll get the gun ready, and then off we go as soon as she texts you.'

'Fine,' said Sarah. 'And you definitely know the way? I've never been there.'

She knew he did. John gave a reassuring smile.

'I'll show you,' he said. 'Odd that you were never asked.'

'Things have always been very odd in that household.'

John's tablet was on the sideboard. He turned it on, went to the Google Earth app again and then to his "recents". The area around Carl's house came into focus, and he zoomed in to quite a tight scale in 2D. Then he sat down at the kitchen table and motioned Sarah to come in close.

'This is the lay-by where we wait for the text and change over as drivers,' he said, pointing. 'It's three miles or so to the gates, but I'll guide you all the way.'

He zoomed in to a larger scale, focused on the house itself and moved to 3D so that Sarah could get a better impression of what it actually looked like. It was the same image he had viewed before, with the drive culminating in the big gravel turning circle.

'So, the French windows must be here?' said Sarah, indicating the wing of the house on the opposite side of the circle from the approach up the drive. They were in shadow, and hard to see.

John had already identified them and nodded his confirmation.

'Drive up to the gravel turning circle, start a right-handed, anti-clockwise U-turn and stop halfway round, directly opposite the French windows, here,' he indicated.

'That'll put me in the passenger seat on the far side of the car from him, which is what I want. Keep the engine running. Get a bin liner ready, and make sure after it's all over that you get your sister's phone in it.'

'And return the gate fob to her.'

John nodded. 'That too.'

'And the actual act?'

'He'll come out, or your sister will send him out. I'll take it from there. Don't look.'

Sarah glanced at him. 'I'll play it by ear.'

John grimaced. 'Up to you.'

'What then?' asked Sarah.

'When I say drive, you drive, whether there's been any shooting or not. Either way, we leave as soon as we can. The gate will open automatically. Hopefully we won't see anybody as we pull onto the road. Tell your sister when you get her phone back not to raise the alarm for fifteen minutes.'

'Why fifteen minutes? Why not longer?'

John sat back and folded his arms.

'It's a feasible length of time for her to have hidden after the shots, and we'll be well away by then on our back roads route to here. Plus, we don't want a big discrepancy between the time she raises the alarm and any time of death indicated by a post-mortem.'

Sarah considered this. It made sense.

'OK, so we get back here. Then what?'

'It shouldn't be later than about one-thirty. Ideally, we're not spotted, but it's not a disaster if we are unless anyone clocks the plates, and that's highly unlikely. The car goes straight into the garage; I change the plates back. Then I clean the gun and return it to the cupboard – not so perfectly that it looks as if it's been recently cleaned and oiled. The spent cartridges go in the murder bags too; any unused ones go back in the cupboard. Finally, I have a bath.'

'To make sure there's no firearms residue on you?' said Sarah.

'Correct,' replied John. 'All that shouldn't take more than half an hour. Meanwhile, you take a stroll to the village shop. Talk to people if you can; reinforce the impression that we've been here all the time.'

'Understood,' said Sarah. 'So, I get back here; you're squeaky clean; we've still got the murder bags.'

'Yes,' John agreed. 'I've thought long and hard about them. So, then we're going sailing, after we've put all the clothes we were wearing in the wash.'

'Sailing?'

'Yes, with the dogs. We make sure first that everything is in those bags: three phones; two tablets; two number plates; two pairs of shoes; any used cartridges, gun cleaning swabs or notebooks; your wig and sunglasses. And also, we put some green plastic bin liners in there and a few bricks. I've got some of those out the back.'

'Whoa, slow down,' said Sarah.

'The bags you bought look pretty much like sailing bags anyway. Put some jeans and sweaters over the top of whatever we put in there as a basic disguise, and I'll take my normal sailing bag too so we can bring all that stuff back. We'll be at Burnham-on-Crouch before 5pm. The dogs come with us, as a distraction. The bags go on the boat. The dogs go on the boat. We go on the boat. We all spend the night there.'

'And then the next morning…'

'Not too early – we don't want to attract attention. But at a civilised hour, when everyone else is beginning to be up and about, we head out to sea, get somewhere well offshore that the echo sounder tells us is pretty deep and then wrap the murder bags in green bin liners, together with three or four bricks apiece. Then, discreetly, over the side they go.'

John looked at Sarah, seeking approval. She was deep in thought.

'We've got to hope the police don't catch up with us before morning,' she said doubtfully, after a pause.

'They'd need to be Sherlock Holmes, Hercule Poirot and Miss Marple rolled into one, with a dash of Usain Bolt,' said John. 'Consider this: they've got to decide we're suspects, when we've got only the vaguest connection with the man through your sister, who'll be pointing them anywhere except towards us. Then they've got to find us, when only Tom knows where we are, and he's away – they don't know where. Then they've got to find the boat. Then they need a warrant to search it. And all that mostly overnight, on a weekend. If we're on the water promptly on Sunday morning, then we'll be fine.'

'Only one thing left, then,' said Sarah.

'What's that?'

'Your bed needs to support that dirty weekend alibi.'

'Damn, you can't expect me to think of everything. I suppose it does.'

* * *

Cynthia did not sleep well, unsurprising in the circumstances. To the maximum extent possible, she'd prepared for the next day before going to bed.

She had already packed the food for Carl's meal in her car, in a cool box; not that he would ever eat it, but if her reason for being at the house was to prepare a meal, then evidence of a meal there must be. She had a notebook too, such as anyone would take to an important meeting, plus her normal mobile phone and her PAYG one, the latter buried deep in her handbag.

She had laid out her clothes, discreetly elegant. Dark, and certainly not white. Just in case.

She ran over everything she had to do the next day in as much detail as she could as she lay wide awake in the small flat. The code Sarah had texted to her made sense. She'd have to claim that she'd lost the key fob and call on her normal mobile to get Carl to open the gate.

Otherwise, it was simply a matter of arriving, summoning Sarah and her Jackal and improvising as necessary to engineer the confrontation with Carl. That bit worried her – it was unpredictable.

She must remember to hand over her phone afterwards and to get the key fob back. Beyond that, in theory at least, her role was pretty simple.

But assisting in the killing of your husband is not at all simple, thought Cynthia anxiously. Sarah had a genuinely straightforward motive and had never had any emotional or physical connection with the individual who was about to die. Neither had her tame Jackal.

But Cynthia had loved Carl, once. Could she connive in his cold-blooded killing? Did he deserve it? How would the children react?

It was ugly; it was untidy, but if it could be done without suspicion falling on her, then logically it was for the best. There was no other way. Not if Carl was to be prevented from wrecking everything.

She knew that everything the family owned came from the proceeds of crime. Though she realised it wasn't noble, she wasn't willing to give all that up.

Ultimately, that trumped everything. Having convinced herself, Cynthia swiftly fell asleep.

* * *

Woody was not a particularly clever man, certainly not bright enough to understand the concept of entrapment, nor to realise that if Frank did anything with his recording, he'd also be implicating himself. Carl's chauffeur was a brave man physically; what he feared above all else was superior intellect, and in Frank, he knew he was well outgunned in that respect.

So, he regarded himself as over a barrel after his lunch with the lawyer, as Frank had accurately calculated that he would. Of course, the financial inducement on offer helped.

He called Frank on the evening of their lunch. 'If you want it done soon, I need to know who.'

'Not on this line, Woody,' came the smooth reply.

They arranged to meet in a multi-storey car park in Bishop's Stortford the following morning. Woody arrived early and watched for the distinctive Jaguar. He slid quietly into the passenger seat before Frank had even switched off, to the lawyer's surprise and disquiet. They were in the world of physical skulduggery now: Woody's world.

'So, who?'

Frank waved such a direct question away.

'It's local. In the countryside, not the town. What will you need?'

'Any relatives about? Will he be suspicious?'

'No. You should be able to get him alone if you time it right.'

'Then either a decent, untraceable handgun, or failing that, a sawn off 12 bore shotgun. And help in getting rid of it.'

Frank was enough of a lawyer to know that "untraceable" meant not linked to any specific individual, nor ideally to any given crime. But he wasn't a firearms expert.

'What's decent?'

'9mm pistol, with a silencer if you can get it. Plus ammunition, obviously.'

Frank made notes. He had his sources, and he trusted them, but time was short.

'I'll get back to you on the details of how we deliver it to you, and then dispose of it.'

'Nothing too bulky. Two magazines.'

Frank kept writing, infuriatingly slowly, it seemed to Woody. 'I have to know who it is, and where he lives. I have to plan how to get in.'

'Oh, that'll be no problem,' said Frank mildly, folding up his notebook. 'You've been there many times and can come and go as you please. It's Carl.'

Woody stared at him, open mouthed. 'What? He's my gaffer!'

'You work for the family, Woody, not for any one individual.'

Woody reflected on this and also on the fact that were he to decline, he'd be a marked man, especially if Carl was no longer around to protect him. That would not be a good situation.

'Carl's head of the family.'

'He is becoming something of a liability. You know how oddly he has been behaving of late. So, I am seeking a solution on the family's behalf.'

'He's my friend, too.'

Frank looked up in alarm. Emotional empathy from Woody was not a factor he had considered.

'I have worked for the man a lot longer than you. He doesn't have friends. He cultivates people who are, or may be, useful. Which you have been, to date.'

'And if I don't?'

Frank sounded regretful as he replied.

'It will happen anyway. You'll get no financial retainer, your disloyalty will be noted and you're on record as saying you'd do it. Altogether, not good.'

Woody knew he was boxed in. He decided on a strategy of "agree now and reflect later".

'Let me know when I can expect the gun.'

'Tomorrow,' said Frank. 'I'll get it to you somehow. Then it must be done within a week.'

David knew that his mother was up to something, and he knew that Frank was up to something. However, he wasn't quite sure if they had teamed up. On balance, he thought it was probably best to keep his distance from both of them and let their plans run their course, whilst appearing generally but vaguely supportive. In other words, go with the flow.

This was rather what Frank had expected him to do. Cynthia too.

He regretted what he imagined was about to happen to his father, but he wasn't emotional about it because he wasn't an emotional individual. In purely commercial terms, the man whom he'd admired for so long was now endangering the business he'd built up over many years. David viewed himself as the heir apparent, and he had big plans for that business, so the threat Carl represented had to be mitigated. It was as simple as that.

He just hoped that the plan to do so didn't bring the roof down on everyone's heads – another reason to keep his distance.

Nothing would be traced back to him.

Plausible deniability – something Carl had always thrived on. David liked that concept.

CHAPTER TWENTY

Saturday morning. John hadn't slept well, and he sensed that Sarah, next to him, hadn't either. He'd set the alarm for 6am but was awake long before that.

He got up and ran himself a hot bath, which he hoped would relax him. It did to a certain extent, but he was far too restless to lie there for long. He was back in the bedroom shortly before the alarm was due and felt Sarah's watchful eyes upon him.

'Coffee?' he asked, as he turned off the alarm. It sounded spectacularly mundane in the context of what the day was due to bring.

He could only see the top half of her face above the duvet but thought she looked worried. She shook herself free.

'Sure.'

John smiled at Sarah wanly.

'You OK?' she asked after a moment, as she digested his taut appearance.

'Fine. Just a few nerves. It'll pass as soon as we start doing things.'

'I could relax you for a bit if you like. It's still early.'

It was clear what she meant. There was no hint of seduction; it was purely a distraction technique, and John knew that neither of them was really in the mood.

'No thanks.' It came out too abruptly, and he softened it quickly. 'Definitely later. Afterwards.'

Sarah forced a tense smile. 'Never done it on a boat.'

'You have to be a bit of a contortionist,' John smiled at her briefly in an attempt at humour. 'I'll get your coffee.'

Once downstairs, he fed Barney and Pip and let them out before making two coffees and heading back up.

They drank together companionably in bed and ran through their plans again, though they'd already done so the previous evening. From time to time they lapsed into silence, each deep in thought.

After about an hour, they got up. John dressed simply, in jeans and a check shirt, wearing his normal ancient loafers around the house. The cheap new trainers he'd bought for what he termed "the event" were already in the back of the Volvo, as were Sarah's; they wouldn't put them on until they had left John's house, to avoid leaving prints there which might match any left at the scene.

Sarah dressed in similarly inconspicuous style and then went into the bathroom to start experimenting with her wig. She didn't feel like breakfast.

John forced himself to have a bowl of cereal whilst digesting the online *Daily Telegraph* on his iPad. Maybe they'd have a new story to report tomorrow, he thought idly. Then he checked the weather forecast in Bishop's Stortford on his murder tablet. Dry and cloudy. That was good: less chance of leaving traceable tyre tracks, though since they would be on gravel at Carl's house, he was fairly relaxed about that anyway.

After a while, he took a deep breath, put away the breakfast things, removed the keys from the safe and unlocked his gun cabinet. He took out the little .410 and opened it, squinting down the barrel to ensure it was clear, a basic safety check, as taught to him by his father, who had been a magistrate. John wondered briefly how he would have viewed the situation, and then blocked the thought swiftly from his mind. He was dead, so thankfully he would never know. Even so, John felt a pang of guilt.

He shut the shotgun and laid it across a nearby chair; then he turned back to the cabinet and took out the box of twenty-five cartridges. He knew already that they were number five shot, unlike the number six that he and Sarah had practised with. That meant fewer but heavier pellets, befitting bigger types of prey. A fortunate coincidence.

John counted out ten cartridges from the box. At an absolute maximum he expected to use half that, so this number gave him an ample reserve; anything more would simply be burdensome and hard to conceal.

He left the rest of the ammunition in the box and locked it in the gun cabinet before returning the keys to the safe. Then he placed his ten cartridges in the deep right-hand pocket of the sleeveless gilet he intended to wear and left it on the chair beside the gun. This had a tailored gun sleeve, which it had taken him a while to find earlier in the week (he detected the hand of Jenny's "tidying"), but he had done so eventually. Now he slipped the gun into it.

It is illegal to transport an uncovered weapon. John didn't want to fall foul of that particular little-known regulation in the remote eventuality that they were stopped by the police, en route either to or from Carl's house. For the same reason, he dug out his shotgun certificate and put it in the gilet's inside breast pocket.

It was still before 9.30am, and having checked everything necessary, there were over two hours to go before they were due to depart. John had no idea what Sarah was doing upstairs, like all men down the ages, and couldn't just sit around.

'Going to take the dogs for a walk,' he yelled up the stairs, receiving a faint "OK" from Sarah.

John was out for about an hour and was seen by several people as he passed the village shop, which he thought was probably no bad thing. He envied the dogs their oblivious happiness as they ran free around the fields behind Tom and Emma's house. Meanwhile, he grappled with an enormous sense of dread, coupled with helpless inevitability. If asked to describe it, he would have said that the nearest he had ever felt was when approaching the end of the holidays after his first term at boarding school, aged eight. It was not an emotion he had ever expected to feel again.

Sarah was downstairs when he returned, seemingly calm, and sipping another cup of coffee. John could see some hairs from her wig creeping out of a plastic bag on the sideboard. A few random clothes suitable for a casual activity like sailing were laid out there too.

'All set?' said Sarah evenly. If she was feeling the pressure, she was concealing it well, thought John.

'Yes. All set.'

'Shouldn't we go now?'

John glanced at his watch. 'Ten-forty-five – too early. We'll be sitting around in the lay-by for too long.'

'I just want to get on with it.'

They sat quietly in silence, as the minutes passed with terrible slowness. John thought that the kitchen clock had never ticked so loudly.

At 11am, John fetched the murder bags and placed the two tablets and his PAYG mobile phone into one of them; he had no use for it anymore, whereas Sarah needed hers to receive the text from Cynthia. He also went outside and fetched the six heavy bricks he'd already selected from the porch, placing three into each bag. The clothes Sarah had brought downstairs were placed on top of the other contents of each bag in a rudimentary disguise.

At 11.15am they could stand it no longer and headed out with the two bags, which went into a dark corner of the garage. John pulled the top cover over the car's loading area to hide the empty space from view before he shut the tailgate.

They returned once more to the kitchen, and John fed each of the dogs a rawhide bone before they shut and locked the front door. The two animals would be alone for about two hours, but there was a flap in the back door, so they could get into the garden if need be. John was holding the gun in its sleeve and wearing the gilet, plus his flat cap, as they headed out to the garage, having checked carefully to see that that nobody was about to pass the front gate as they did so. Sarah held the plastic bag with her wig and wore the big-brimmed hat with sunglasses.

'Stop,' said John briefly, as they opened the garage door.

'Put everything in the car and go to the gate. No headgear – if anybody sees you now, we want them to recognise you as being here. When it's clear, wave me out.'

Sarah nodded, dropped her belongings on the back seat and headed for the gate. John placed the gun in the rear seat footwell and reversed out, before stopping to close and lock the garage doors behind him.

He looked at Sarah as he got back into the car and could see her peering carefully either way from the gate. She turned and beckoned.

Slowly, John drove his Volvo past the Fiat and the Golf so obviously parked close together in front of the house. Sarah got in as he reached the gate.

They drove off completely unobserved, as they had hoped. Within a mile or so, John pulled briefly into a field gateway whilst Sarah put on her wig, sunglasses and hat, and they both changed their shoes. John pulled his flat cap further down over his face before pulling out into the lane again.

So far so good. They were on their way.

* * *

Woody lived in a rented house in a village about five miles from Carl's home. He fondly imagined that nobody in "the organisation" knew where, but of course they did.

His marriage had been stable once, before he went to prison, but now it was more on and off. Carol had become distressingly independent during his time away. At the moment, it was off – she'd got fed up with Woody being under her feet over the period whilst Carl had been on remand, compounded after his acquittal, when her husband had still been under-employed. So, she'd decamped to her sister Wendy, temporarily Woody hoped because he wasn't good on his own. Not so much lonely as not self-sufficient. Cooking, washing, cleaning: these were all women's work in Woody's world.

There were no children, so he had been alone in what was by then a fairly untidy house when the doorbell rang on Friday evening. Woody had a peephole in his front door, which was always locked, and kept a cricket bat behind it. Though he was expecting a delivery, he didn't like the look of what he saw as he peered through: a motorcycle helmet with a dark visor on a tall, leathered figure.

'Who is it?' he yelled through the door, and then stepped swiftly to one side: a basic precaution against shots being fired through it.

'Package for you, mate.' He could see a wrapped box in the gloved hand held up to the peephole.

'Who from?'

'No idea, mate – I just deliver.'

It didn't sound like something that had to be signed for. Woody thought fast.

'Leave it by the door.'

He could see the figure hesitating and then coming to a decision.

'Suit yourself,' he said, in a "some people" tone of voice. The biking boots stomped heavily down Woody's front path.

Woody waited for the motorcycle to start, and for another couple of minutes after it had gone, then he unlocked the door, stuck his head outside and peered cautiously around. Nobody. He retrieved the package, stepped back inside and locked the door again.

It was about the size of a large chocolate box, though considerably heavier and wrapped in brown paper. Woody knew immediately what it was and removed the paper carefully.

It was indeed an actual chocolate box. Woody opened it,

and inside was an automatic pistol, resting on a bed of cotton wool. There was a small cloth bag too, which Woody took out first and opened. He took out one of the items inside: a 9mm bullet. Peering inside, he could see more.

He turned to the pistol and took it from the box: Walther P38, with the old-style wooden grips. He knew the type but had never fired one. German service issue in World War 2, and indeed for a long time afterwards; quite a few of them had made their way back to Britain as post-war "souvenirs", together with the earlier and more famous Lugers, and thence into the underworld.

The weapon looked weathered, as well it might, given that it was over seventy years old, but as he cocked the mechanism, Woody could see at once that it was in good working condition. He thought that it probably had a few tales to tell.

Where problems might arise was if the ammunition was of similar elderly vintage. Woody picked up the 9mm bullet and examined it critically. Then he took a saucer from the cupboard and poured the remaining contents of the bag into it. There were sixteen bullets in all, and they looked reassuringly bright and new, also, two inert, black painted drill rounds so he could practise with the mechanism. Someone knew their stuff: a P38 used an eight-round magazine.

Turning back to the box, Woody found what he was looking for. There were two magazines beneath the cotton wool. He examined them critically to see if the lips which held the top bullet in place when they were loaded were in any way bent or deformed – that was often the Achilles heel for an automatic pistol and could easily lead to a jam. But they both looked pristine.

Woody filled the magazines with eight rounds apiece and then gauged the spring pressures as he unloaded them again. He was checking the other significant risk with an automatic: a magazine spring which had been compressed for too long and would then exert insufficient pressure to chamber the next round once the previous one was fired. He gave a small grunt of satisfaction afterwards. He wouldn't charge the magazines with bullets again until shortly before he needed to use them.

Despite the absence of a silencer, which he knew had been a tall order at short notice, Woody was satisfied. The 9mm calibre was still in widespread use with police and armies around the world after many years, being both powerful and reliable. The only way his P38 was inferior to a modern pistol was in magazine capacity, but Woody didn't expect to need more than two shots to achieve his objective, and hopefully only one. It was a bit heavier than ideal too, but that would make no difference.

He was boxing the pistol up carefully, after putting the bullets back in their bag, when his mobile rang – number withheld.

'You have it?' said Frank.

'Yeah.'

'OK?'

'It's fine,' said Woody.

'This weekend then. He'll be home alone throughout as far as I know.'

'What about afterwards? The gun?'

'Get rid of it.'

Frank rang off without waiting for a reply, and Woody looked at his handset in disgust. Then, he carefully put the chocolate box on its side behind a pile of golf journals, pulling the top one across so that it couldn't be seen from above.

He sighed heavily and ambled into the kitchen to take a beer out of his fridge.

He'd need a plan, and that required thought. Or maybe cunning, which was more Woody's line.

* * *

Carl spent Saturday morning clearing up. He was aware that the house was not in a state which Cynthia would approve of, and he also knew that he should have started this chore the day before, rather than allowing himself only a couple of hours.

His plan had been to get the maid to do it on Friday, but of course the wretched girl had called in sick. For a moment he'd nearly sworn at her – he could sense the fear in her voice – but then he remembered the new leaf he was supposed to be turning over. He'd confined himself to an abrupt grunt and a "Get well soon – see you on Monday" before slamming down the phone.

Everything was as good as it was going to be by 11am, and Carl had been thinking as he hoovered and polished. His aim was to show that he'd made an effort rather than to achieve Cynthia-like standards of perfection, which were probably beyond him anyway. Whatever the provocation when they met, he was determined to be friendly and conciliatory; a bust-up would probably lead to his wife flouncing out, and that would solve nothing.

He wanted her back, not out there looking for a divorce lawyer.

After his cleaning efforts, Carl had a shower and changed out of his scruffy jeans into some white chinos and a pale blue shirt which Cynthia had given him, one that he knew she liked. He added some tasselled loafers and a smart gaucho belt, before examining himself in the mirror: marginally overweight due to the junk food he'd been eating recently, he concluded ruefully, but otherwise a damn sight better preserved than most men of his vintage. He also tidied up the bedroom. Though he was a natural optimist, Carl didn't really expect to end up there, but he certainly didn't want to ruin the chance if it presented itself because of a few clothes left carelessly strewn around and an unmade bed.

He went downstairs and took a couple of expensive champagne flutes from the set of twelve in the cupboard, putting them on the silver tray in the drawing room. Then he checked the temperature of the bottle he'd put in the fridge the previous night before shutting the door again. He knew that Cynthia would notice that it was vintage Taittinger, rather than Prosecco. He'd take it out and open it about ten minutes before she was due, might even help himself to a preliminary glass.

Finally, he walked around outside the house just to make sure there was nothing untoward on the lawn or lying on the gravel. It was all perfect, and there was even a sunny break in the cloudy weather.

Carl looked at his watch. 11.40am. Whistling happily, but tunelessly, and betraying just a hint of nerves, he headed back into the house.

* * *

Cynthia had left at 11.15am for the thirty-five-minute drive from Chelmsford to her home. That morning, she took some time with her make-up, dressed smartly in the dark trouser suit she'd chosen and wore an expensive brooch which she knew Carl would recognise. Her hair had been freshly done on Friday. She wore her wedding ring too, for the first time in a while. Everything that would please Carl, and nothing which would put him on edge or rile him – that was her intention. Even her Audi had been through a car wash, after she'd filled it with petrol, and was gleaming. Carl had grumbled when she insisted on ordering it in white, because it showed the dirt so easily.

She didn't hurry and felt surprisingly calm, despite her restless night. Her planned steak meal for Carl was packed. Her role in the plan was relatively simple, and she'd thought it through carefully. She had reconciled herself fully to the necessity of what was going to happen.

Cynthia was early because she'd allowed a safety margin and hadn't needed it. She stopped in a pub car park a couple of miles short of the house for ten minutes, checked her make-up and then took her PAYG phone out from her handbag. It had been fully charged overnight.

It was a couple of minutes before 11.55am. Cynthia waited patiently and typed out her short text. At precisely that time, she sent the single letter "A" to her sister.

As she started the car, she heard her phone ping immediately in response and picked it up. A thumbs up emoji.

Sarah and Jackal must be nearby.

Everything was on track. She drove off.

CHAPTER TWENTY-ONE

Sarah looked at John after sending the reply. They had been parked in the lay-by for nearly ten minutes, after a silent journey, both lost in thought. There was nobody else there, as they had hoped.

'That's it. "A". She's going in.'

Without a word, John opened his door, got out of the Volvo's driving seat and then opened the rear door behind him, whilst Sarah got out of the car on the other side. He removed the .410 from its sleeve, returning that to the footwell. Then he walked behind the car to the front passenger door. Sarah had meanwhile walked around the front of the car and settled into the driving seat. As John got in on the passenger side, she gave him the gate fob, still in the plastic bag Cynthia had put it in. They had talked this procedure through exhaustively the night before.

John sat quietly, with the gun across his lap. Now they would wait. There was nothing to say, though John looked across briefly. Sarah seemed absolutely calm. No sign of nerves at all, he thought.

Mind you, he didn't think he was showing any himself, but he could clearly feel his heart thumping, and his mouth was dry. As with any ordeal, the waiting was the worst part.

After ten minutes, Sarah thumped the wheel with both hands in frustration, betraying her own internal tensions.

'What's gone wrong?'

John was about to reply when her phone pinged again. Sarah grabbed it eagerly from the central coffee cup holder where she'd placed it.

'Yes! "B". She's there, and so is he.'

They waited in strained silence. The phone pinged again, about five minutes later.

"D". Sarah started the engine.

'Drive carefully,' said John, calmly. Sarah gave him a filthy look as she pulled away.

'It's my car, and you haven't driven it before,' he smiled, with a feeble attempt at humour. Sarah said nothing but did indeed drive with caution as she pulled out of the lay-by onto the A1184.

'Just under a mile down here, turn right,' said John quietly. 'I'll tell you when.'

The junction sign was visible after a minute or so. 'That's it.'

Sarah made the turn a couple of hundred yards later. John carefully broke open the shotgun on his lap as she did so and fished one of his ten cartridges out of the deep gilet pocket. He inserted it and closed the gun; the sound was loud in the confined space of the car.

'Won't fire till you thumb back the hammer, right?' mumbled Sarah.

John nodded. 'Well remembered.'

Sarah drove at a steady 40mph along the country lane, passing nobody, and it was less than three minutes before John warned her. 'On the left – a couple of hundred yards.'

They pulled slowly into the entranceway, with the electronic gates looming twenty yards or so ahead of them. John had the fob at the ready. The gates began to swing open immediately as he pressed it but slowly, and Sarah was forced to pause the car for twenty seconds or so. Both of them wordlessly took off their safety belts as they'd discussed. Being a Volvo, it then refused to move off; they'd forgotten this, and since she was unfamiliar with the car, Sarah gave John a wild look of panic until he calmly pressed the manual override on the electronic handbrake.

'OK, here we go,' she said, once the gap was sufficient. John squeezed her left arm briefly with his right.

With the seat belt alarm bleeping in protest, the Volvo crept slowly onto the gravel drive through the gates. John sensed them closing behind them once the car was clear. They couldn't immediately see the big parking circle outside the house from where they were, because of the crest in the drive, just the roof. Gradually, however, more and more of the building came into view.

They were in.

* * *

Woody left home just after midday in his own car, an ageing silver Vauxhall Astra. He was pretty sure he'd catch the boss getting ready for lunch then, and he knew he'd be alone.

He'd pondered it all carefully the night before. He could get into the house grounds, because he had a gate key fob, and if he was seen doing so, he had a perfectly valid reason: that's where he worked. If that happened, he'd abort and either turn around unseen or manufacture some reason for being there if Carl detected him: retrieving something from one of the cars, probably. He didn't think his car would leave identifiable tyre marks on the gravel, but if it did, again, so what? He drove to the house regularly or at least had done, until Carl had become virtually housebound. And he knew that the security camera didn't work.

He'd familiarised himself carefully with the Walther before he left, using the inert drill rounds, and liked what he found.

It was surprisingly modern for such an old design. He could chamber a round by pulling back and releasing the slide, pushing the safety de-cocking lever on the left down with his thumb to lower the hammer safely and then releasing the lever so that it came to rest in the interim "safe" position. From there, he could immediately render the pistol ready to fire by nudging the lever to a horizontal position with his thumb. The first shot would then be double action – pulling the trigger would both cock the hammer again, and then release it. Each subsequent shot would be single action, as the hammer was automatically cocked by the recoil of the previous one. Alternatively, he could thumb back the hammer so that the first shot was single action, requiring a much less forceful trigger pull. It was a more up-to-date mechanism than the Browning 9mm he had learnt to use in his army days, which was single action only. To be ready to fire, the hammer had to be back, with the safety on ("cocked and locked"). There was more scope for accidents that way.

Woody knew that pistols were renowned for accidents and had even witnessed one during his brief military service, when someone had shot himself in the foot. He always treated them with respect.

He decided that he'd carry the Walther with a round chambered and the hammer down. After several practice attempts, he concluded that once he drew the weapon it would be best to thumb the hammer back if he had the time, because the lower trigger pressure necessary to fire the initial round would hopefully result in a more accurate shot. But it wasn't essential.

So, when he set off, the weapon was in this "hammer down" state, in the deep inside left pocket of his old Barbour jacket, which he kept unzipped – he could easily reach it with his right hand there. In the left-hand outside pocket was the spare magazine, loaded with eight rounds, like the one already in the gun.

He was quite calm, but there was one big uncertainty. He hadn't quite decided what to do.

It should be pretty easy to finish Carl off, and then make a quick getaway, but Woody wasn't entirely sure how he'd react when he confronted his boss.

Probably, he would kill him, but he didn't like the thought of that moment of betrayal he was sure he would see in Carl's final expression if he couldn't catch him from behind. The man had been good to him.

Part of him was tempted simply to reveal Frank's treachery, and then hopefully bear witness to the comeuppance which would no doubt be visited upon the lawyer.

But he was decidedly uneasy about trying to outwit Frank and the repercussions which might result.

Eventually, like much else in his life, Woody decided to play it by ear.

Carl looked at his watch again at about 11.50am, though he knew Cynthia was seldom on time. He felt excited to see her, teenage date style. It had been nearly six weeks, and then only for the briefest time after his period on remand. She'd been gone in a huff by the next morning.

The landline rang at just before midday. It was her. Don't say she's not coming…

'I've forgotten my gate thing. Can you buzz me in?'

Carl knew her well, of course and sensed her nervousness. His old self would have made a pretty robust response to such ineptitude. But today he was on best behaviour, so he bit his tongue.

'No problem, doll. See you in a minute.'

He swore quietly under his breath once he'd got off the line and went over to the gate control panel in the kitchen. Once he had pressed the button, and seen the green light flash, he went outside to greet his errant wife.

The white Audi seemed to pause for a few seconds as it came into sight over the crest, but it arrived within half a minute or so, and Carl could see Cynthia's smile. She gave him a little wave through the glass as she stopped on the gravel, keeping well to the left-hand edge of the parking circle. He'd missed those little gestures.

By the time he reached the car, Cynthia was already ferreting around in the boot with the food. She stopped briefly as he approached.

'Hello Carl,' she said non-committally, offering her cheek for a chaste kiss.

'Hello, love,' her husband replied and then stood back

to look at her in genuine admiration. 'You look fantastic. It's great to see you.'

Cynthia hesitated for a second. 'Yes, well, help me inside with all this, would you?'

'Sure.'

Carl swept up the two cool boxes and led her into the house through the French windows. They passed through the big, formal drawing room to the passage beyond which led to the kitchen, and he placed them on the island.

'Champagne?'

'Love some. I'll just get these steaks on, then I'll see you in the drawing room.'

Carl nodded contentedly and retreated. Cynthia glanced quickly at the security panel and could see that the TV screen monitoring the gate camera was blank, as she expected. Good. She duly placed the two steaks in a pan, put it on a low simmer, then walked back down the passage and stuck her head around the drawing room door.

Carl was standing there grinning, with two brimming champagne flutes.

'Just going to powder my nose. Won't be a sec.' She smiled and retreated before Carl had a chance to respond.

Once in the loo, she locked the door and quickly took her PAYG phone from her handbag. She was certain that her husband hadn't spotted her send the "B" text from the car when she first saw him. The second text took only a second to prepare, for again it was only one letter, though she took another second to put the phone on silent before she sent it. "D". Come now.

Cynthia put the phone back into the depths of her handbag, flushed the loo and took a deep breath. She knew that her sister and Jackal were only three miles away.

Carl didn't seem remotely suspicious, and she was confident that she could string him along till they arrived.

CHAPTER TWENTY-TWO

As they topped the rise in the drive, Sarah spotted the parked Audi on the left of the circle.

'That's Cynthia's car.'

'She'll shoo him out somehow,' replied John, his voice tightly clipped. 'Get the car into position. Not too close.'

There was plenty of room on the gravel to get past the parked Audi, and Sarah was keeping to the right anyway so that she could begin a left-hand U-turn. She stopped the Volvo exactly halfway through that manoeuvre, with the engine still running, directly opposite the French windows but about thirty feet from them.

The passenger door was now furthest from the house, and John opened it but stayed seated in the car, the gun out of sight on his lap. The seat belt alarm still gave off its monotonous chime.

Cynthia had delayed re-entering the drawing room as long as she decently could. As she did so, she first heard, and then saw, the Volvo through the French windows as it approached. It stopped directly outside.

'Carl – someone's in the drive,' she said, with as much alarm in her voice as she could muster.

Her husband had heard the car too and was already spinning round, mystified; the gates should have shut automatically after Cynthia had passed through them.

'What the hell?' he exclaimed, placing the two champagne glasses on a sideboard and then making for the open French windows.

Cynthia moved quietly into the passage and headed back towards the kitchen – she didn't want to witness what was coming next. Once there, she turned off the steaks and waited.

John saw the obviously angry figure, thirty feet away, coming through the French windows towards the car. He sensed Sarah, who was closer, recoiling in her seat. He'd rehearsed this scenario in his mind too often to count. Slowly, he got out of the Volvo; the gun was still out of sight to the man approaching on the far side.

Aside from being mystified, Carl felt affronted – who were these bloody strangers on his property when he was trying to reconcile with his wife? Well, they were going to leave and soon.

He could see the female driver of the grey Volvo looking at him through her closed car window: sunglasses and dark hair. She looked scared, silly bitch. He'd give her reason to be.

On the other side of the car was a man, standing now and beginning to move around the rear of the vehicle. Carl continued his aggressive march towards it but took in the figure as he approached. Middle aged – certainly over fifty. Flat cap. Trainers, which was odd, didn't look the type. No physical threat.

Carl didn't break step. And then suddenly, he did.

As the man emerged from behind the car, it became obvious for the first time that he was carrying a firearm of some type. Carl was now only a dozen feet away.

'Who the fuck are you?' Carl yelled uncertainly, as he stopped. All he heard in response was a click.

Carl had heard weapons being cocked before and grasped in a second all too clearly what was about to happen. He would probably have done better to rush the gunman, but that would have been counterintuitive in the face of such an unexpected threat.

Instead, he turned to run indoors.

Though prepared for a rush, John had predicted this reaction. He knew that the .410 was unlikely to kill with its first shot, so at all costs he had to prevent his victim from running out of its very short effective range. He took careful aim at the back of Carl's right knee and fired at the fleeing figure from no more than fifteen feet. He saw the shot smack against the white chinos: a tight spread of only a few inches, with an instant splash of blood.

Carl went down like a sack of potatoes, screaming in defiance, pain, rage and fear.

'You fucking bastard. Oh shit…'

Sarah was now emerging from the car too. As Carl rolled around in agony on the gravel, grasping his bloodied knee, John walked calmly towards him, breaking the smoking gun open and carefully putting the spent cartridge into the left pocket of his gilet. Transferring the gun to his left hand, he took a fresh cartridge from his right pocket, inserted it and closed the gun. Sarah heard the click as the hammer went back again. It had taken him less than four seconds to reload.

'Please – no.'

Carl turned on his back and rose onto his elbows to confront his attacker. Then he sensed that there would be no mercy, and something of the original East End hard man in him reappeared. At least go out with a bit of style.

'Like that then is it, you pig? Just one thing first – who was it?'

John was now only six feet away and moving to one side. Carl saw that there would be no answer. He also sensed instinctively that what was going to happen would be quicker, and probably less painful, if he stayed still rather than thrashing around. He flopped down onto his back and extended his arms, crucifixion style. John was now five feet from his right side.

Carl twisted his head to look at his attacker, who was beginning to crouch down on his haunches, raising the gun into his shoulder.

'Keep calm, and shoot straight,' he said quietly to the gunman.

He saw his assassin's eyes narrow briefly in surprise. Then it all went black forever.

John shot Carl in the side of the chest from his low position, just beneath the right armpit, exactly where he had planned to if he got the chance. He'd calculated beforehand that a shot there would avoid the protection of the breastbone, maximising the chances of hitting something vital.

The impact blasted Carl onto his left side, so that the wound was uppermost, and he lay motionless. John thought that the gaping rent in the bloodied pale blue shirt almost certainly concealed a fatal injury if the shotgun pellets had penetrated to any depth. At that range, they had hardly dispersed at all.

It had to be put beyond doubt though. John carefully repeated the loading procedure as he rose to his feet, pocketing the old cartridge again, and this time, he held the little shotgun out one-handed, to the full extent of his right arm so that the muzzle was less than a foot behind Carl's exposed right ear. It wasn't heavy.

He had to keep away from any blood spatter. At that distance, there would be plenty.

He cocked the hammer for a third time, steadied himself carefully and gently pulled the trigger. The result was even more sickening than he expected. He looked briefly at the shattered skull and turned to Sarah, who was frozen still, gaping at the scene in horror. She was clutching one of the bin bags.

It had been an execution. John had planned it that way.

'Buck up. Find your sister,' he ordered in a clipped tone. 'And remember, don't go inside.'

Sarah looked at him, startled, and headed towards the French windows. John took the third spent cartridge out of the gun, put it into his left-hand pocket and went back to the car, where he quickly returned the .410 to its sleeve. Then he placed it into to the rear seat footwell before getting into the front passenger seat. He put on his seat belt.

From the kitchen, Cynthia had heard the third shot, around fifteen seconds after the first, and then the hysterical yells of her sister. Surely it must be over.

'Cyn! Cyn!'

She collected herself, took her PAYG phone from her handbag and made her way quickly from the kitchen down the passage back into the drawing room.

For a moment, her heart leapt at the unfamiliar figure by

236

the open French windows, before realising that it was Sarah in a wig and wearing gloves.

She paused. 'It's done?'

Despite the sunglasses, she could see that her younger sister was weeping.

'Yes. Horrible.'

At least one of them was calm. Cynthia proffered the phone without comment, and then indicated the green bin bag Sarah was holding. It took her younger sister a moment to come to her senses, but then she opened the bag to receive the phone, handed over the plastic-wrapped gate fob from a gloved hand and turned back towards the car.

'Fifteen minutes,' she shouted over her shoulder, sounding panicked.

Cynthia stepped out of the French windows. Whoever Jackal was, he was already in the passenger seat of the car, looking away, and visible only in silhouette through the tinted glass. The seat belt alarm continued like a metronome. Sarah slung the bin bag into the back and hurried into the driving seat. She put on her seat belt, finally silencing the alarm, and within seconds the Volvo was completing its U-turn and passing close by her Audi as it headed back down the drive.

The bloodied corpse lay on the gravel, twelve feet or so away, seemingly smaller to Cynthia than her husband had been in life.

There were some dark lumps around the head, which she didn't want to think about too much. She didn't go any closer and felt surprisingly calm and unemotional, though she was glad that she couldn't see Carl's face.

Fifteen minutes, then she'd call the police. Cynthia turned back into the drawing room, where she couldn't see the body.

The two glasses of champagne were still on the sideboard. She drank them both, straight down.

* * *

Woody was still in a quandary about what to do as he turned into the driveway and pressed the key fob. He felt the comforting weight of the Walther in his pocket whilst he waited as the gates swung slowly open. If the circumstances were wrong, he knew he could always abort.

He was approaching the gentle crest in the drive when he was forced to swerve as a grey Volvo estate came over the top towards him. It was being driven quite fast, but in a controlled fashion, and Woody could see that the couple inside were as surprised as he was. He had no idea who they were and didn't recognise the car.

Woody cursed, but he also felt a momentary sense of relief. Those people had seen him, and his car, and would no doubt testify as such if they had to. They'd clearly just visited Carl. No question of going ahead with the shooting now.

That relieved feeling lasted only seconds. As he approached the gravel turning circle in front of the house, Woody was surprised to see a white car he recognised as Cynthia's on the left, and then a pile of rags near the French windows directly ahead of him. Suddenly, he realised with mounting shock that it was something else. He braked hard, jumped out of the car and ran across before abruptly stopping a few feet short of the body, with his hand to his mouth.

There wasn't much left of the head, but Woody knew Carl's hair colour well enough, even though it was matted with blood.

'Jesus.'

Woody stared wildly at the scene of what was obviously a murder: one that had pre-empted the killing he had intended himself.

Suddenly, he felt eyes upon him and swung around in a panic, fumbling in his Barbour pocket.

It was Cynthia, standing in the French windows. Woody could see that she was shocked, though whether that was on account of his own sudden appearance or because her husband was lying dead in front of her, he didn't know.

'What the fuck happened?' he shouted at her, aggressively. He could see the panic in her eyes.

'I was in the kitchen, making lunch,' said Cynthia quickly. 'There was shooting; I hid. And then a car drove off.'

'I know. I nearly hit it. Volvo. Who?'

'Never saw it.'

Woody thought fast. Maybe he was just the backup, and Frank had run another plan in parallel. Or perhaps Cynthia was in on it; he'd been told Carl had become a family problem. Whatever the truth, Carl was now dead, and Cynthia was very much alive. Woody had never underestimated Cynthia. He decided to level with her.

'Frank sent me to kill Carl,' he said.

'What?' Cynthia gaped at him disbelievingly from the doorway.

'Yes. Look.' Woody pulled the Walther out from his Barbour pocket and saw Cynthia shrink back in fear.

'Don't worry. I've not come for you,' said Woody with as much reassurance as he could muster; as a rule, he wasn't great at reassurance.

He put the pistol back out of view and looked quizzically at the woman opposite. He seemed to be expecting direction.

Cynthia's mind was racing.

'Look, Woody,' she said, guiding him into the drawing room. 'It's as I said. Carl and I were going to have lunch together to talk things through, you know, our marriage. I was in the kitchen when I heard him go out. Then shooting: three shots. I hid till I heard the car go. I was about to call the police.'

Woody stared at her uncertainly. She didn't seem very upset at the death of her husband. But then, they were separated. He didn't know what to think.

'Now, let's not make this any more complicated than it already is. Forget the Frank angle. You were just coming here to clean the cars.'

'They'll suspect me. The police.'

'Perhaps. Initially. But you haven't fired a gun, have you? Let alone the one which killed Carl. It's a fluke that you got here just after it happened. I'll tell them that. And it's true! They can't pin anything on you.'

Woody thought hard and pulled out the pistol again. Cynthia's heart lurched for a moment.

'OK. What about this?'

'We'll hide it. Now let me call the police, and then stick to the story when they get here.'

Woody nodded, and then trailed awkwardly after Cynthia as she returned to the kitchen, where the nearest house phone was. She took a deep breath, and then dialled 999. Woody listened.

'Hello,' she paused, listening to the operator. 'Police please.'

There was silence: only a few seconds. 'My husband's been shot. He's dead. Please come as fast as you can.'

Woody thought that she was very calm and in control.

'No – I didn't see anything; I was in the kitchen. Just heard three shots and then hid.'

A further pause.

'About fifteen minutes ago.' It was less actually, as she knew.

She gave the address, listened for a moment, said, 'Fine,' and then rang off, turning to Woody.

'They'll be here in under twenty minutes. Give me that gun.'

She reached out. Woody hesitated, took the loaded Walther from his pocket and then made it safe by removing the fitted magazine and ejecting the live round from the chamber. He put the loose bullet back into the magazine, took the spare from his pocket and then placed the pistol and the two magazines into Cynthia's outstretched hands. She was taken aback by his professionalism.

'You meant business.'

Woody nodded. 'Frank meant business. He got it for me, gave me no choice.'

Cynthia looked at him grimly. 'I see.'

She turned on her heel and headed through the far door to the hall, where the stairs were.

'Where are you going to put it?' Woody called after her. It sounded lame.

'Somewhere only I know,' called Cynthia confidently over her shoulder. 'Now, wait outside for the police. I'll join you in a minute.'

* * *

The gates still hadn't quite closed from Woody's passage through when John and Sarah approached. The sensor detected their car and clumsily reversed the mechanism, but they were static for nearly half a minute before the gap was big enough. It seemed like an age.

'Who the hell was that?' said Sarah, smacking the dash viciously as they waited.

John shook his head as Sarah began to drive through. 'Don't know. A man. He won't have recognised us.'

'The car – he'll know it was a grey Volvo.' Sarah pulled out onto the road.

'Nothing we can do about that.'

They drove back in silence, carefully and slowly. There was not a lot to say, and they were both coming down fast from huge surges of adrenalin. About five miles from home, whilst they were on a quiet lane, John turned to Sarah.

'Take the wig off. If we're spotted now, it's just you and me coming back from somewhere. We're far enough away not to be connected.'

He threw his cap on the back seat for the same reason, and they pulled into a gateway whilst Sarah removed her wig. Then they both changed their shoes, putting the ones they'd been wearing into the bin bag with Cynthia's and Sarah's phones.

'But the plates?'

'Nobody will notice them. I'll put the originals back on in the garage as soon as we're home.'

Sarah knew this. They'd talked through the procedure often enough, and anyway, nobody saw them pull back into John's drive.

Thereafter, they were a well-oiled machine.

The Volvo went straight into the garage, which was closed up whilst John performed his first task: feeding the dogs.

Then it was into the garage again to change the plates back behind closed doors: a five-minute job. The old ones, which might link them to the vicinity of Carl's house, went straight into his murder bag, already in the garage. Into hers, Sarah meanwhile placed the plastic bag containing her PAYG phone, plus Cynthia's, the wig, the three expended shotgun cartridges and the shoes. Suitable sailing clothing was replaced on top of each.

Finally, both bags went onto the back seat of the Volvo; the rear loading area would be left for the dogs.

John then returned to the house to clean the .410, making sure any evidence that it had been fired recently was removed. He was careful not to leave the gun too oily and dried it thoroughly so that it appeared to have been unused for a while. Then back into the gun cupboard it went, together with the seven unused cartridges, which he returned to their box. Nobody could tell when that had been opened; if anyone asked, they were leftovers from Sarah's shooting lesson a fortnight or so before.

They wouldn't mention any of this unless they had to, but it was a truth they could fall back upon if need be, and it would also explain any recent prints upon the gun or the cartridges.

However, before he closed the cabinet again, John made a last-minute change to this plan: three missing cartridges from a full box was not a coincidence he would want to explain if ever suspected of a killing where three shots had been fired. He took seven live cartridges out of the box again and locked up.

John then made a quick trip to the garage to put the soiled gun cleaning swabs into his bag; he added the seven live cartridges too. He thought for a moment about wiping down the contents of both bags for prints but decided that if he and Sarah were caught with them, then it was probably all over anyway.

They simply had to get rid of the bags altogether, fast, and beyond realistic recovery. They already had a plan to do so. So, stick to it.

He locked both bags with the cheap padlocks they had come with and pocketed the keys.

Sarah made them both a very welcome cup of tea, and they checked their normal mobile phones. There had been no communication to either of them, apart from a couple of marketing emails and a text to remind John that his Barclaycard bill was due for payment shortly. Then Sarah headed off on foot to the village, where John knew she would ask the first person she met the location of the nearest post box: the aim was to fix their location in White Roding.

Meanwhile, John had a hot bath and scrubbed himself thoroughly to ensure that there was no trace of any firearms residue or gun oil. Sarah took a quick shower on return from the village; the chance of her having been contaminated during the shooting was minute, but a chance was still a chance.

Finally, all the clothes both of them had been wearing went into the wash.

All this took less than an hour. Well before 3pm, the Volvo was out of the garage again, back on its normal plates, and the two delighted dogs were in the back.

John took a picture with his phone of Pip and Barney staring out happily from the car, with Sarah doing her best to look casually cheerful beside it.

Just before they left, he texted it to Tom, with the caption: "Going sailing".

* * *

The police were quick; Woody gave them that, and they came in strength: two patrol cars, each with a crew of two (one of the four being a WPC), and a detective inspector, plus two sidekicks, one of them a sergeant, plus a scene of crimes officer.

A few minutes later, an ambulance came up the drive too, though one glance at what was left of Carl was enough to convince the paramedics that a hearse would have been more appropriate. The body was left in situ whilst the SOCO got into his white forensic suit and took pictures from every conceivable angle.

Woody came under immediate suspicion from the detectives, as he expected, even though Cynthia vouched loudly for the fact that he hadn't arrived until whoever had shot her husband had already left. The police were obviously considering the possibility that they were in cahoots.

'Take her inside,' said Inspector Barry to his Sergeant.

Cynthia resented the dismissive tone but had little choice in the matter. The WPC accompanied them. Sergeant Athill asked to be shown the kitchen and where Cynthia had hidden when she heard the shooting. Cynthia had all this pre-prepared, including the evidence of the half-cooked meal and the open bottle of champagne.

'I drank both the glasses Carl had poured,' she explained, apologetically. 'Afterwards, you know. I bet you would have done too!'

Detective Sergeant Athill noted this silently and began probing the story of the marriage breakdown: the supposed reason behind Cynthia's presence at the house. It was at least a worrying coincidence that her estranged husband had died within minutes of her first visit for nearly six weeks, but as he was experienced enough to know, coincidences did happen.

The Sergeant knew that he needed more than mere suspicion, and Cynthia's story appeared impressively solid. Her apparent lack of shock would have been surprising to a layman, but Sergeant Athill had been a detective for a sufficiently long time not to be surprised by much anymore.

Outside, Woody was getting the third degree from Inspector Barry and Detective Constable Lees. It was undoubtedly a grey Volvo estate that he had met in the drive (one of the jacked up, four-wheel drive ones), but his default approach to any interrogation by the police had long been to muddy the waters as much as he could. All he would admit to them was that it was a dark car.

Inspector Barry looked at him cynically. 'And you tell me you were the victim's chauffeur?'

'Amongst other things, yes.'

'Trained, were you?'

'I did a course, if that's what you're asking.'

'Know a bit about cars, then,' interjected Lees. It was a statement of fact, not a question.

Woody shrugged uncertainly. 'Yeah.'

'And you're telling me that you can't do better than "a dark car"?' The Inspector again. 'You're not doing yourself any favours here. Think again.'

'Look, the sun was in my eyes; I wasn't expecting them;

they came over the top of the rise in the drive. It's a blind crest – look for yourselves. I barely had time to swerve.'

The Inspector indicated briefly to one of the uniformed constables, who ambled unhurriedly down the drive. Then he turned back to Woody.

'Them?'

'Yes. There were two people in the car.'

'Ah, now we're getting somewhere. Describe them.'

Things were going rather faster than Woody would have liked.

'Man and a woman,' he said, unhappily. 'She was driving: dark hair and sunglasses. He had a cap on, didn't see his face.'

'What sort of age?'

'Couldn't tell. It was only a glimpse.'

'Under thirty?'

'No, older.'

'Under forty?'

'Possibly. Don't think so.'

'Under fifty?'

'Around that age. She was maybe a bit younger. But I'm not sure.'

The two detectives looked meaningfully at each other. Lees was writing methodically in his notebook.

'You confirm that you definitely did not fire a weapon?'

'I didn't fire any fucking thing.'

'Then you won't mind taking a forensic test, will you?' said Lees, in a "checkmate" type of voice.

'No,' said Woody, calmly. 'Gunshot residue check, I assume. Bring it on.'

The detective looked discomfited at both his suspect's knowledge and his apparent confidence; in fact, Woody was

247

more worried than he appeared, because he had handled the Walther.

It occurred to him that he should probably have washed his hands after handing the pistol over to Cynthia and before the police arrived. But he hadn't fired it. He hoped that this would put him in the clear.

The test took about five minutes to complete, from a kit, and Woody feigned boredom as it was conducted. Wearing forensic gloves, Lees took careful swabs from both his suspect's hands and bagged them – those would go to the lab. Then there was a field test, which could give a provisional indication if chemical droplets were applied to a second set of swabs.

It was negative. Woody stared insolently at the detective, who struggled to contain his disappointment.

'You should listen to people more, mate,' he said.

Barry had meanwhile been talking to the SOCO and the paramedics. He took a further close look at the corpse.

'Bring him over here,' he called across to Lees.

Woody was guided across to the body and turned from close-in to face the remnants of the head.

'Look at that,' ordered Barry.

Woody did so – it was indeed shocking. He tried to remain calm but failed.

'Look, he was my boss. He paid my wages. Why would I kill him?' he demanded angrily. 'You've just proved I haven't fired anything.'

'What did that, do you think?' said Barry, impassively.

Woody looked again, as briefly as he could. He had little doubt.

'Shotgun, I reckon. From close. But nothing to do with

me. I've told you what happened. I met a car in the drive. I saw the body. I jumped out of my car, and I met Mrs Barrow immediately. No idea who did this.'

All this was true, which made it believable. Inspector Barry realised with a sinking feeling that unless Cynthia had shot her husband herself (and there was scant evidence of that, though he'd ask her to take a forensic test too), they were indeed probably looking for someone else.

'If I am not under arrest I'd like to go, please. Nobody should have to see that,' said Woody, gesturing at the body without looking at it.

Woody sensed that he had the upper hand. Without waiting for police assent, he moved away to stand beside Cynthia, who was now in the opening of the French windows.

'Take it from me, he didn't do it,' she said defiantly. 'And neither did I.'

CHAPTER TWENTY-THREE

It was just over an hour to Burnham-on-Crouch, and John and Sarah travelled in silence: both were badly fatigued, and the enormity of what he had just done was beginning to weigh heavily on John. There was, of course, no going back.

Deep in thought, he drove badly.

'Ever been sailing?' he said at one point, trying to initiate conversation in response to Sarah's instinctive flinch as he braked late, behind a queue of traffic.

Somehow, he'd never asked her. The tone of Sarah's weary "no" soon put paid to that. He turned on the radio instead and tried Radio 3, in the hope that it would calm his racing mind. It didn't.

At one point, just outside Chelmsford, John spotted a garage with a drive-through car wash. He hadn't planned it, and the outside of the Volvo appeared clean enough, but he pulled in anyway.

'Can't be too careful,' he said. 'It should get rid of anything that might link the car to the scene. Dirt traces, or something.'

Sarah stared glumly ahead, exhausted. She only began to perk up as they approached Burnham Yacht Harbour, surprised by the size of some of the vessels out of the water in the assorted boatyards as they drove past.

'How big is this boat of yours?' she asked curiously, as they passed a particularly ostentatious specimen.

John saw where she was looking and smiled in wry amusement.

'Not as big as that one,' he said drily. 'But don't worry; there's space enough for us and a couple of dogs.'

'Won't they fall in?'

'No – they love it. At least Barney does, and Tom says Pip does too. We just clip them on.'

It was just approaching 5pm as they reached the marina, and the earlier cloudy weather had given way to a glorious evening. The news came on the radio. John thought nothing of it till an item late in the short bulletin.

Carl Barrow, allegedly one of the leading organised crime bosses in Britain, has been shot dead at his home in Hertfordshire.

John reached immediately for the mute switch. Sarah looked across at him in surprise.

'We don't listen to anything about it; we don't read anything about it; we don't comment on it; we don't discuss it with anyone; we don't react to it,' said John firmly. 'As we discussed. Too many people have given themselves away like that.'

'I just thought it might be useful to hear anything the police said.'

'No. We behave normally. Easier if we don't know what they're saying.'

They lapsed into silence again, until John stopped in the marina car park a couple of minutes later. The dogs started barking as soon as the Volvo's engine was switched off. They were let out under supervision on their leads after their hour in the car, then John put them back in.

'Just till we unpack,' he explained to Sarah. 'Come and have a look.'

He led her down by the hand, a hundred yards or so through the trees, where there was a walkway leading onto the pontoons of the marina. Upwards of a hundred boats were moored there.

On such a sunny weekend afternoon, there were plenty of other owners and families around. Some were seemingly packing up after a day on the water, others arriving, or going back and forth to the Chandler a couple of hundred yards away, buying rope or clothing or life jackets or whatever the latest nautical gadget was. John and Sarah were just another couple in the crowd and attracted no attention from anyone.

It was all new to Sarah, and John could see that her spirits were reviving amongst the sights and sounds in the fresh sea air. After about thirty yards, he turned right, off the central access pontoon, onto one of the mooring ones which ran at right angles. He stopped at the third boat along: a sailing yacht, with a motor cruiser moored either side.

'Well,' he said and then gestured rather hesitantly. 'Here she is.'

Thomasina had been named after Tom because John and Jenny didn't have a daughter. She was about as old as he was and had been bought second hand when he was four, an extravagance which John could ill afford at the time, though he had never regretted it. Jenny and he had spent some of their happiest times on her. She had always been wintered out of the water and kept in fine shape, largely these days by Tom, who had known her forever and was thus a keen sailor.

Her thirty-five-foot fibreglass hull was dark green, and her rigging clinked lazily in the faint breeze against the aluminium mast. Her woodwork looked immaculate despite her age; her metalwork shone; and John felt proud of her. She was built more for comfort than for speed, but cruising rather than racing was always the sort of sailing that he and Jenny had enjoyed.

He could see that Sarah was enchanted. He helped her over the rail onto the boat and unlocked the door to the cabin, which he knew would impress her: it was surprisingly well equipped.

'You stay here and look around once it's aired a bit,' John said. 'I'll get our things.'

The first items he fetched from the car were the two locked bags. He slung the handles over each shoulder and headed back. They were very similar to yachting bags, like many others he could see around the marina being carried hither and thither, and though they were heavier than most because of the bricks inside, there was no way that anybody else could tell that.

After that, there was a bit of food (and rather more booze) in a cold bag and finally the two excited dogs.

Sarah had fixed them both a strong gin and tonic by the time John got back from his third trip to the car and was sitting contentedly in the cockpit. Both the boats either side of them were unoccupied, so there was no danger of being overheard.

'We should do this more often,' Sarah said.

'You haven't been to sea yet. You might get seasick.'

He was delighted when she flashed him one of her old smiles. 'I won't.'

'Do you like Thomasina?'

'I love her.'

'I'm glad. We all do in my family; she's part of it. Well, just Tom and I now. I think Emma's coming round, too.'

He paused reflectively, and Sarah quickly picked up on it.

'Here's to us,' she said, raising her glass. 'And to Peter.'

John smiled tiredly and raised his drink too.

'Us and Peter. And Thomasina.'

'Yes. And thank you.'

'Let's not talk about it now.'

Sarah accepted this, and they sat in companionable silence, watching the sun go down over the course of a second gin.

Eventually, John took the two dogs for a quick walk whilst Sarah washed up ('I want to try everything in here out.'). Then they locked Barney and Pip inside, with plenty of ventilation, before heading off to the spacious marina restaurant for an early supper.

The Swallowtail, it was called. Conversation was awkward: they couldn't talk about the obvious topic for fear of being overheard, and anyway, John didn't want to. Instead, they had a rather stilted discussion about the rudiments of sailing, with John using table mats and condiments to illustrate the principles. But their hearts weren't in it; they were both shattered.

By 8pm they were back on the boat for a quick stroll with the dogs and a final drink as the sun set. By 8.45pm, they were snuggling down into their sleeping bags to the sound of water gently lapping around the hull. Their toes were touching where their sleeping berths merged as they narrowed into the bow of the boat.

'I'm going to sleep like the dead,' said Sarah, before the realisation of what she had said hit her.

She bit her knuckles in the resulting protracted pause, unsure of the reaction.

'Goodnight,' said John.

* * *

The next morning dawned fine and calm. John had slept surprisingly well and woke early due to the unfamiliar sounds of the sea and the gentle swell. Then the crushing realisation of what had happened the previous day hit, and for a moment, he felt a wave of misery sweep over him.

He looked across at Sarah – she too was wide awake, staring vacantly at the roof of the cabin. He reached across for her hand.

'It'll be OK,' he said gently. 'Promise.'

Her reaction was sufficiently encouraging for him to make his way across the central aisle to her narrow berth. They both badly needed an escape from their dark thoughts.

'Now I know what you mean about having to be a contortionist,' Sarah smiled breathlessly up at him a few minutes later. Their two sleeping bags lay entangled on the floor, where they had been cheerfully colonised by the dogs.

John sat up suddenly, banging his head on the overhead locker and cursing loudly.

'You're a wicked temptress,' he stated flatly, rubbing the bump. 'Come on. We've got lots to do.'

'I'm a temptress? You're the one who's over here; I didn't ask you.'

They bickered happily as they got dressed; then John fed the dogs in the cockpit and took them for their morning constitutional whilst Sarah put on the coffee. They had a bit of fruit to accompany it at the little table in the cabin and pointedly did not switch on the radio. John spoke as they ate.

'I want to get under way early but not early enough to be noticeable,' he said. 'Before most people are up and about, though. It'll be less crowded offshore then, which will make things easier, and we'll catch the tide.'

'How far out are we going?' asked Sarah.

John reached behind him into a rack and pulled out a local chart, which he unfolded.

'Look here,' he indicated. 'These lines are like map contours. They indicate depth rather than height, sometimes in metres, but this is a traditional one in fathoms. A fathom is six feet.'

'OK,' said Sarah cautiously. 'Can't we be tracked?'

'Well, there's a GPS. But we're just sailing, like everybody else here. No reason anyone should be interested.'

Sarah looked unconvinced. John ignored this and returned to his chart.

'This area out here is pretty deep for these parts,' he pointed.

'Six fathoms. Thirty-six feet. It's about five miles offshore, east of Foulness Island. That's further out than most people sail unless they're heading to the Continent. It should put us beyond casual observation.'

'How long will that take?'

'Not much more than two hours, including about five

miles from here to the estuary of the River Crouch. So, ten miles in all. There's a nice gentle breeze.'

'Thirty-six feet doesn't sound very deep,' said Sarah, doubt written all over her face. 'Won't the bags be spotted?'

John shook his head and smiled.

'This isn't the Caribbean,' he said. 'There are no tourist divers out there, and even if there were, they wouldn't be able to see more than five feet in front of their faces. It's murky as hell, plus thirty-six feet is deep for anyone other than a pro. They'll never be found.'

John unlocked the two weighted bags, removed the few items of clothing they'd put in as a rudimentary disguise, and then locked them again. Both of them then went into separate green bin liners, which he tied tightly shut.

It took very little time after that to get Thomasina moving: John had sailed her by himself often enough before. Strangely enough, the last time was the day six weeks or so ago when he'd first remet Sarah in The Swan, he reflected, as he cast off from the marina.

Usually, John sailed down the River to the open sea, which was as much a matter of pride as anything, but today there was an easterly wind, and if he did so, he would have to tack into it. He didn't want to waste time on such complications with the river banks close either side. Accordingly, they motored along at a gentle five knots in the sunshine in their orange life jackets. Nautical amateur Sarah steered under John's supervision, with the dogs happily and loosely restrained in the cockpit. It was not yet 10am, and there were few boats about.

As they approached the estuary, the breeze began to pick up, and John decided it was time to introduce Sarah to sail power. Initially, he could see that she was concerned by the seemingly uncontrolled flapping of the sails as he raised them electrically and then by the extent to which Thomasina heeled over as they caught the wind and began tacking in a zigzag pattern into the easterly wind.

But gradually, he could see that she was beginning to enjoy it, yelping with pleasure as spray broke over the cockpit. He explained again the basics of sailing to her and why no boat could head directly into wind, hence their zigzag course. She seemed to grasp it immediately and was soon happily spouting terms like "ready about", scurrying to winch in the jib as the boat changed onto the opposite tack. They must look just like any other happy couple enjoying a bracing sail, thought John, and of course, that was exactly the intention. Looking at them, nobody would suspect their ulterior purpose.

After about forty-five minutes, John consulted his chart and then his echo sounder, which gave a pleasingly deep reading. He eased course several points away from the wind to the north-east and loosened off the sail so that Thomasina was proceeding flat, on a gentle reach, the wind coming from her beam. Then he looked carefully around.

There was no boat nearer than a mile, and that was a big blue Catamaran heading away from them, south-west towards Burnham. Otherwise just coastal traffic, three miles or so inshore. In the opposite direction, out to sea, there was nothing.

'This is it,' said John. 'Now, hold that course; point straight at that large red navigation buoy on the horizon. I'll only be a moment.'

Sarah took the helm with mild alarm but nodded firmly once she had identified the buoy. John dived down into the cabin and was back in the cockpit with the first of the bags in its bin liner within seconds. He looked around again, carefully. On the starboard side of the boat, facing out to sea, still nothing.

He pitched the heavy bag over the rail without any further ado. Then he looked back in Thomasina's wake for twenty seconds or so; it appeared to vanish without trace. Within a minute, the second bag followed it, together with both the padlock keys.

John descended yet again and returned smiling, with two cans of lager.

'A bit early in the day, but it's a celebration,' he said as he handed one over to Sarah. 'Cheers!'

'I think we've done it,' she said, laughing. 'The perfect murder.'

John affected not to hear, and she looked at him quickly when he failed to reply. He wasn't quite ready yet to acknowledge the blunt reality of what they had done by using that word.

With the immediate tasks that had kept them busy now completed, they lapsed into thoughtful silence at the enormity of it all as they sipped their cold beers.

Thomasina flew back; with the wind almost behind her now, John could sail right up the river. He dropped the sails and motored in only for the last couple of hundred yards.

It was about 1pm before the boat was packed up to John's satisfaction, knowing that his son would no doubt be assessing his efforts soon with a critical eye. He suggested lunch at the Swallowtail before heading home. They'd leave the dogs in the car, with an open sunshine roof.

'Sounds like a plan,' said Sarah.

They only needed to make one trip from the boat with their much-reduced baggage, each of them with a dog on a lead. A couple of minutes later they emerged from the trees, into the car park.

Then they stopped dead in shock.

'Oh shit,' said John. Sarah leaned fearfully into him.

There were two police cars there, not fifty yards away, and very close to their Volvo. One of them still had its blue lights flashing.

It took John all of twenty very long seconds to spot the ambulance hidden behind a large camper van. Whatever accident or emergency had befallen someone, it was clearly nothing to do with them.

He sensed Sarah relax as the same realisation hit her.

'About that lunch…' she began.

'I agree. Let's get the hell out of here.'

* * *

The bracing sea air and the mental toll of their activities that morning had tired Sarah out, and she soon fell asleep in the car, leaving John alone with his thoughts as he drove. He didn't want to wake her by listening to the car radio and so endured an unwelcome period of forced reflection.

The last two days now seemed like a fantastic nightmare. Should the truth ever come out, then a long prison sentence inevitably awaited, together with the disdain of his son and all of the many friends he'd shared with Jenny over their long married life.

He could hear the gist of the sarcastic comments now and even picture some of the individuals who would make them: 'It didn't take long for him to go off the rails once Jenny died.'

John felt vaguely surprised that these aspects seemed to matter more to him than the ethics of the actual killing. Carl Barrow's final words to his killer, with their calm acceptance of the inevitable, did merit something approaching an uneasy sense of respect. John knew that he would certainly never forget them. However, he decided that he would make himself bear down hard on this feeling – the man was a ruthless criminal, who had driven Sarah's husband to a miserable end. He wasted little more sympathy on his victim's family; after all, his own wife had been complicit in the murder.

He realised that he'd focused wholly on the successful planning, achievement and concealment of the murder and hardly at all on the aftermath, which would cast a very long shadow – that was now the stark reality.

Driving home on autopilot, John forced himself to think about the future.

Normality: that was what it was all about. Preserving appearances. He knew it would be difficult and glanced across at the sleeping woman next to him.

Would she give the game away? And beyond that, where was their relationship going, now that he'd helped her to achieve her objective?

They were back at White Roding shortly after 2.30pm, and John woke Sarah gently from a deep slumber once the Volvo had come to a halt in front of his garage. He recognised the same symptoms cross her face as he'd felt that morning: first the sleepy smile of contentment, followed suddenly by the harsh shock of memory. She grasped his hand in panic.

'Oh God...'

'It'll be alright,' John said quietly, cradling Sarah's head to his chest and helping her out of her seat.

'Go inside and put the kettle on. I'll unload the car.'

Sarah nodded tiredly, took the keys and headed into the house. Oblivious to the sombre atmosphere, the dogs bounded out of the back of the car as soon as John opened the tailgate and followed her inside happily. John heard her snap at one of them in her exhaustion; the strain she was under was obvious, and that was a concern.

He took their one remaining bag out of the car and left it in the hallway before heading for the kitchen. Sarah gave him a wan smile as she handed over the steaming cup of tea.

'Sit down,' said John gently, doing so himself.

He waited till she was settled at the kitchen table.

'Now, listen,' he said. He could see that she was welling up and took her hand in his.

'We've done very well. We've achieved what we set out to do, and we've disposed of the evidence. It couldn't have gone better. Agreed?'

Sarah nodded, her lip wobbling.

'Afterwards, it was always going to be like this. We can't look back. We've just got to put it behind us.'

'How can we?'

John smiled indulgently. 'A little late to think of that. It's nothing to do with us – we mustn't give anyone cause to think differently. So never, ever, mention it.'

'Yes, you're right.'

'Starting this afternoon.'

Sarah looked at him uncomprehendingly.

'Tom and Emma will be over to pick up Pip before long. They'll be full of the wedding, and we must show interest.

And we've just had a wonderful time sailing, haven't we?'

Sarah reflected for a moment, then drained her cup before making for the stairs.

'You're right,' she said, over her shoulder. 'I'll go and freshen up. Don't worry; I won't let the side down.'

John was semi-reassured. He busied himself tidying up and unpacking. Sure enough, it was only thirty minutes before he got a text from Emma: "On way home – u back yet?".

He replied immediately: "Yes – Pip ready anytime". A thumbs up and "30 mins" arrived in response.

'Half an hour,' he shouted up the stairs.

Sarah was down in less than ten minutes, by which time John had laid out some tea. He looked at her approvingly: lightly made-up, but with her newly acquired tan very evident, and wearing a gaudy new top. She saw him appraising her and smiled back.

'Do I look happy enough?' she asked lightly.

If she was still stressed, then it was very well hidden.

'You do,' said John. 'Deliciously so, in fact. Hold the thought.'

It was well under half an hour before Tom's VW Passat estate pulled up outside. He'd always been a fast driver, so John had half expected the early arrival. He met his son and daughter-in-law, whose bump he fancied was just beginning to show, on the doorstep.

He sensed Sarah close behind him. She gave him a little pinch, which made him smile without having to force it.

Tom claimed to be slightly hung-over, though he appeared right as rain. He greeted Sarah with a kiss on the cheek, which pleased John. They moved inside for tea, Pip all the while noisily greeting his owners.

Emma seemed back in her shy mode, saying nothing until she interrupted Tom's lengthy wedding anecdotes over the second cup. John wondered briefly if she'd detected his flagging attention.

'Enough, Tom,' she said fondly, laying her arm on his. She turned to John and Sarah.

'So, how was your weekend?'

John looked quickly at Sarah, who didn't hesitate for a moment and flashed her most radiant smile.

'Unbelievable,' she said.

EPILOGUE

The police investigation into Carl Barrow's death petered out after a few weeks.

None of his criminal associates would talk, and Detective Inspector Barry's private assessment is that, despite the image of "in the know" self-importance they all like to project, none of them knows anything anyway. Well, somebody may do, but he (or she) isn't talking.

As for the family, all of them seem upset, and the pretty daughter may even mean it.

The eldest son is less convincing and seems to be relishing his new business responsibilities. Might have had a hand in it then, but no proof and a cast-iron alibi.

The wife is very controlled, suspiciously so in Barry's view, but although she was at the scene, she has her story, and she's sticking to it. Formidable woman.

So, an organised crime boss has been killed by another member of the underworld, it seems, possibly at the behest of someone in his own dubious family.

The case got a fair bit of publicity for a month or so,

and as a result, the Chief Constable in particular was anxious to solve it. However, Barry's private opinion is that nobody (himself included) really cares much when bastards like Carl Barrow get their just desserts. Indeed, the consensus of the general public, politically incorrect though it may be, is probably "good riddance".

That's not his publicly expressed professional opinion of course; being unsolved, the case must remain open.

* * *

David isn't sure who did it but doesn't underestimate either his mother or the family lawyer, Frank, who he thought had agreed to cooperate with him.

They may have been in it together for all he knows, though they appear to dislike each other cordially as much as ever, endlessly squabbling over his attempts to legitimise the business, Cynthia supportive but naïve; Frank making the right noises but always finding reasons for things not to happen.

He's not gone completely cold on the old methods yet: an attempt by Jimmy Laing and his people to muscle in on an area where their territories adjoined after Carl's death was quickly seen off in the traditional way, plus through the "emigration" of somebody whose loyalty appeared to be in question. Such a robust response has reassured Carl's old guard.

Respectability is the ultimate direction of travel for David though, like Michael Corleone in *Godfather II*, a film he watches every few months.

He had a few hiccups along the way too, didn't he?

Frank Paton is mystified, dating from when the inquest found that Carl had been killed by a shotgun, rather than a pistol. He once asked Woody about it but got his head bitten off: 'Look, you wanted it done then, and it was, OK?'

He left it there and has made sure that Woody is looked after financially by the family, as promised. Best not to cross a man capable of something like that.

Frank's days of influence are limited to when he ceases to become invaluable, and he knows it, hence his resistance to change.

In retrospect, he misses the simple certainty of the old days under Carl. Things are a lot murkier now.

* * *

Having got it back from Celia, Woody keeps the Walther somewhere safe, despite slight unease that it might link him to unsolved crimes of the past. If he's caught with the pistol, he's in big trouble with the law, certainly, but it's worth it as insurance and for the pleasure it gives him to hint occasionally to Frank that he still has it. And may use it.

Cynthia has kept him on at his increased salary; she pretty well had to. He's even got Carol back, though sometimes that seems a mixed blessing.

In as much as he reflects on it at all, Woody thinks that Cynthia was probably involved somehow in her husband's death.

But she pays him now, so he doesn't lose sleep over it. Easy come, easy go.

* * *

Cynthia knows that a lot of people suspect her, including her own daughter, but she takes comfort from the fact that she's the only one who knows how the jigsaw fits together. Of course, she keeps such knowledge close to that impressive chest.

Very much the power behind the throne in the organisation now, Cynthia is selling the showy house she shared with Carl, who gave her so little say in its design. Indeed, she rather relishes playing the grieving widow, who can't bear to live anymore at the place where her late husband met his untimely demise. She wants something more discreetly upmarket, and she can afford it, being the sole beneficiary of his will. Additionally, Carl had substantial life insurance, a prudent precaution in his line of work.

Cynthia sees Sarah (she's stopped calling her Bim) very occasionally, on neutral territory, but they keep their distance from each other, knowing that too close an association might prove dangerous. Certain topics are tacitly recognised by both of them as being off limits.

Carl's widow has never met her sister's new man and has no plans to do so.

* * *

As for John and Sarah, they've never been questioned, or come under the slightest suspicion, and are still very much an item; indeed, they're bound together, as both know that any open disagreement between them could prove fatal. Each can destroy the other.

268

On the surface, their relationship remains in rude health – people are pleased for them, an announcement seeming likely any day. Tom has cheerfully accepted it as an inevitability.

Occasionally, however, John catches Sarah giving him a strange, sideways glance when she thinks he's not looking.

At that moment, he knows she's not seeing him as her lover, or as the avuncular, cheerful, soon-to-be grandfather he knows himself to be; nor indeed as a prospective husband.

She's looking at the man she's seen shoot most of somebody's head off. It's not a romantic vision, but it's one she'll never be rid of.

So, though it is unspoken, there will always be a "Before" and an "After" for them.

A Clean Kill it may well have been, but, as ever in life, actions have consequences.